FAUX PAS

FAUX PAS

A Paws and Pose Mystery

Shannon Esposito

This first world edition published 2015
in Great Britain and the USA by
SEVERN HOUSE PUBLISHERS LTD of
19 Cedar Road, Sutton, Surrey, England, SM2 5DA.
Trade paperback edition first published 2016
in Great Britain and the USA by
SEVERN HOUSE PUBLISHERS LTD.

British Library Cataloguing in Publication Data

Esposito, Shannon, author.
  Faux pas. – (A Paws and Pose mystery)
  1. Murder–Investigation–Fiction. 2. Yoga teachers–
  Fiction. 3. Pet grooming salons–Fiction. 4. Detective and
  mystery stories.
  I. Title II. Series
  813.6-dc23

ISBN-13: 978-0-7278-8539-5 (cased)
ISBN-13: 978-1-84751-642-8 (trade paper)
ISBN-13: 978-1-78010-699-1 (e-book)

All Severn House titles are printed on acid-free paper.

Severn House Publishers support the Forest Stewardship Council™ [FSC™],
the leading international forest certification organisation. All our titles that
are printed on FSC certified paper carry the FSC logo.

MIX
Paper from
responsible sources
FSC
www.fsc.org   FSC® C013056

Typeset by Palimpsest Book Production Ltd.,
Falkirk, Stirlingshire, Scotland.
Printed and bound in Great Britain by
TJ International, Padstow, Cornwall.

ONE

*O*h no . . . *no, no, no!* My heartbeat sped up as I lay stretched out in sphinx pose and watched my deceased, childhood dog saunter into my doga (doggie-yoga) studio. A low whimper came from Buddha, my seventy-pound bulldog mix, who had been demonstrating an excellent canine version of the pose next to me. *He could see Angel, too.* We both watched in fascination as Angel weaved her little, ghostly terrier self through the dozen human and dog clients in various states of the pose on their mats.

This was not good. Not good at all. I was finally starting to feel like I had my life, my career – my insane mother – under control. Angel fancied herself my guardian angel, so her showing up today only meant one thing: a crap load of trouble was about to hit the fan in my world.

As Angel came to sit on the other side of me, her soft spirit eyes shining, her tongue lolling in her signature happy-to-see-you smile, I glanced around at my clients to see if anyone else could see her. All humans and canines seemed oblivious to the new ghostly presence in the room. Only Buddha – now recovered from the surprise – eyed Angel with the uninterested gaze he doled out to most everyone. That's what made him such a good assistant in my classes. Not much ruffled his feathers . . . or fur. Still, I found it curious he could also see my little childhood BFF. Was it because of his connection to me? I shook myself free of that tangled web of thoughts. Those kinds of questions only led to more questions, not answers.

'OK, everyone, let's slowly lift our hips back up into our last downward facing dog.'

As I pushed my hips up – and my heels to the mat – my calves, back and shoulders stretched in a delicious way, inspiring an audible moan and then a sigh. I glanced at Angel's ghostly form, then frowned. I loved the little bugger, but did not love what usually happened after she paid me a visit.

'Thanks for the warning,' I whispered to her. 'I'll watch my back.'

She sneezed.

I took that as: 'Yep, good idea.' Then she stood, gave me one more shiny-eyed stare, turned and disappeared into the mirrored wall behind me. I eyed the spot for a moment and then lowered myself to the mat.

'OK, ladies and pups. Time for *savasana*.'

These words also elicited an audible sigh of pleasure from the small circle of pampered, plumped, peeled and Botoxed women. I smiled to myself. If they only knew how easy I made my doga classes. It actually didn't even feel like work, so sometimes I felt guilty for taking their money. Mostly we spent an hour doing a lot of stretching and twists for the ladies and massages for the dogs. Some of them would never come back if I put them through the challenge of a real yoga class. But, it did have health benefits for both them and their pets, so I tried not to feel too guilty. Plus, I needed the money. If I didn't move out of my mother's house soon, I was going to end up in a padded room or jail cell. I was thirty-five and done with her guilt trips, codependence and manipulating ways of controlling my life. Not to mention her serious Twinkie addiction. At least, I really, really wanted to be.

Sighing, I patted Buddha on the rump, letting him know it was corpse pose time. '*Savasana*, Buddha.' I'd been practicing yoga with him butting in on my mat time since I rescued him five years ago, so he knew the basic commands. He happily obliged, belly up, all modesty out the window, wiggling and snorting. I left him and picked my way through the room, rubbing a few dog bellies as I went to dim the lights.

A hushed argument suddenly broke out on the right side of the room. Celeste Green's Chihuahua, Princess, began yipping. I rolled my eyes and cursed under my breath. Not very yogi of me, I know, but this feud between Celeste and Zebina was getting out of hand. I needed to nip it in the bud before I started losing clients who came here to lower their blood pressure. Of course, I couldn't imagine why anyone living full-time on Moon Key would have stress. *No, that's not fair, Elle.* Money doesn't solve all problems in life. Even obscene amounts of money.

Moon Key is a Gulf coast barrier island that you can only get to via private ferry. There are around a thousand permanent residents here during off season. That triples during snow-bird season. My best friend, Hope, got me this job teaching doga classes at the Pampered Pup Spa & Resort, but I have to give up the glass slippers every evening and return to my childhood home in the ghettos of Clearwater. Actually, it was *our* childhood home. We both grew up there. Hope just happened to marry into money and so now enjoys Moon Key as a full-time resident.

I'm saving up though. I have my eye on this beach bungalow that had an electrical fire a few months ago. Luckily, no one was there at the time but word around the island is Mrs Yates refuses to use it for their vacation house now. The only real estate agent allowed to sell property on Moon Key, M.J. Morgan, told me personally he's already put an offer in on one of the condos for the Yates when they come back in October. Says he might be able to convince them to ditch the two-million-dollar bungalow cheap. I'm crossing fingers and toes that by *cheap* he means what they paid for the LED lit, climate-controlled, blessed-by-the-Pope refrigerator inside the bungalow. A girl can dream.

'Ladies.' I crossed my arms and plastered on a smile as I stared at the feuding women. 'Can I see you both outside, please.' My voice cracked. Celeste snapped a thin leash on Princess's bejeweled collar and smiled up at me, though her eyes glowed like radioactive embers. 'Of course, Elle.'

Zebina growled, flicking her silky, dark ponytail over a toned, exfoliated shoulder and scooped up her plump Boston terrier, who grunted as she tucked him under her arm.

I started my deep breathing exercises as I led them out through the studio's French doors. They both followed me into the hallway, and I shut the door on the gossiping whispers already starting behind us.

'That's it, I'm getting a restraining order and filing harassment charges, you crazy cow!' Zebina's dark eyes flashed dangerously.

Celeste, a petite blonde in her early fifties, smiled up into the taller woman's face and moved her French-manicured hands on to her hips. 'Go ahead and try it, you selfish, home-wrecking slut. This is the United States of America. Home of the free to do whatever the hell I want, wherever the hell I want to do it!'

I held up a shaky hand between them as the familiar rush of anxiety coursed through my blood. I fought the urge to claw at it. The anxiety, not the women. 'Whoa, let's take a few deep breaths here, ladies. We're all adults. Surely we can figure out how to deal with this um . . . situation peacefully.' I took a few deep breaths of my own, trying and failing to stop the tightening in my chest and my quivering stomach. 'Please?' I wasn't above begging.

'No, no we can't.' Zebina shifted Max in her arms. He grunted. I swear his bulging eyes were pleading with me to help him escape. I'm sure my eyes were saying the same thing to him. 'We can't because she doesn't want peace. She wants to harass me, to drive me insane.' She poked an accusing finger into Celeste's face.

'Not a very far drive,' Celeste spat back. Princess yipped again and turned circles nervously at Celeste's bare feet, getting tangled in her leash.

I pinched the bridge of my nose, counting to ten. Today, I was definitely earning my money. This was going downhill fast, and I was only one more finger poke away from a full-blown panic attack. 'Celeste, please. Princess can feel your energy, and you're making her very nervous.' I pointed down at the little panting, white dog. 'This is the exact opposite of the purpose of doga.'

Celeste's eyes flicked to me. 'Elle, you . . . you OK?'

'I'm fine. Just bad with confrontation.' I straightened my spine and did my best impression of exuding confidence. *Fake it until you feel it, right?* 'OK, here's the deal. Celeste, I understand your anger with Zebina . . .'

'The husband stealer!' She screeched, her focus off of me and back on the other woman.

'Yes. OK, the husband stealer.' I shrugged helplessly at Zebina as she shifted her glare to me. 'But that's none of my business. And I can't have this kind of energy in my class. It's not good for anyone.' My breathing was so shallow now;

words were riding on short puffs of breath. 'So, I simply can't have you two in the same class any more. Zebina, you've been coming here the longest. You choose. Morning or afternoon session?'

Her eyes darkened behind layers of expertly applied mascara as she glared at Celeste, a mean little smile pulling at the corners of her pink, glossed lips. 'I'll keep coming to the morning session. Since my *fiancée* needs me in the afternoon.'

Oh crap. I leaned against the wall for support. My whole body went into fight or flight mode as I watched the murderous look morph Celeste's delicate English features. I did understand where the rage was coming from. After all, Zebina was the reason Celeste's husband of twenty-some years had just divorced her. And Zebina rubbing it in her face by calling him her 'fiancé' was just cruel. But, I had classes to run. And I had no idea how to deal with all the complicated drama people created, except to keep them separated.

'It's settled then.' I pressed a hand to my chest, trying to steady my heart rate. My face felt like it was on fire and sweat had beaded up around my hairline. I noticed all this in the background as I pushed the words out. 'Celeste, you are welcome to bring Princess to the afternoon sessions. They start at four.' I wasn't sure she'd be interested in coming at all if she couldn't harass Zebina. It seemed to have become her singular purpose in life. She hadn't even started taking my classes until two months ago when her divorce was final. So, I had probably lost a client but gained some sanity. 'Please . . . gather your things for today.'

To my surprise, Celeste didn't resist. Maybe it was out of pity. She eyed me sideways with a frown. 'Fine, Elle.' Scooping up Princess under one arm, she yanked the French door open, then turned back to Zebina. Her eyes narrowed to glittering slits as she bared her pearly teeth in a pseudo-smile. 'See you at Zumba.'

I busted into the gift shop, sending the crystal dog bones on the door crashing into one another and sucking in air like an asthmatic horse. I'm sure my eyes were wild as they met

Bonnie's. One glance at me and she abandoned her customer and ran to the back room, emerging with a paper bag.

As she grabbed my elbow to steer me behind the counter and pressed the open bag over my nose and mouth, all I could think about was how I was going to die while still living with my mother.

'Come on, sugar. You got this. Just concentrate on slow breathing.'

I nodded gratefully as Bonnie helped me slide down the wall and put my head between my knees. Her take-charge attitude really helped. Giving up control of the body that was trying to kill me was exactly what I needed.

'Just breathe slowly in and out. That's all you have to do right now. Just breathe.'

Her voice sounded far away, muffled behind the wall of pure terror my mind had erected and the concert-worthy drum-beat of my heart. *Was it possible for a heart to burst through a person's chest?* The scene in *Alien* flashed in my mind. *If an alien could do it, surely a human heart beating this hard could? No. Stop it, Elle. Focus. In and out.*

I sucked in stale air and blew out shallow, hot breaths, expanding and contracting the paper bag. The crinkling sound it made, and the fact I had eaten horseradish with my eggs for breakfast, distracted me quite nicely. Bonnie grabbed my face between her hands and made me look into her eyes.

'Slow your breath, Elle. Breathe deeper.' She demonstrated with her own breath. Her eyes were gray-blue with specks of gold around her pupils. They were earnest. Fierce. I should obey. 'That's it. In and out.' She moved one cool, dry hand to push the damp hair off my forehead and neck. Then she began to hum and rub my arms. A single tear of humiliation rolled down my face and neck. I moved my attention back to my breath, followed it as it filled my lungs and then the paper bag. Again. And again. Until finally my whole body shuddered and the panic attack released its hold on me.

The back of my head hit the wall as I collapsed in exhaustion, dropping my arms and enjoying breathing like a normal person again. I had survived. Now I was just embarrassed.

Bonnie squeezed my hand. 'That was a pretty bad one.'

I opened my eyes and rolled my head to look at her concerned expression. 'I'm OK now. Thanks, Bonnie.' This wasn't the first time she'd had to deal with one of my panic attacks in the nine months since I'd been working here. I was grateful she understood and never judged me for it. That made one of us.

She cocked her head and smiled. 'It was Celeste and Zebina, wasn't it?'

I rolled my head back and forth and finally smiled back at her. 'Yep. Those two are going to be the death of me.'

'Or each other. I wondered how long they were going to last in your class together. Celeste is harmless, though I'm not so sure about Zebina. Those Greek women can be . . . passionate. I keep warning Celeste she's playing with fire but she's obsessed with revenge. What can you do?' She chuckled and stood. Her long, blonde hair slid over one shoulder, clad in a butterfly print Valentino dress. 'I've got to check on Mrs Tinsley, then I'll run and fetch you some wet paper towels. Sit tight.'

'Thanks, Bonnie.' I watched her move gracefully back on to the shop floor. She truly was the most put-together, take-charge woman I'd ever met. She was in her mid-fifties, had the energy and body of a thirty-year-old and the confidence that came with experience. Maybe if I would've had a mother more like Bonnie to model myself after, I wouldn't be such an emotional basket case. I squeezed my eyes shut and forced myself to stop thinking about my mother as my chest began to tighten again.

TWO

The next morning I led the class with a renewed sense of calmness by repeating my mantra. Today was a new day. Today I wouldn't let other people's drama affect my own sense of peace. Today the anxiety would not win. I sighed with contentment as my thumbs massaged Buddha's rough paw pads and then moved in between his toes.

'Good Lord in heaven, Violet! What are you feeding that mutt?' Elsa, my oldest client at eighty-two and not one for subtlety, scooped up her Chihuahua with arthritic hands and dragged her mat to an empty spot at front of the studio, mumbling as she went. 'Smells like somethin' crawled up there and died . . .'

I glanced up to see the other women in the area of Violet and her Weimaraner, Ghost, covering their noses and chuckling. Ghost was on his back, enjoying his paw massage, oblivious to the dirty looks being tossed his way.

I smiled to myself and did the only thing a yoga teacher could do in the face of client flatulence. Ignored it. 'Let's move to the back legs now . . .'

A blood-curdling scream cut me off.

A few of the dogs growled or jumped up in surprise. Everyone froze. We stared at each other, wide-eyed. The owners began trying to calm their pets.

'What in the name of all that's holy was that?' Violet asked, her green eyes wild with alarm.

'Someone probably just saw a spider,' Whitley offered, always the voice of reason.

'I'm sure it's nothing.' But my curiosity still got the best of me. 'Just continue the leg massage, try to keep the dogs calm. I'll be back in a sec.' I motioned for Buddha to stay and then hopped around the mats and dogs, making my way quickly to the door. As I opened it, one of our three security guards, Marvin, ran by. *What in blazes? Could that kind of scream come from just seeing a spider?* I had my doubts. A snake . . . maybe. I ran through the possible snake culprits as I padded on my bare feet behind him. A diamondback rattler would be the most likely. Or a cottonmouth. Nah. Maybe a pygmy rattler? They would be small enough to go unnoticed slipping into the building. And they all eat small mammals. Maybe one was going after a small dog?

We ended up at the doorway to the mudbath room. I gasped as I stood on my tippy-toes to glance over Marvin's wide left shoulder. He seemed frozen in shock or disbelief.

I had been so focused on my snake theory, I was having a hard time comprehending what we were actually looking at. 'What the . . .?'

The large, white bathing tub had been tipped over, and Dead Sea mud had spilled all over the floor, splattered on the walls and covered some poor creature shaking in the corner. I shifted and peered over Marvin's other shoulder. In the middle of the room with its arms and legs stretched out, was a small figure face down in the mud. A delicate rose gold bracelet hung off of the one foot that had escaped the avalanche of mud. I knew that ankle bracelet. I clutched Marvin's arm. 'Holy crap, Marvin. I think that's Celeste Green!'

Marvin didn't answer me. He pushed me gently back with his big paw. 'Stay back, Elle.' Then he pulled out his phone.

There's no hospital on Moon Key, just a small emergency clinic that can't handle much more than a sunburn. And we didn't have an actual police department, either, but we did have a pretty heavy security force that patrolled the area in golf carts shaped like police cars. Despite this, the 'public security officers' took their jobs seriously.

Who would he call, I wondered. Moon Key security station? Or the Clearwater Police Department, who actually had jurisdiction here?

I listened in on his call. Clearwater PD it was. They'd respond, bringing all necessary personnel to the island by boat, but it'd still take about twenty minutes to gather everyone and get here. I glanced sadly back at Celeste. Not that it mattered. Time meant nothing to her now.

I suddenly felt like we should be doing something. 'Maybe someone should move her face out of the mud, at least?'

Marvin shook his head. 'I don't think we should touch anything.'

I glanced up at Marvin. *Did that mean he thought her death was suspicious?*

Maria – the lady responsible for both giving the dogs their mudbaths and the blood-curdling scream – had apparently recovered from the shock and was now sobbing uncontrollably. I slipped into the room and went to comfort her while Marvin moved out of the doorway to try and clear the hallway of curious onlookers. I wrapped my arms around her shaking body. She was so warm. I pushed her thick hair away and checked her forehead for fever. 'Shh, it'll be OK, Maria. Do you know what happened here?'

She shook her head with her hands covering her mouth. Her words came out attached to violent sobs.

'Me enteré de que estaba muerto!'

I had a limited knowledge of Spanish so I tried to encourage her to speak English. 'Maria, can you tell me in English?'

'Si . . . I find Miss Green! Dead!' She then reverted back into a hysterical string of Spanish. I rubbed her back, giving up on getting any information from her for now. My own heart was racing and I felt a bit woozy.

Above Maria's sobs I could hear Marvin arguing with the workers and clients in the hallway, trying to field questions and get them to leave the area.

He came back in, shaking his head and stared at Celeste. By the noise in the hallway, I gathered he had failed at his quest. I held Maria and we watched him expectantly. He seemed to be wrestling with something. Finally he shrugged. 'Suppose I should check to make sure she's really dead.'

I raised an eyebrow. Unless the woman had found a way to breathe mud, she was clearly dead.

He walked over and lowered himself awkwardly to his knees in the mud. After a few long seconds of hesitation, he pressed two meaty fingers to her neck beneath her chin. His head was bowed as he shook it. 'Yep. Dead.' He raised weary eyes up to the people now pressing in on the doorway, trying to get a better view. 'Everyone please, for the last time, stay back. We need to keep this area undisturbed for the police.' He looked down at the mud on his crisp, blue uniform and then stared at his hands. I think he just realized he had been touching a dead woman.

The mud creature in the corner suddenly darted and tried to scramble out of the room. Unfortunately, it only succeeded in slipping and sliding and slinging Dead Sea mud into Marvin's face.

'Whoa, whoa, little guy!' Marvin scooped up the mud creature and, as he held it close to his chest, he stared at something hard on the floor. 'What the . . .?' He slowly rose and handed the creature off to Maria, his eyes still focused on the floor. 'Here.'

Maria pulled the small animal into her body and began rubbing its face with a towel, speaking to it softly in Spanish between sniffles. It was good she now had a job to keep her mind occupied.

I stared at the emerging features of the animal in her grasp. *Oh no!* It was Princess! Poor thing. Did she have her mudbath interrupted by her mom collapsing and dying right in front of her? No, she must have come in with Maria. Either way, she was going to need a canine therapist. Luckily, we had one of those here, too. I grabbed a second towel from the shelf and began to help Maria soothe the shaking dog while keeping an eye on Marvin. He had taken out his cell phone and was aiming it at the mud by Celeste's right hand.

'What is it?' I moved carefully to stand behind him, the mud squishing between my toes. I tried not to enjoy it out of respect for Celeste.

'Looks like she tried to write something in the mud.' His flash went off again as he took another picture. 'You should stand back, Elle.'

Ignoring his warning, I leaned over his shoulder. 'Huh. Looks like the letters B and O. What could that mean?'

'Botox.'

We both looked up to see Bonnie pushing her way through the crowd in the doorway. Tears were streaming down her face. My eyes widened. I'd never seen her upset before. But,

I knew Bonnie and Celeste had become pretty good friends over the last few months. And I imagined, like me, this was her first time seeing an actual dead body.

'Botox?' Marvin repeated, pulling his six foot four frame up to face her.

She nodded. A sound like an injured animal escaped her lips as she stared down at Celeste. 'She came here to pick up Princess straight from the plastic surgeon's office. She was getting Botox injections done today. We were supposed to meet in the café for an early brunch ten minutes ago. I waited. She never showed up and she's never late. That's when I knew something was wrong.' She shook her head and swiped at her nose, her eyes narrowing, her face turning blotchy. She gasped. 'He did this to her!'

'Who?' I asked, though I had a sinking feeling I knew who.

'Dr Craft. He . . . he killed her!' Her shoulders shook as her whole body deflated, and she sobbed quietly. Two of the ladies moved in to comfort her.

Yep. Dr Ira Craft. My best friend Hope's husband. The most popular, and by that fact alone, the most sued plastic surgeon in the Tampa Bay area. *Fantastic.*

Just then Rita Howell, the spa manager pushed her way through with Alex Harwick, head of Moon Key security, on her heels. I scooted myself further behind Maria, trying to hide my five foot seven frame behind her five foot two one. I'd always been bad at math, but I was desperate.

Alex was a forty-something ex-football player and typical good ole' Florida boy. He also didn't understand or accept rejection. I had stopped counting the number of times he had asked me out in the nine months since I'd been working on Moon Key. Every time I declined he would smile and say, 'Maybe next time.' It was unsettling.

Three more security officers marched up behind them, their grim faces and purposeful demeanor helped move everyone out of the way.

Rita Howell clapped her hands. 'OK, everyone. Show's over. The spa will be closing for the day. Everyone out!'

The voices grew louder as the crowd of curious women began to disperse and talk amongst themselves. Most of my doga class was among the looky-loos. I started to leave with them.

'Not you, Elle,' Rita Howell barked, waving her cell phone at us. 'You, Maria, Marvin and Bonnie will stay here and explain this to the police. They're pulling into the guest marina now, so they should be here in a few.'

'Me?' I choked, feeling the heat crawl up my neck. 'I don't know what happened. I got here after she—' I pointed helplessly at Celeste on the ground – 'ended up like that.'

Rita waved off my concern. 'Just answer their questions. It'll be fine.' She snapped her fingers at the safety officers. 'Don't just stand there. Get this place emptied out and locked up. And one of you go wait by the door to let in the ME and the real law enforcement. Go!'

As always, everyone scattered like cockroaches when Rita snapped her fingers.

'Unbelievable.' I stepped outside the mudroom to get some air. I needed to go check on Buddha. Though I'm sure he was taking his after-doga nap, completely oblivious to the human drama unfolding. Sometimes I really envied him.

Bonnie came and slid an arm around my shoulder. 'You OK?'

I raised my chin to look up at her. Her mascara had run and left black tear trails on her cheeks. I wondered if I should say something, then decided she probably wouldn't care right now. 'Yeah. Fine. I should be asking you that, though.' I squeezed her hand. 'I'm so sorry.'

'Thanks.' She squeezed my hand back. 'I'm really going to miss her. She was a good friend. And a good client. Dr Craft has to be held accountable for this.'

I glanced back up at her. 'Why do you think it was Ira's fault? Maybe she had a heart attack, or tripped and hit her head when she pulled the bath tub over on herself . . . or something that didn't have to do with her Botox injections.'

'No.' She shook her head. The light, coconut scent of her shampoo drifted from her. It smelled expensive. 'I warned her. You don't go back to a doctor who you've threatened to sue. Especially not for a procedure like Botox to the neck.' She raised a perfectly plucked brow. 'Plus the fact she was trying

to write Botox in the mud? I'd say he's as good as in prison.'
She shrugged. 'It will be easy enough to prove, that he killed
her. Accidentally . . . or not.'

I stared at her. Her mouth was set in a grim line. She was
serious. She really believed Celeste died from her Botox procedure. Could Ira really be capable of murder over a lawsuit? I
thought back to all the time I'd spent with him and Hope since
their wedding two years ago. No. He was a nice guy. A bit of
a nerd, sure, but sweet. So, surely if Celeste did die from her
Botox injections . . . was that even possible? Surely, if she
did, it was an accident. But, even that was unacceptable.
Couldn't that be considered manslaughter? At the very least,
he could lose his license. *How was I going to tell Hope?*

My stomach churned, twisted and I suddenly felt my breakfast burrito about to make a second appearance. A group of
official looking people in uniforms rounded the corner and
marched toward us. I slapped my hand over my mouth and ran
for the trash can.

THREE

'And you work here?' A portly man in an ill-fitting suit, who introduced himself to me as Detective Farnsworth, was scratching my information on his notepad. Sweat dripped from under his chin and splattered on to the pad. I tried not to visibly cringe. He pulled out a handkerchief and swiped at his neck and then the notepad.

'I do work here, yes.' They had taped off the mudroom and separated us all for questioning. I would have preferred a little more distance from Celeste's body. The surreal element to the situation that had kept me numb until this point was quickly falling away. It was all beginning to sink in. Celeste was gone. Camera flashes were lighting up the orange sorbet wall in front of me. I felt dizzy. 'I teach doga classes.'

His eyebrow pushed up into greasy hair desperately in need of a cut and his dull brown eyes sharpened their focus on me. He smelled like cheese doodles.

'People bring their dogs to do yoga with them. It's healthy for the both the humans and dogs.' I repeated the defensive mantra absent-mindedly as I rubbed my palms roughly on my thighs. He was still staring at me expectantly. How much did he want me to explain? 'I'm also on salary. I help clean up where needed, check on the dogs when they're left alone in the suites, help walk them in the garden, things like that.'

'Suites?' He shook his head and mumbled something about rich people under his breath. 'OK, Miss Pressley, please walk me through what you remember.'

I talked through the whole thing with him. When I got to the end I hesitated, but then realized Bonnie would be spilling the beans about Ira anyway, and I didn't want it to seem like he had anything to hide. 'So, Bonnie, the tall blonde, was supposed to meet Celeste in the café for brunch after Celeste's Botox appointment. That's where she was coming from.'

'And do you know where the deceased had this Botox appointment?'

I bit my lip and sighed. 'Yes. She went to Dr Ira Craft, two buildings over, next to Royal Dry Cleaners. But I know him personally and I can tell you, he's not capable of murder. He's a sweet guy and very professional.' I stopped when I noticed the intensity with which the detective was now staring at me. He reminded me of a bulldog.

'Who said anything about murder, Miss Pressley?'

My face flushed. My heart fluttered like a bat against my chest. *Oh. I guess I just did.* 'I just meant that if it was the Botox injection that killed Celeste . . . he didn't do it on purpose. I'm sure it was an accident. Who would risk Botox in their neck anyway? Or maybe it wasn't the Botox. She could have been checking to see if Princess, her dog, was in the mudbath room and slipped. Pulled the tub over on to herself. Hit her head. Something accidental like that . . . could have easily happened.' I really needed to shut up. I clamped my lips together and nodded like I had just proven my point.

The detective narrowed his eyes. When he spoke, his tone had grown cold. 'I'm going to need a number where we can reach you.'

'Pick up, pick up,' I whispered into the phone as I stroked Buddha's side. He had napped through all the drama just like I thought he would.

'Hey, Elle. What's up?'

'Hope! Listen, something awful has happened. The police are still here. Celeste Green is dead.'

'What? Dead? Celeste Green? Oh, the lady who started coming to your class to torture her husband's mistress?' Hope asked.

'Yes, her. She's in the mudbath room, face down . . . dead. But that's not the worst part.'

'There's something worse than dead?'

'Most definitely. You have to call Ira and warn him the police will be there to question him soon. Celeste had come here straight from a Botox appointment with Ira before she died.'

Hope went silent for a moment. 'I don't understand. So the

police think Ira had something to do with her death? That's ridiculous.'

'I don't know yet. I just know it's been pointed out to them that's where she was before she died, at her appointment with Ira.' I didn't mention I was the one who had pointed it out. No need for her to be worried and mad at me. 'OK, doing it now. I'll call you back.'

I collapsed back on to the polished wood floor. My hair fanned out into a sweaty, auburn halo around my head. Buddha rolled over and pressed himself against me with all four paws in the air.

'Goofball.' I rested one hand on his belly. The steady heaving of his breath against my ribcage, along with the palm-shaped fan whirling on high above me, started to normalize my heart rate. I took a few slow breaths, moving my mind with the air in and out of my lungs to calm my nerves. It was automatic now.

Poor Celeste. No one deserved to die like that. And what about Princess? Maybe her ex-husband, Robert, would take her. Oh no. That would mean Zebina would be Princess's new mommy. Celeste would roll over in her grave if that happened. I probably should have told the police about her ongoing fight with Zebina. If anyone had a motive for murder, it was Zebina.

My phone vibrated in my hand, and I about jumped out of my skin. It was Hope.

'Hey.'

'I told him. He tried to sound like everything was fine, but I could hear it in his voice, he's worried. He's going to stay there and wait for them. Oh God, Elle, what does this mean. I'm picking you up. When can you leave there?'

I pushed myself off the floor. I still needed to make the rounds and check on the second-floor dogs whose owners were out. It was my shift. There shouldn't be too many, though. 'The police are done interviewing me but give me thirty minutes to make my rounds upstairs.'

'Be there in twenty.'

By the time I finished walking our six canine guests in the 'gardens' out back and stashing Buddha in one of the suites with his lunch, Hope's black Jaguar was waiting behind the security golf carts.

She grabbed me as I slid in and squeezed me tight. 'Thanks, Elle, I'm so scared.'

'Hey.' I patted her back. 'Everything's going to be fine.'

'I don't know.' She sniffed. 'First we lose Jelly-Belly and now this. What if we're cursed?'

'Jelly-Belly had a good long life, Hope. I know you miss him but losing him last month wasn't a curse, it's just life.' Pulling back, I grabbed her face in both hands and stared into her watery eyes. 'And as for this mess, we both know Ira didn't do anything wrong so let's just hold on to that, OK?'

'You're right.' She blew out a deep breath. 'You're so right.' She smoothed down her glossy, brown bob and threw the car into drive. 'Come on. Let's go to the resort spa until Ira calls. I need some therapy.'

I would have settled for a meal, since I had lost my breakfast, and a glass of Cabernet to calm my nerves. But Hope had developed quite the taste for being pampered since marrying Ira. Don't get me wrong, she truly did love the guy. She just enjoyed the perks of his money, too. I couldn't really blame her.

We ended up side by side at The Nail Bar at the Country Club Resort, our feet resting in hot, bubbling water; our backs being massaged and kneaded by the large leather chairs we sat in.

Just throw some toad legs and witch's wart and we could cast a spell to bring back Celeste. Clearly I was getting delirious.

I glanced at Hope. She was clutching her Swarovski crystal-encrusted phone like a lifeline. My heart hurt for her. 'Hey, Hope, don't you guys have an anniversary coming up?'

She nodded absent-mindedly. 'Yeah. We've got a trip booked to Greece at the end of the summer.' She threw me an attempted smile. 'I hope this doesn't mess up our plans.'

'It won't,' I assured her. A petite, young lady with silky, dark hair arrived and lifted one of my feet out of the hot water. Her eyes crinkled in greeting above the mask. I returned the smile. 'I'm sure it'll all get straightened out soon.'

'I don't know.' Hope shook her head. 'What if the police tell him not to leave town?'

I shook my head and gave her what I hoped was an encouraging smile. It felt forced. 'They only do that in movies. Besides, it's not going to do us any good to speculate until we find out more . . . like how she died. We both know her Botox appointment had nothing to do with her death.' *We did, right?* The girl stopped scrubbing my heel vigorously with a pumice stone and glanced up at me. I forced another smile and then turned my attention back to Hope. 'Let's just try to relax until Ira calls, OK?'

She nodded and then checked her phone. I stared at the fish tank in front of us. It ran the entire length of the room and held the most brightly colored fish I'd ever seen, giving some professional aquariums I'd seen a run for their money. I pushed down the panic bubbling its way up into my chest. Maybe it was just the fact I saw my first dead body today, but I didn't have a good feeling about any of this.

'You like the caviar?'

I stared at the girl, my brain trying to switch from death to caviar. 'I'm not hungry, thank you.' I mean, I was hungry, but not for fish eggs. Nice of her to ask though.

Hope chuckled for the first time since she'd picked me up. 'For your feet, Elle. They do a caviar mask and massage.'

Staring at my friend, I tried to process her words but was having a hard time. 'Why?'

She shrugged. 'It has a lot of protein. Supposedly your body absorbs it and plumps up your skin.'

That's it. I was officially confused. 'So, she wants to use fish eggs to give me fat feet?'

Hope stifled a laugh as she nodded.

I turned my attention back to the young girl now massaging my calves with fingers that felt like iron bars. 'No fish eggs. Thank you.'

'Elle?'

I rolled my head toward Hope. 'Yeah?'

Her smile was gone. 'What if it was a mistake? What if Ira did something wrong in the procedure. Even if it was an accident, someone is still dead. He would be devastated, and he'd lose his license to practice. He'd have no future. We'd have no future.'

I reached over and grabbed her hand. 'Don't worry. If you guys lose everything and can't afford to come to these fancy places that give you fat feet with fish eggs, I will torture your feet and paint your toes ugly shades of eggplant for you.'

'Hey!' Hope tried to look indignant through her tears. 'Don't make fun of my purple fetish. Because if you want to go there . . .'

'No.' I held up my hands in surrender. 'You're right. Fetishes should never be brought into a fair fight.' After a few beats, I said, 'In all seriousness though, you don't really believe Ira could make a deadly mistake like that, do you? You know Ira is the best at what he does and obsessive about safety.'

Hope wiped at her eyes and took a deep breath. 'No. You're right. I know Ira isn't capable of being that careless. I'm just worried.' She nodded. 'Thank you, Elle. I don't know what I'd do without you. I'm so glad Dad and I moved to that crappy, little neighborhood of yours in eighth grade.'

This had us giggling more than it should have. One of those kinds of giggle fits that are basically a tension release valve for your soul and involve tears.

Finally I sighed. 'Me too, Hope. Me, too.'

My second foot was getting its coating of NYC Mystic Pink polish when Hope's phone buzzed. I watched her face grow paler as she quietly listened. After a moment she whispered, 'I love you, too.' Then she turned to me, her doe-caught-in-the-headlights eyes glistening with tears.

I leaned toward her. 'What did he say?'

'They told him not to leave town.'

FOUR

By the time Hope had finished her 'therapy' with a good dose of shopping and treated us to a five-course dinner, night had fallen and so had my resolve as she begged me to help get to the bottom of Celeste's death. I wasn't sure how in the world I could help, but I couldn't deny my best friend anything . . . especially with a stomach full of rock oysters and crème brûlée cheesecake. Besides, she was right, I was kind of already in the middle of it seeing as she died at my place of employment.

When she dropped me back off at the Pampered Pup Spa & Resort, the security golf carts were gone. I hoped that meant so was Celeste's body.

Hope grabbed my arm as I opened the car door. Her voice cracked as she held up her pinky. 'Swear you'll help Ira?'

Nodding, I wrapped my pinky around hers. 'Pinky swear.' This had been our ritual since eighth grade and was like a blood oath to us . . . without the need for actual blood. I hugged her. 'Now go get some rest.'

She swiped at a tear that had broken free. 'Thanks, Elle.'

'Hey, Marvin.' I gave the guard a tired wave. 'Did Rita go home for the night?'

He nodded, shifting his substantial weight from one foot to the other. He had to be exhausted. I hoped his shift was over soon. 'Yes ma'am. All clear in there.'

'What about Maria? Was she OK?'

Marvin's cheeks sagged as he nodded. 'She had stopped crying by the time the police were done questioning her. She just needs some time to process it. We all do, I reckon.'

I nodded my agreement. 'So, what did she say happened exactly?'

'Well, apparently she had prepared the mudbath and then gone upstairs to fetch Princess from the suite. When she came back down about ten minutes later, she found Miss Green like

that, with the tub pulled over and mud everywhere. Said she
knew she was already dead by Princess's reaction. The dog
was terrified, jumped out of her arms, slipped and scampered
through the mud to hide in the corner, away from the body.
She screamed and you know the rest.'
    'I do. Unfortunately.' We shared a tired sigh. 'Just going to
pick up Buddha then. You get some rest yourself.'
    'Night, Elle.'
    Buddha was stretched out on the bed amidst bone-shaped
pillows when I entered the room. His stubby little tail was the
only thing that moved when he saw me. The urge to collapse
next to him was strong. But, I had promised Mom I'd stop at
the grocery store on my way home.
    'Come on, lazy bones. Time to go.' I scratched his belly
and then clipped the lead on to his harness. He groaned like
an old man as he hoisted himself off the bed, giving me one
last sad sack look. 'I know. Me too.'
    I stopped by the mudbath room on my way to the elevator,
just out of curiosity. Sure enough, it was cleaned up and already
back to normal. The ladies who worked here were scarily
efficient. I stared at the polished Mexican-tile floor, feeling a
wave of sadness wash over me. No trace of death remained.
No trace of Celeste remained. She was just . . . gone. 'May
you find peace wherever you are, Celeste.' I wondered where
Princess was staying tonight. I'd have to find out tomorrow.
    The elevator doors opened up into the parking garage. The
spa employees had assigned parking spaces and guests could
also pay to have their own space close to the elevator. One
thing I've learned from working on Moon Key: everything
was available for a price.
    During summer days, this popular second level of the
parking garage was usually about half-full. During season all
three garage floors would be packed. During both seasons in
the evening it was dark, eerily quiet, and stale from the lack
of air flow. I hurried Buddha to the end row and my personal
parking space where my rusty, blue VW Bug waited silently
like a discarded remnant of the seventies. I always left the
convertible top down here, not something I dared to do at
home.

The passenger door creaked as I pulled it open and Buddha hoisted himself into the front seat with a grunt. The car noticeably sunk. 'I think we need to cut back on some of those treats, big guy.' I kissed him affectionately on the nose as I buckled him in his harness, not really upset he had put on a few pounds in the last nine months. Much better than the skin and bones he was when I found him five years ago. He glanced up at me with hopeful brown eyes and licked his jaw, recognizing the word 'treat'. I shook my head as I rounded the car to my side. If people only knew how smart dogs really were.

I was on autopilot as I slid into the driver's seat, started the car with a few twists of the key in the ignition and slowly backed out of the space.

Crunch!

I hit the brakes, coming out of my thoughts with a jerk. *Good grief, what now?* I hoped whatever I just ran over didn't puncture a tire. A new tire was not in my budget. Forcing my tired bones back out of the car, I squatted beside the car to check.

What the . . .? Glass? Who would leave glass in the parking garage? My irritation and fatigue were reaching their limits. Lowering myself to my knees, I carefully picked up a piece of the crushed glass flattened by my back tire. A white label held some of the pieces together. As I read it, a cold chill crept up my spine.

'Botulinum toxin type A.' *Botox.*

Standing slowly, I glanced around the parking deck. Somewhere in my tired brain, a connection was trying to form. Celeste. Her Botox appointment before her death. Did this have something to do with it? Finding Botox here tonight seemed too much of a coincidence.

'Mommy will be right back,' I said to Buddha. I could hear him whimper as I quietly padded back toward the elevator, where the rich usually paid for parking. After nearly reaching the elevator I stopped and stared at the sign above an empty space: RESERVED FOR CELESTE GREEN. I'm not sure why my gut had to be right so often. *But, what did it mean?* My tired brain was having trouble with logic. A noise on the deck above startled me, and I sprinted back to the car. Shoving the broken bottle into the glove box, I tore out of there in a puff of exhaust.

Once we were off the ferry, over Memorial Causeway and navigating the familiar streets of downtown Clearwater, I eased off my white-knuckled clutch of the steering wheel and forced myself to relax. At a light, I dug a rubber band out of my bag and pulled my hair off my damp neck and forehead. The air conditioning didn't work in my car so we counted on the movement to cool us off. In the summer months we were pretty much baked. Even in the evening, the humidity made the air feel like its main component was glue. Luckily Buddha didn't complain much. I reached over and scratched beneath his ear, my fingers gentle on the bald spot where mange had left a permanent scar. I was careful to avoid his wide, panting mouth and foamy tongue. The only thing worse than being sticky from the humidity was being sticky from the humidity *and* covered in dog slobber.

'Who's my handsome boy?' I spoke soothingly to him. He really was handsome. His body was all white except for a tan patch of fur right above his tail in the shape of Australia. His face was half white, half tan with expressive brown eyes and ears that flopped over at the tips. Luckily whoever docked his tail as a pup left those ears alone. I loved those ears. The light turned and I pressed the gas, feeling grateful for the millionth time that he was a part of my life.

Pulling into the cracked cement driveway where weeds had found an undisturbed home, I stared at the small, lime green cracker-box house. 'Crap.' I sighed. 'Buddha, you didn't remind me to stop at Publix. Mom isn't going to be happy with us.' I unbuckled both our seat belts. 'Come on, she'll just have to understand it was a rough night.'

'Mom?' I called, throwing my bag and mat by the front door. I could hear the TV on in her bedroom. Buddha went to the kitchen to find his water bowel and left me to fend for myself. I knocked softly on her door and pushed it open a crack, a move I had performed so many times it was pretty much muscle memory. 'You awake?'

'You pick up the groceries?' Her voice rose over the sound of gunfire on TV.

I pushed on the door and walked deeper into the room. A half a dozen empty beer bottles littered her nightstand and an open box of Twinkies sat beside her on the bed. 'I didn't have time to stop tonight, sorry. Something really awful happened at the resort.' I moved closer, ignoring the string of expletives she launched at me. 'A woman died tonight, Mom.' I sat down on the edge of her bed. 'I saw her. She was laying there in our mudbath room. Dead. I had to talk to the police and then . . .' I stopped. I didn't want to get into the whole thing about Ira being involved. She hadn't had anything nice to say about Hope's choice for a husband in the first place. 'There was just a lot to take care of.'

She pulled her gaze away from the TV long enough to throw me a bloodshot look of disgust. 'I knew when you got that job, it'd become more important to you than I am.'

My body jerked as if she'd slapped me. 'How could you say such a thing? That's not fair.' I felt tears prickling my eyes. My emotions were already raw from the day, and I knew I shouldn't be taking the bait, but I couldn't help it. Hurt morphed to anger in two point five seconds. My stomach clenched and blood roared in my ears. I felt all the tension of the day release with a snap. Standing up, I balled my hands into fists. 'Without my job, you wouldn't be able to lay here watching TV all day, drinking beer and eating Twinkies.' I clamped my mouth shut, but it was too late. The words were out. There was no taking them back.

The air in the room seemed to go still. The horror on my mom's face as she turned to me made me want to crawl into a hole. Her cry of despair made Buddha peek his head in the room.

'Is that what you think of me?' she cried, tears already forging tracks down her puffy face. 'I don't need your money!' She was breathing hard now.

I needed to calm her down before she had a heart attack. I collapsed back on to the bed beside her. 'Mom . . .'

'No! You listen to me. I raised you all by myself. I didn't have help from anyone!' Her arms were swinging around now. I backed up so I didn't get clocked . . . accidentally or not. 'No man stuck around to help change your diapers or do your homework.' I didn't feel like this was a good time to point out *she* had never helped me with my homework either. Or that I'd been paying most of the bills since I graduated from high school. I just sat there silently and let her rant. 'So, if you think it's too much to ask of you to help out the woman who gave birth to you and raised you, then by all means, get the hell out and find your own way in the world. I'll be just fine.'

I stared at her in disbelief. 'You don't mean that.'

She crossed her arms. 'I do. I don't need nobody living in my house judging me.'

I stood up like she'd pushed me off the bed. I had reached my limit. 'You're absolutely right, Mom. It's nobody's business but yours if you want to keep yourself holed up in this bedroom, destroying your arteries and liver while the house crumbles around you. Certainly not your daughter's. The only person who has ever stood by you and wanted you to be happy!' I pushed my hands through my hair with a growl of frustration. 'I'm out of here. You know my number if there's an emergency.'

I stormed out, slamming her bedroom door. I heard something hard crash into the door behind my head and cringed. Probably a beer bottle. 'Unbelievable.'

Still in a white hot rage, I threw my clothes into a suitcase. As I squashed them down to make room for underwear and flip-flops, I realized most of my clothes were yoga clothes. *Well, now that I wouldn't be paying for Mom's bills and groceries, I'd be able to get some real clothes.* I stomped to the kitchen to get some grocery bags for my bathroom stuff and stopped at the sight of dishes in the sink and trash on the counter. *Nope. I'm not cleaning that up any more.* I yanked open the cupboard where I kept my stash of health food, tossed the items into two of the bags, pivoted and marched back to finish packing.

With my life stuffed in the tiny back seat and Buddha once again strapped in, though looking a bit confused, I headed back to Moon Key. I'm sure Rita wouldn't mind me crashing in a room with Buddha for a few days until I found a place.

By the time I reached the ferry, the rage had simmered

down. Now I was just hurt. And sad. *What would she do without me?* I straightened my slouched shoulders. She's a grown woman with her own life. It's not my responsibility to buy her Twinkies and wash her dishes. And it was time for me to have my own life, too. Still, I knew the guilt would come, fast and thick . . . it always did.

FIVE

An hour before class was to start I sat in lotus pose hoping to calm the monkey mind that had kept me up until three this morning. I should've gotten the best sleep of my life considering I'd been lying on the most comfortable mattress ever made. In fact, everything in the suite – from the solid gold bath fixtures to the custom furniture – was the best money could buy.

Priscilla Moon, billionaire heiress and dog lover extraordinaire, had spared no expense redecorating and revamping when she bought this island nearly fifty years ago. The story was, while vacationing with her three Yorkshire terriers, she'd been told she couldn't bring them into establishments. So, she simply bought the island and fired everyone, creating a dog-friendly slice of paradise and turning this once posh human-only hotel into the Pampered Pup Spa & Resort.

Paintings of her Yorkies still hang in the lobby today, even though she passed on quite a few years ago. They're a part of the island's history and folklore. I've even heard some of the staff talking about Priscilla and her dogs haunting the Pampered Pup, but I've never personally seen them.

I rolled my shoulders. My back felt fantastic but the argument with Mom intruded and made me tense once again. *Was she right? Was I judging her?* The only thing I'd ever fought with her about before this was keeping Buddha. She had begrudgingly given in then. But, this was different. *Let it go.*

I took a deep breath and tried to follow the air slowly back out of my lungs, but my attention went immediately back to Mom. *Oh god. Was I being judgmental?* I was. Guilt kicked the door open with one giant foot and it slammed me in the face. My eyes opened in defeat. I had no right to judge the way she lived her life. My stomach rolled and clenched. A growl of frustration escaped my lips. I didn't have to be there to watch her self-destruct though. *I can help her without doing that. I'll just mail her some money every month.* I shook my head. This wasn't working.

Untangling my legs, I pushed myself up, giving my back a long stretch on the way. Buddha silently watched me from his own version of a meditative position: sprawled out with his back legs stretched out behind him and his jowls melting on the floor.

'We need to bring some calming energy into this space, Buddha.'

My deceased dog Angel's visits had really brought home the idea of everything being about energy for me. Energy is neither created nor destroyed, just changed. Got it. No science books needed. Though, how it worked was still beyond my comprehension. I grabbed my keys and unlocked the large closet where I kept supplies: extra mats, rolling balls, straps. And in a separate smaller closet were my incense, candles, CDs and various other tools of relaxation. Grabbing my sage smudge stick and a lighter, I proceeded to perform a cleansing ceremony of the studio. Making sure I moved to each corner, I reverently moved the negative energy out of the room with the smoldering bundle. Watching the smoke curl up into the space, expand and then dissipate was a meditation in itself. When that was done, I turned down the lights, lit all the candles around the room and popped in my favorite *Sounds of the Rainforest* CD.

By the time the first clients came through the door, I was seated once again on my mat with a smile and a calm sense of well-being. 'Good morning,' I greeted the ladies easily as they filed through the French doors.

That feeling didn't last long, however, as little Shakespeare the shih-tzu took advantage of Beth Anne turning away to roll out her mat, and began to assert his dominance over Ghost, the passive Weimaraner.

'Shakespeare!' Beth Anne gasped, jumping up to stop the little white and gray dog's vigorous pumping on Ghost's rear end. 'Good Lord in heaven, Sweet pea. Stop that!'

Poor Ghost lay there frozen. The whites of his eyes showing in a way that made him seem both startled and comically horrified. His owner, Violet, had her hands on her hips, shaking her head of fiery-red hair as Beth Anne finally separated the dogs.

Beth Anne's cheeks had pinked and she was breathless. 'Sorry, Violet. He's been extra ornery this morning.'

Violet waved a hand, sending her bracelets clinking together, a smile pulling at the corner of her mouth. 'So was Fredrick. Must be somethin' in the air.'

'Fredrick? Is he your new flavor of the month?' Whitley smirked, casually leaning back on her hands.

Violet shrugged and began to run her hands down Ghost's smooth, gray fur to soothe him. 'I'm not sure he's going to last that long. He's got a very annoying habit of whistling through his nose when he sleeps.'

Whitley rolled her eyes. 'With as many men as you've gone through, Violet, I'm surprised you haven't learned by now that all men do something annoying in their sleep.'

'Well,' Violet smirked back, 'I don't usually let them sleep.'

'Y'all, maybe it's the candles and the romantic lighting in here.' Beth Anne grinned at me as she made Shakespeare lay down on the mat in front of her. She also began to run her hands along the length of his small body in a soothing manner. He barked and tried to get up. 'No. Stay.'

I waited a few minutes and then rang a bell to get everyone's attention. I didn't know exactly how fast news traveled in their circles, but I figured we should say a few words about Celeste since this had been the class she attended for the past two months. When the chatter quieted down, I cleared my throat.

'Everyone, if I could have your attention, those of you who were present for yesterday morning's class know what happened. For the few of you who weren't here, I regret to inform you that Celeste Green was found in the mudbath room here yesterday afternoon. She's . . . well, she's deceased.'

I waited for the buzz of questions, including how it happened, to die down. 'I know it's shocking. I don't really know any more than that. As for how she died, that'll have to be determined by the ME's office. But, I thought we could start class with a moment of silence to remember her and wish her peace wherever she is.' Everyone nodded in agreement. 'So, let's close our eyes.'

The rest of the class went smoothly. It was unusually quiet as everyone worked through their own thoughts and feelings about Celeste's death. Or maybe they were thinking about their next shopping spree, who knew. I chose to think they were affected by the woman's death so she wouldn't be forgotten. Maybe I should make something for the studio in remembrance of her? I got a sudden image of Zebina setting whatever I made on fire. Speaking of Zebina . . . I glanced around the room. She wasn't here today. I guess I shouldn't have expected her to be. Surely Celeste's ex-husband was notified about her death and so Zebina would know. I wondered how she was taking it. Was she glad her arch nemesis was gone? Or did she feel guilty that she treated her so badly? Or maybe . . . she had a hand in Celeste's death. I thought about the smashed bottle of Botox in my glove box.

'OK, everyone, let's do one more happy baby before we end with *savasana*.' I walked around the room as the ladies lay back with their legs in the air and grabbed their big toes. 'That's it. Rock back and forth if you like, massaging your spine.' I liked to be ready to help if a dog decides not to cooperate while their owners are in this vulnerable pose. All but two dogs were resting quietly at the ladies' feet. I let the mini dachshund and young poodle play. They didn't seem to be disturbing anyone. It had been a learning curve for us all, having the dogs in class. Especially me being new to teaching. But, I had to say, it was working out better than I could have hoped. For the first time in my life I felt like I was doing something worthwhile . . . and enjoying the heck out of it.

After class was over I brought out a box of dog toys and dumped them in the middle of the floor so the dogs could have playtime. Some of the women gathered around me while their dogs were occupied to hear more about Celeste's death.

'I really don't know any more, sorry,' I said. I wasn't about to tell them she had come from an appointment with Ira. I'm sure that information would get out soon enough.

'Maybe she finally pushed Zebina over the edge,' Violet offered as she grinned mischievously. 'I've dated three Greeks and they all had fiery tempers. Especially when you're dating them all at the same time.'

That got a few chuckles.

'Did the police think it was natural causes?' Beth Anne asked, holding the end of a stuffed flamingo in a game of tug of war with Shakespeare. 'Or maybe someone did kill her.'

'Killed her? Good grief, Beth Anne.' Violet shook her head. 'I was only joking about Zebina. You need to lay off those murder mystery novels.'

'They didn't say anything about murder.' Nope, that would've been me. I cringed inside. 'I mean, I don't know. Like I said, we'll have to wait and see what the ME says.'

'Was there blood?' Beth Anne asked, undeterred. She was normally a quiet, southern introvert. But, her dream was to write murder mysteries, so I could see the intrigue and possibility making her eyes shine.

'No!' I held up my hands. 'Look, ladies, you're asking the wrong person. I've told you all I know.' I reached down and accepted the tennis ball being pushed into my calf by an eager pug, grateful for the distraction. I tossed the ball and straightened back up.

'Well, I bet if she was murdered, that private investigator she hired to follow her husband around would know something about who'd want her dead,' Whitley added. 'Besides Zebina that is.'

Violet shifted her yoga bag on her shoulder, nodding. 'Yep. He probably knows everything about her. Except the fact she's dead.'

A private investigator? They were right. He'd be a great place to start to find out who would want to harm Celeste. Maybe he could even help figure out who killed her . . . if in fact it was murder. Or maybe I was worrying for nothing and the ME would find out she just had a heart attack or something else less nefarious than murder. But just in case, I decided to pay this PI a visit and see what he knew.

I hurried through my chores at the spa – which included performing capture and release on a spider for Novia, a young maid with a serious case of arachnophobia – so I could try to find the PI before my afternoon class started at four o'clock. Violet couldn't remember his name but said he was the only PI on Moon Key.

After a quick stop to grab a veggie wrap and some fruit for lunch at De Luca Deli, Buddha and I headed out to find him. Didn't turn out to be too hard. There's only one main road that runs around the island, Moon Key Avenue, and only two office complexes on the island. His office turned out to be located in the first one, next to the fire station.

I parked my Beetle between a black Jeep and a white Range Rover, downed the last bite of my wrap with a swig of water and grabbed a banana. I peeled the banana and broke off a piece for Buddha. 'Here ya go.' They were his favorite treat and he swallowed it in one gulp. 'Let's try chewing next time, huh, big guy?' He licked his chops and eyed the rest of my banana with determination. 'Nope, the rest is mine. All right, let's go see what we can find out about Celeste.'

The office door had been painted a bright lemon yellow and sported a shiny, brass handle. All that brightness and shininess, however, hid a stubborn streak. It seemed to be stuck. I shoved Buddha's leash between my knees and the half-eaten banana in my mouth, so I could use two hands to grab the handle and push.

Unfortunately, as I pushed, someone on the other side of the door pulled, the door flew away and I was suddenly staring up at a man. A really, really attractive man with the deepest blue eyes I had ever seen. Time seemed to stand still as we stared at each other from mere inches away. And then I watched in fascination as one corner of his incredibly sexy mouth turned up, producing a dimple.

'Just got the door painted. Sometimes it sticks.' His eyes traveled to my lips and his smirk grew wider.

Then, it hit me. In horror, I realized I still had the banana shoved in my mouth. Slowly, painfully, I reached up and removed it, feeling the heat begin to crawl up my neck and cheeks.

'Sorry, I . . . um . . .' Luckily, at that moment, a large brown dog with white paws and a tail like a whip appeared at our feet. He greeted me and Buddha with a hearty sniffing expedition. Smiling, I scratched under his chin, being careful to keep the banana out of both dogs' reaches. 'Hey there, cutie.' I motioned to my own dog. 'Oh, um, this is Buddha. Is it all right if I bring him in with me?'

The man was still clutching the top of the door with one hand, his other hand planted on his jeans-clad hip. 'Sure, Petey's dog-friendly as you can see. And you are?'

'Yes, I'm dog-friendly. Oh, right.' Mentally smacking myself, I switched the banana to my left hand and held out my right. 'Elle Pressley.'

He slid his hand into mine. The warmth and solidness of his grip brought the heat back to my face.

'Devon Burke. Nice to meet you. Come on in.'

I followed him deeper into the office, scolding myself for the way my body was reacting to him. *Get a grip, Elle. You've seen an attractive man before.* But, I couldn't turn it off. There was something primal about the way this man made me feel . . . alert and drowsy at the same time, aware of my own body and the fact I hadn't bothered to even glance in a mirror before coming. I was suddenly so self-conscious; I almost turned and bolted for the door. Instead I gave in, dumped the banana in a trash can by his desk, admired the smattering of framed photographs on his walls and sat down awkwardly in one of the two white wicker chairs positioned in front of the desk. I began to compulsively twirl a stray wave of hair on my neck. He leaned down to give Buddha a good scratch before he took a seat at his desk, folded his hands in front of him and then stared expectantly at me.

'What can I do for you, Elle?'

You can say my name again. What was that accent? Irish or Scottish? I cleared my throat and forced myself to sound calm. 'I was told Celeste Green was a client of yours?' I ran my hands over my green Lycra yoga pants, wishing he would stop staring at me so intensely. Was he judging me? I'm sure everyone else who entered his office did so in something that didn't come off the Walmart sales rack. Dressing could be considered a sport on Moon Key.

His mouth was set in a grim line, but his eyes were soft and kind. 'I can't talk about my clients, I'm sorry.'

If he were judging me, at least he wasn't treating me with contempt. I returned his kind gaze. 'Even if they're deceased?'

Though his body remained still, his eyes flashed with surprise. Then he shook his head as if clearing his ears. 'Celeste Green is dead?'

I nodded. I had the feeling this man didn't get caught off guard too often. 'I work at the Pampered Pup Spa & Resort where her body was found yesterday.'

Devon Burke leaned back in his chair. 'I've been off the island on business. What happened? Was it a heart attack?'

I tried to keep my attention on his face, but I now had a perfect view of the black dress shirt pulled taut over his muscular chest and arms. I'm sure the concentration it took not to stare made me look constipated. 'I don't know.' My voice cracked. 'She was found face down in our mudbath room.' I knew I had to be up front with him if I was going to get him to help me. 'Here's the problem. She'd just come from a Botox appointment minutes before her death, with Dr Ira Craft. You know of him?'

'Dr Craft? Yeah, sure. I also know Celeste was planning on suing him for a thigh lift she felt made her look worse than before. Why would she go back to the bleedin' man for another procedure?'

I shrugged. 'That's one of the questions. The other question I was hoping you could answer . . . is there anyone you became aware of during your investigation who might want to harm Celeste?' I didn't want to put Zebina's name in his mouth.

He leaned forward once again on the desk and his eyes met mine. 'Do you think she was . . . harmed on purpose?'

I crossed my arms. My foot wiggled nervously. 'I don't know. But, Ira Craft is a friend of mine and the police told him not to leave town. So, I promised his wife, Hope, who's my best friend, I'd help get to the bottom of Celeste's death to clear Ira.' Pinky promised. But I wasn't about to explain to this beautiful specimen of man the significance of a pinky promise.

Devon blew out a breath and ran a hand through his dark, wavy hair. 'Well, she was fond of suing people, so I'm sure there's a long list of folks who wouldn't shed a tear at her death. And I'm sure her ex-husband and his mistress won't be too distraught, either. But, to actually commit murder. That's a whole different ball game.'

'Exactly. He's not someone who would cross that line, even

if angered. That's why, even if she was suing Ira, he shouldn't
be a suspect. Unless . . .'

'Unless what?'

I fought to keep the tears at bay, but I knew my eyes were
glistening with them. I didn't dare blink for fear of sending
them cascading down my face. 'Unless Botox *is* what killed
her.' In my heart I knew Ira wasn't responsible for her death,
but if Botox did kill her, Ira would be the only rational suspect.

Devon stared at me. I could see him chewing on the inside
of his cheek. Then he seemed to come to some conclusion as
his expression softened. 'So what do you need from me?'

My mind flashed on what it'd be like to slip into his arms.
Stop. It. I forced the thought away. 'If it turns out Celeste
didn't die from natural causes or some freak accident . . .
which seems likely considering their warning to Ira not to
leave town, I'd like to hire you to help me find out the truth.'
I mentally smacked myself as I questioned my motives on
this, considering my savings account now needed to be spent
on deposits and rent for a new place. I had been hoping by
staying with my mother and taking care of her, I'd be able to
save enough to buy my own place. That wasn't happening
now. Complete hormone-induced lunacy.

'Even if your friend did have something to do with it?'

My chest tightened but I nodded. I had faith in Ira. 'Yes.'

Devon was silent for a moment as he stared at something
in the corner of the office. When he spoke, his voice was quiet
. . . unsure. 'I understand you want to help your friend, Elle.
But what you're askin' . . . It's really a job for the police.'

It seemed like he wanted to help me, he just needed some
convincing. 'But, you know Clearwater police are busy with
their own crimes off island. We're kind of on our own here
on Moon Key so who better to look into Celeste's death than
the people who knew her? Oh!' I jumped up, suddenly remembering what was in my glove box. 'I have something to show
you. Be right back.'

I was breathless by the time I returned from the car and
handed him the crushed Botox bottle. His fingers brushed mine
as he took it, sending a tingling sensation through my body.
I involuntarily checked his hand for a wedding ring, relieved

beyond reason there wasn't one. Maybe deciding to swear off men had caused some damage to my hormones.

'I found this under my tire in the Pampered Pup parking garage. Celeste had a parking space there just a short distance away from mine.' I began to pace back and forth in front of his desk, to think but also to keep from looking at him and short-circuiting my brain. 'What if someone attacked Celeste when she got out of her car *after* her visit with Ira and injected her with this Botox, killing her and framing Ira?'

I pivoted on my heels to face him and caught his gaze on my legs. And . . . the self-consciousness was back. Tucking a stray wave of hair behind my ear, I slid back on to the chair. 'Tell me what you're thinking. Please.'

He shifted his gaze to the two dogs that had curled up side by side on the rug, then shook his head and turned back to me. He still held the crushed bottle in his hand. 'There are a lot of issues with that . . . theory. Someone would've had to know Celeste, know her schedule and that she was coming from Dr Craft's office. And why would someone go to all the trouble to frame Dr Craft? Seems to me there's easier ways to kill someone if that's your intention. It's an interesting puzzle to be sure. If, in fact, she was murdered.' He paused then rubbed his chin roughly. 'But, to be perfectly honest, I've never investigated a homicide other than . . . well—' his face paled noticeably – 'anyway, mostly my clients just want to catch a spouse cheatin' or catch someone in insurance fraud.' He smiled then, but somehow it only enhanced the pain now burning like a cold, blue fire in his eyes. I wondered what could cause a man to look like that. Did he lose someone? 'But, if indeed someone took her life and my limited experience doesn't bother you, which I'll of course take into consideration by discounting my rate . . . I'm in.'

'You are?' I didn't realize it, but I had already prepared myself for rejection. Him agreeing to help took me completely by surprise.

He chuckled and his expression shifted to amusement. 'Well, we shouldn't start our relationship on a note of doubt, Elle. I'm a man of my word.'

He was teasing me. I tried to fight off the blush by ignoring

that fact. 'Right.' I sat up straighter. 'Right. Good then. Where
do we start?'

'Well.' He pushed himself up from his chair and slowly
stalked around the front of his desk. With a deep exhale, he
leaned against it and crossed his arms and ankles. Once again,
I had to fight to keep my attention on his words. 'I'll start
with a call to the Clearwater medical examiner's office to see
if they've found cause of death. Maybe it was natural causes,
and you won't need my services. But, if you do, first thing
I'll need you to show me is where the body was found. Also, I'll
need to figure out what Celeste did in the last twenty-four
hours, where she went, who she was with. I have a copy of
her usual schedule, so if anything is out of the ordinary, I'll
know.'

'And what can I do in the meantime?'

'You can start by setting up a meeting for me with Dr Craft
so I can hear his side of things, especially if he knew Celeste
was planning a lawsuit.' He reached behind him on the desk
and then held out a card. 'One thing, Elle. If I find any evidence
that Dr Craft did in fact have something to do with her death,
I'll not be coverin' it up. Clear?'

'Yes. I wouldn't ask you to.' I stood, covered the ground
between us in a few strides and took the card from his hand.
It was plain black with 'Devon Burke PI' and a phone number
on it in block silver letters. When I looked up, he was watching
me with that intensity again, his eyes full of questions.

I pulled my own gaze out of his grip by looking down at
the card. 'Thank you, Mr Burke. For agreeing to help.'

'Devon, please.' His expression had grown serious as he
held my gaze.

'Devon.' I was fighting to pull myself away from him. Did
the man possess supernatural gravity? I had to get out of there
so I could think straight. 'Thank you, Devon. I'll call you after
I talk to Ira.' I broke our eye contact and looked at our dogs
curled up together. 'You don't see many mutts on Moon Key.'
When I realized how rude that sounded I jerked my gaze back
to Devon. 'I mean, he's a beautiful dog. It's just most people
here buy designer dogs . . . purebreds. He really is lovely.'
The heat was crawling back up my neck.

The dimple appeared beside the corner of Devon's mouth as he smirked again. 'You don't see many women who get easily flustered here either.'

I couldn't help but laugh then. 'Touché.' *Time to go.* 'Come on, Buddha. Say goodbye to your new friend.'

SIX

During the short drive back to the Pampered Pup, I called Hope to tell her about my meeting with Devon Burke. The sky was a pure blue with a smattering of wispy clouds like pale commas hanging in mid-air. Thin palm trees lined the perfectly paved main road around the island. The sun blazed down on us like it intended to fry us for lunch. I blamed this for my current agitated state.

'He wants to get together with you and Ira. Do you think Ira will cooperate?'

'I don't know, Elle. You know how he feels about private investigators. He's had nothing but bad experiences with them.' Hope sounded exhausted. I waited for her to think. 'I have an idea! We're going to the Thirtieth Annual Pause for Paws charity auction Saturday night. I didn't want to go, but Ira says we need to keep our lives normal right now. Why don't you bring this PI there as your date? That way Ira has to talk to him.'

'My date?!' My heartbeat picked up along with a flood of anxiety. 'I . . . I can't ask him to be my date, Hope.'

'Why not? It's a perfect solution. Getting them together to talk without making a big deal about a meeting and also, it's for a good cause. It's settled. I'll get you two tickets.' I started to protest, but she cut me off. 'Nope. This time it's to help Ira. You're not turning me down.'

I groaned. She'd been trying to get me to go to this event for the past two years. But, at fifteen hundred dollars a ticket, I couldn't afford it, and I had refused to let her pay for my ticket. 'I don't know, Hope.'

I pulled into the parking garage, barely noticing the speed bumps that always rattled my teeth and made me fear for my old car becoming a pile of parts right there on the spot. *I couldn't just ask a man like Devon Burke to be my date. That would be like throwing myself at him. I needed an excuse Hope would understand.* 'I don't have anything to wear.'

'That's not a problem. We're the same size in dresses. Come over tonight and you can raid my closet. I've gotta go. See you around sevenish.'

'Hope?' She had hung up. I pulled into my parking space and stared at Buddha. 'She hung up. How am I supposed to call Devon and ask him to be my date?' Buddha's brown eyes watched me intently. Then he licked my elbow. I sighed. 'You're right. I have to remember it's not an actual date. It would just be to get him in the same room with Ira. OK. I can do this.'

I pulled the black card out of my bag and dialed the number.

'Devon Burke.'

The sound of his voice made my heart skip. I closed my eyes and tried to make my voice sound calmer and more confident than I felt. 'Devon, it's me, Elle.'

'Missed me already have you?'

'No! I mean, no that's not why I'm calling.' I clamped my mouth shut as I heard his low chuckle. I had to stop entertaining him with my nervousness. 'I just spoke with Hope and she thinks it would be a good idea to meet them at the Thirtieth Annual Pause for Paws charity auction this Saturday night. Ira's not a fan of private investigators so she didn't want to make a big deal out of the meeting with you. She said she can get us tickets. What do you think?'

Silence ticked by for an uncomfortably long time. I bit my lip to keep from blurting out how this definitely would not be a date. I was definitely not asking him out on a date.

'OK. It's a date. Where and what time should I pick you up?'

Did he just say, 'It's a date?' Just answer him, Elle. 'Eight o'clock at the Pampered Pup?'

'Fine. See you then.'

Groaning, I let Buddha out of the car and we made our way to the elevator. There were so many emotions running through me, I couldn't tell if I was excited or horrified. I hadn't found myself attracted to anyone in ten years, let alone this flustered by someone. How was I supposed to spend an evening next to this man without making a complete fool of myself?

*　*　*

'OK, try this one.' Hope emerged from her mall-sized closet holding a glass of white wine in one hand and a sea-foam green beaded gown in the other. 'It'll bring out those sinfully beautiful green eyes of yours.'

I rolled said eyes. I was perched on her bed with my own half-empty glass of wine and a pile of discarded gowns around me. Sliding off with a sigh, I took the gown from her and held it up in front of her full-length mirror. I was completely over trying on dresses and had decided showing up naked would be preferable to trying on one more. 'It looks like it'll be too tight.'

'Stop whining. And it's form fitting. Try it. Last one, I promise.'

I shot her a look of doubt and then resignation. 'Fine.' I sat my glass down on the edge of her dresser and then unzipped the back of the dress, being careful not to catch any of the delicate beading in the zipper.

'So what's he like?' Hope plopped on the bed and watched as I slid the weighty dress over my head.

'Who?' I managed through the heavy fabric over my face.

'Your date.' I freed my head and shot her an annoyed look in the mirror. She laughed. 'Fine. What's your non-date date like?'

'He's . . .' *Gorgeous. Charming. Dangerous.* 'I don't know. Just a guy.'

'Whoa!' Hope slid off the bed and sauntered over to stand behind me. 'Elle, are you blushing? This guy is hot, isn't he? Like Hayden Sykes hot?'

Hayden Sykes was the guy in our high school every girl wanted. *Devon was way hotter.* I glanced at my face in the mirror. *Crap.* I was furiously blushing. But . . . wow. I let my gaze fall. This dress was amazing. It fit me like a glove, accentuating my yoga-induced tight core and curved hips. And I had cleavage. It was a miracle dress.

'Holy sweet mother of pearl, Elle. *That* is the dress!' She swept my layered, auburn waves into a quick up-do and held them above my head. 'Just look at your eyes. I told you it would bring out those green cat-eyes of yours. Perfect. You'll knock his socks off.'

'That's not why we're doing this.' I shook my head as she completely ignored my protest and went to dig around in her jewelry, mumbling about having the perfect earrings. Sometimes I wished she didn't know me so well.

SEVEN

Luckily, Rita had no problem with me staying in a suite with Buddha until I found a place. She had a tough exterior, but was a softie at heart. So, Saturday night I stood out in front of the Pampered Pup in the green, beaded gown; my hair piled into a sophisticated updo and studded with tiny emerald pins courtesy of Hope's hairdresser. The nude strappy shoes Hope had paired with the dress were higher than I was used to, so I implored to the universe's sense of empathy to help me stay upright tonight.

I was also trying not to touch my face. The women at the spa had been instructed by Hope – who had surprised me and prepaid for everything – to give me a full makeover. An order they really took to heart. I was treated to a makeover that involved plucking my brows, curling my eyelashes, lining my lips and eyes and applying various containers of color and powders to my face until I didn't even recognize myself. My usual beauty routine involved two items: soap and sunscreen, which, upon hearing this, sent my make-up artist into a tizzy. I was given tiny sample packs of cleanser, toner and moisturizer with an admonishment to stop using soap.

It was as I stood there – blinking furiously to keep from rubbing at my eyes, which itched from the heavy layers of mascara – that a black Jeep suddenly whipped around the fountain and pulled up to a stop. Devon and I stared at each other. Feeling a bit like Cinderella must have felt when seeing her magical coach for the first time, I approached the Jeep's passenger door.

'Hang on.' Devon slid out and came around to open the door for me. Dressed in a well-fitting black tux, his face shaved smooth and smelling like man heaven, he grinned down at me. 'You look beautiful.'

My gaze followed the words from his mouth. Being so close, I could see a tiny scar on his upper lip. I fought the urge to reach up and touch it. Instead I cocked an eyebrow and let my eyes meet his. 'You look surprised.'

His smile widened as he opened the door for me to climb in. 'Stunned is more like it.' He held out a hand to help me up into the Jeep. 'Oh, hope you don't mind the top off. Sorry, I didn't think about your hair being blown about.'

This made me laugh. 'No, it's fine.' I slid my hand in his and stepped up as graceful as the unfamiliar shoes would allow. 'I prefer the open air.' I actually was grateful. I already felt overheated in his presence. I didn't need to be shut in a tight space with him. As he hopped back up into the driver's seat, I thought about his comment. Wait a minute . . . Stunned? Did he say stunned? Good grief. I must have looked like a hot mess when we met in his office.

Devon navigated the short fifteen-minute drive to the Country Club Resort at a speed of twenty-five miles an hour. I presumed to keep my hair from 'being blown about'. It was fine with me, though. I wasn't in any hurry to get there. The warm summer air and stars twinkling above made me sigh with gratitude. I felt little tendrils of my expensive updo being pulled free by the breeze but I didn't care.

Devon cleared his throat. 'So, what is it you do at the Pampered Pup, Elle?'

I turned to him and studied his profile. Even shaved smooth, his strong, square jaw just screamed 'rugged'. Self-consciously, I adjusted the spaghetti strap on Hope's gown. I realized I'd been dreading this question. This is where I wished I had some fancy job with some fancy degree that would impress him.

Mustering enough fake confidence as I could, I answered. 'I teach doga classes, mainly. And help out around the spa when needed. It's sort of a family environment there.'

He stopped at a red light and met my eyes. There was no judgment, only curiosity. I felt the rest of the world fade around me. His gaze had real power. It pulled me into him and cracked me open at the same time. I felt vulnerable and a bit terrified.

'What's doga?' It was asked as a simple question, no snark, which I appreciated.

Feeling more at ease, I said, 'It's yoga but my clients bring their dogs to class with them. Yoga's not just for people, you know.' I let myself smile, really smile because his attention was making me giddy, like I'd already had a few glasses of wine.

His gaze fell to my mouth as he grinned. 'No. I didn't know.'

A golf cart shaped like a Mercedes tapped what sounded like a clown horn behind us. Devon's eyes went to the rear-view mirror and he held up a hand in apology, resuming the drive.

'So, what made you get into the private investigating business?' I asked.

I shifted in my seat to face him because the silence had suddenly grown heavy. I watched as he gripped the steering wheel so tight his knuckles turned white. I wanted to reach out and take his hand, caress it and release whatever tension had just consumed him by my question. Instead, I waited.

'My parents had a winter place here. My mum fell in love with this little sandbar. I think it was the privacy afforded her here.' His lip twitched and he sighed. 'Five years ago, they were involved in a boating accident. They were both thrown from the boat and drowned.'

'Oh god, Devon, I'm so sorry.' I felt terrible for asking.

'Thank you. There's a fella in prison for it. Supposedly a drunk boater. His sentence is almost up, so he'll be free to do as he pleases while my parents . . .' His voice trailed off.

'What do you mean supposedly?' I asked. 'You don't think he was drunk?'

He glanced at me. 'Well, he may well have been drinkin' but it was no accident.'

I saw the pain in his tight-set jaw. I felt both surprised at his belief his parents were murdered and empathetic at how horrible losing both parents like that must be. 'Are you saying you think someone . . . killed them on purpose?'

He nodded slowly. 'I was working as a travel photographer so I was in Laos when it happened. I dropped everything and came here. There are just some things that don't add up. This fella who rammed their boat, he's got ties to Dublin. Too much of a coincidence for me, especially considering some of the things going on with my da's business right before their death.

Plus, witnesses say there was another boat that left the scene, but the driver who was charged denied it. I got Clearwater PD to open an investigation and tried to help out as much as I could. There just wasn't any evidence from the scene to suggest anything other than an accident. So I went through the two-year program to become a PI, hoping it would give me more access to information. It's helped me make some connections.' He sighed. 'Anyway, my parents were my first case.' He glanced at me and shrugged. 'Unsolved so far.'

That just deepened the growing sense of respect I had for this man. He definitely didn't let anything stand in his way. And he took those amazing photos in his office? There had to be a major flaw somewhere, I was just blinded by hormones at the moment. I didn't know if I should pry. Would it be rude to ask questions about his parents? Maybe he'd like to talk about them, to remember them. I took a chance. 'What were your parents like?'

The slight smile my question received made me glad I asked. 'Da was a building and racehorse tycoon from Dublin. He was a quiet man. No nonsense, spoke his mind sort. Ma . . .' The pain turned to sadness as his expression softened. 'Ma was brilliant in investing and bloodstock. Her da was a famous jockey, that's how they met. She was sharp and fearless and fair. Always fair. The kindest woman I've ever known.' We were pulling up to the line for the resort valet. He threw the Jeep into park and turned to me, his eyes a storm of emotion. His hand reached up and fingered a stray wave by my cheek. Tucking it softly behind my ear, he said, 'Her hair, it was the same color as yours.' His hand brushed my cheek. His gaze caressed my face, when it met my eyes, an almost unbearable ache began at my core.

Whoa. What was happening? Was it possible that he felt the same attraction I did? There was suddenly something I needed to know. 'So, if you find out who killed your parents, would you go back to being a travel photographer?'

He smiled. 'Traveling's in my blood, Elle. Seeing and recording the world, its beauty and its dark side. I do miss it.'

My heart dropped like a stone. 'Yeah, dumb question,' I mumbled.

'Can you pull up, sir?' The valet's voice came from behind me.

My heart was still heavy when the valet opened the door for me. Even though we were under the open night sky, I felt in need of air. Then Devon was there, holding out his arm and I took it, slipped my hand around his bicep and the world titled right side up again. This fact left me uneasy. This man I barely knew should not have such an effect on my world.

As we approached the glass doors, someone stepped right into my path. My face hit a solid chest and I bounced off it with a small squeak.

'Elle!' The large blockade in a blue security uniform said cheerily. 'I don't usually see you at these events. Wow, you look like an angel. How are you?'

I had let go of Devon's arm to check my throbbing nose. I glared up at Alex Harwick. 'Well, I was fine,' I mumbled. Deciding my nose wasn't broken, I glanced over at Devon, who was watching Alex with a certain stillness that reminded me of a predator staring at their prey.

'Alex, this is Devon . . .'

'Burke. Yes, we know each other.' Alex's eyes narrowed as he looked from me to Devon. Neither one of them said a word.

Not being good with uncomfortable silence, I grabbed Devon's arm. 'Oh, there's Hope. Good to see you, Alex.' I pulled Devon forward through the doors, tripping myself in the process. Devon caught me before I hurt my nose again, and we shared a conspiratorial smile.

'Not a big fan of Alex Harwick either?' I asked.

'That's one way to put it.' His blue eyes darkened. There was definitely history there. I'd have to find out later what exactly was between the two men. Tonight we had a different agenda.

We moved deeper into the crowded lobby, and I spotted Hope making a beeline for us.

'Elle!' she squealed. 'You look like a goddess! Doesn't she look like a goddess?' She was shaking Devon's hand vigorously and grinning at him like an idiot. 'Hi, I'm Hope.'

I tried to give her the eyes . . . the ones that said: Chill out, you're being an over-the-top-psycho best friend. But, she wasn't paying a bit of attention to me. I needed to get her away from him pronto.

'Devon Burke. Nice to meet you.' He shot me a questioning look as she kept a hold of his hand, scrutinizing him like a piece of artwork.

'Hope, come to the ladies room with me.' I grabbed her hand. 'Go on in, Devon. We'll find you.'

'Oh. My. God!' Hope squealed at me as the door closed. Startled, an elderly lady who'd been washing her hands at the sink, glanced over at us. I mouthed 'sorry'. Hope was too busy gaping at me to notice.

'Elle Pressley, you were totally holding out on me. That man is one gorgeous hunk of flesh! Those shoulders! And those eyes! Oh my lord in heaven, those are eyes a woman could lose herself in. I didn't see a ring either, Elle,' she sang.

'Shhhh!' I pulled her to the far corner of the bathroom. 'Would you please not start your matchmaking tonight? Please! This is a business deal. We are here to help Ira, so don't make this into a thing for me, OK?'

She crossed her arms under her perfect cleavage, one of the perks of being married to a plastic surgeon . . . no more bra stuffing. We had some pretty embarrassing locker room moments in eighth grade due to this practice.

'You're no fun. You know I need a distraction. I have to keep my mind busy, or I'll go crazy. Besides, what's the problem? Is there something you don't like about him?' Her brow shot up accusingly. 'You don't like his sexy Irish accent?'

'No,' I groaned. Feeling deflated, I leaned against the wall. 'I mean yes. He's perfect. I just feel out of control around him. Like I lose myself completely. And I refuse to end up like my mother. I'm not losing myself for any man.'

'Oh, Elle.' Hope pulled me into her arms. 'You could never end up like your mother.' She pulled back and grinned at me, her eyes full of empathy. 'You hate Twinkies.'

Feeling suddenly emotional, I wiped the dampness under my eye with an index finger and gave in to a chuckle. 'There is that.'

She grabbed my hands and made me look at her. 'Seriously, you can't keep running away from every eligible bachelor who comes across your path. Especially one who looks like he just stepped out of foreign cologne commercial.' Sighing at my lack of response, she held up her hands. 'Fine. I won't interfere in your love life any more. Or lack thereof.' She moved to the mirror and dabbed at the corners of her mouth. It was unnecessary, her lipstick always stayed in place. 'But, if you don't go for this one, I'm going to seriously question your sanity.'

I moved to stand beside her and wiped the smeared mascara from beneath my right eye. This is why I, on the other hand, didn't wear make-up. Keeping it in place was definitely a talent I didn't possess. Our eyes met in the mirror and I shrugged. 'I already do that daily.'

EIGHT

'Looks like Georgia has found her target for the evening.' Hope shot me an amused grin after scanning the ballroom. I followed her gaze and couldn't help but smile. Georgia Waters – Moon Key's most notorious, sculpted-to-perfection female player – had Devon cornered between the bar and a giant cardboard cut-out of Reed Spelling, the Pause for Paws founder. 'You better go help him out, Elle. I'll find Ira.'

Help him? I don't think so. This was going to be too entertaining to stop. Georgia didn't get her reputation as a 'man-eater, southern belle style' for nothing. I couldn't wait to see how Mr Smooth handled this.

I sauntered over to the bar slowly, being careful not to slip on the polished wood floor in these ridiculously high heels. 'White wine, please.'

I was only about ten feet from Georgia. She had her back to me, which was completely exposed due to a neckline that plunged low enough to make one question if she wore underwear. I had to pull my eyes from the yellow rose tattoo where her underwear line should have been. Devon, however, was staring straight at me. I held up my glass to him in silent salute, making no move toward him.

His eyes narrowed for a moment, became calculating and then he broke out in a laugh, as if whatever Georgia had just said was the funniest thing on earth. I watched in utter fascination as he turned on the charm, beaming himself at the woman like he was light itself. Georgia had her hand resting lightly on his chest, her ample cleavage pressed into him as she leaned in and whispered something in his ear. Devon's attention was suddenly on me again, holding my gaze over her head. He let a slow smile spread across his lips and whispered something back to her. Peals of soft laughter poured from her and hit me like a cold bucket of sweet tea.

That was it. My body (or was it my heart?) overrode my
idea of watching him squirm, and I found myself moving to
stand beside them. Devon's smile morphed into one of barely
concealed triumph. Georgia eyed me suspiciously, sliding her
hand down to rest on Devon's hip.

'Elle Pressley.' Her voice dripped with southern sugar but
her deep blue eyes were not so inviting.

'Georgia.' I purposefully let my gaze fall to her hand and
then met her stare head on.

'Hi Elle. I wondered where you'd gone off to. You two
know each other then?' Devon sounded amused.

Georgia looked up at Devon and then back at me, getting
the message. She removed her hand but didn't put any distance
between them. 'Yes,' Georgia drawled, eyeing me like she was
seeing me for the first time. Seeing me as competition for the
first time was more like it. 'Elle. So good to see you again.
How is that charming little dog thing you do going?'

Wow. Straight for condescension. 'Great. It's going great.
You should come try out a class, Georgia. It's really beneficial
to dogs.'

She flashed her bleached smile at me. 'I don't own a dog
at the moment. I'm way too busy.'

I know. I pressed my lips together and forced a smile. She
wasn't worth it. I moved my attention to Devon. 'There's
someone I'd like to introduce you to.'

'Certainly.' He motioned with his bottle of Guinness for me
to lead the way. 'Lovely chat, Miss Waters.'

'Call me Georgia,' she threw at him as we walked away.

There were hundreds of people there. Luckily the auction
tables seemed to be attracting most of the tux- and gown-clad
swarm. Our search for Ira was still interrupted along the way
by a few of my doga clients. Whitley, Violet and Beth Anne
were there, along with a half-a-dozen others. It was nice to
see them all sans fur-covered yoga clothes. I introduced them
to Devon and had to practically pry him back out of their
hands as they ogled, caressed and flirted with him.

As we moved through the crowd once again I shook my
head. 'I would say sorry, but I have a feeling you were enjoying
that. You should probably check your pockets for dollar bills.'

I smiled up at him as we searched for Ira. I was five foot nine counting the two inches of heel and still had to look up at him. That was another check in the pro box.

Yeah, the wine was hitting me. All that practice of monitoring my thoughts flew right out the window in the presence of Devon Burke. They were taking a good romp in the mud, and I was powerless to stop them. I tried to give myself a pep talk. *Don't be so hard on yourself. Obviously you're not the only one he has this effect on so let yourself feel what you're feeling and then let it go.* Letting go. That was a hard one for me.

Devon chuckled beside me. 'Your clients are very . . . friendly.'

I thought about Celeste Green. 'I'd say passionate is probably a better word.' I pointed in front of us. 'There they are.'

We approached Hope and Ira, who were in conversation with another couple. Ira smiled as we drew near, but it didn't reach his eyes, which sagged with dark circles. He really didn't look good.

'Hey, Elle.' Hope clinked her wine glass with mine and gave me a look that said she needed rescuing from the conversation. 'Ira, Mr and Mrs Berry, this is Elle's date, Devon Burke.'

They all exchanged pleasantries as I glared at Hope. She purposefully didn't look at me. I couldn't believe she used the word 'date'. I took a big slug of wine, emptying my glass.

'Hi, Elle . . . Mr Burke, nice to meet you,' Mrs Berry said, slipping her arm around her husband's waist.

I went in for the kill. 'Hope, I forgot to mention what a lovely *purple* gown that is.'

She swiveled her attention to me with a tight smile, knowing me too well to miss the payback for the date comment. 'It's lavender and thank you.'

Mrs Berry caught the tension between us, which was the second reason for my comment, though not as satisfying as the first. 'Excuse us. We'll leave you youngsters to talk. We're going to go check out the silent auction items.'

Before I could do anything to start a conversation between Ira and Devon, Bonnie barreled up and stood seething beside me in a lovely pale-yellow gown. Her focus was fixed on Ira.

'How dare you show your face here. I know what you did, Ira Craft!' Bonnie spat at him. 'And don't think you're going to get away with it.'

Ira paused mid drink, his pale face now blooming with red splotches. 'Sorry?'

Bonnie moved her hands to her hips. 'Yes. You will be!'

'Bonnie . . .' I rested a hand on her arm. 'I know you're upset, but I don't think this is the right time for this.'

She turned to me, her eyes swimming in unshed tears. 'You're right, Elle. Tonight is about helping the animals. But—' she jabbed a finger into Ira's chest – 'you are the real animal. I know you killed Celeste and the police are going to figure it out soon enough.'

Hope stepped in front of her horrified husband. Since I knew her so well, I could see the tension in the way she held herself, but she kept her voice low and calm as if she were speaking to a spooked animal. 'Bonnie, I don't know why you think Ira would've hurt Celeste but he didn't, I assure you. And you're right, the police will prove that soon enough.'

Bonnie made a growling sound, turned on her heels and stomped away. We all silently watched her disappear into the crowd.

Now seemed a good time to bring up the real reason Devon was here. I stepped over to stand beside Ira. When I placed my hand on his arm, he startled. Hope slid her hand into his and nodded to me in support. I waited for an announcement someone was making over the loudspeakers to end before I spoke.

'Ira, I have a confession. Devon Burke isn't really my date. He's a private investigator. I brought him here tonight in hopes that you would talk to him, so he could help prove your innocence.'

Ira's expression shifted from the shock of Bonnie's confrontation to confusion as he eyed Devon. And then the unmistakable blush of anger. His eyes fluttered closed, and he downed the rest of his drink, the ice clinking against his teeth.

I had never seen him angry before and it unnerved me a bit that I was the cause of it. My stomach clenched under my gown as I waited for his reaction. Hope and I shared a concerned glance.

Finally, he opened his eyes and focused on Devon. 'I appreciate the offer, Mr Burke, but I *am* innocent so I don't need anyone to *prove* it.'

Devon rocked back on his heels. He had one hand shoved in his pocket, the other holding the beer bottle at his side. He nodded at Ira and spoke softly. 'Actually I think you do. I spoke to the Clearwater medical examiner's office this mornin'. They've determined cause of death for Celeste Green.'

I felt us all collectively holding our breath. Ira lifted the hand that Hope wasn't clutching. 'Well?'

Devon's eyes flashed with emotion, betraying his calm demeanor. 'Botox . . . to the neck.'

Ira's eyes grew wide. He let himself fall back against the wall. 'But . . . that's impossible.'

'Yes, well I was skeptical, too, but they assured me it's quite possible. The official cause of death is asphyxia, as the muscles needed for breathing were paralysed by the toxin.' Devon took a slug of beer. Still watching Ira carefully he added, 'And I would suggest contacting your lawyer. They'll probably be coming at you with an arrest warrant in the next few days.'

NINE

We were seated at a round dinner table, quiet and in shock from Devon's news. Unfortunately, it didn't help that Zebina and Robert Green were two of the people who'd been seated at our table. Zebina acted friendly enough, but Robert eyed Ira wearily. I knew Robert and Ira had been golf buddies, so I was a bit surprised he wasn't being supportive of Ira right now. Of course, it was his ex-wife that had died. Still, did he really consider Ira capable of murder?

A thought wiggled its way into my wine-soaked brain: was it a coincidence Celeste was killed so soon after their divorce went through? What if Robert didn't want to pay Celeste alimony? Is he capable of something as devious as blackmailing Ira to get Celeste out of the way? If so, maybe now Robert was afraid Ira might spill the beans about his involvement to the police if Ira gets arrested for her death. Maybe that's where the tension between the two men was coming from.

I glanced at Ira, who was staring into his drink, deep in thought. Hope had clutched on to his arm and was whispering something to him. No, I just couldn't bring myself to believe Ira was capable of murder. I was usually a pretty good judge of character, and nothing I'd ever seen in Ira suggested murderer. Robert, on the other hand, I had no idea what he was capable of.

'Ladies and gentlemen, our kind servers will start to bring dinner out in a moment but before that happens, please welcome our founder, Reed Spelling, who'd like to say a few words.'

Applause broke out as a tall, salt-and-pepper haired man took the podium.

Devon leaned into me. 'Going to the bar, can I get you a refill?'

I closed my eyes against the sensation of his breath on my ear. 'Yes, please.'

As the servers brought around the salads, and Reed Spelling gave his speech about all the fabulous things donated, encouraging us to walk around and bid on them, I scanned the ballroom. I had a pretty good view of the bar, and I didn't see Devon there in the cluster of gowns and tuxes. *Maybe he went to the restroom?* And then I spotted him, sitting at a table talking to Bonnie. Actually, she seemed to be doing the talking while he listened. After a few moments, he shook her hand, picked up our drinks and headed back to our table.

'Bonnie was fairly close with Celeste,' I said as Devon handed me the wine and slid back in his seat. 'She's just upset. You can't take what she said to heart.'

'Just doing what you're paying me to do. Investigate.' He clinked my glass with his Guinness bottle. 'Slainte.'

Ouch. Right. I was paying him to be here. This wasn't a date. As much as I kept reiterating that to Hope, I seemed to lose sight of it somewhere between feeling jealous of him making Georgia laugh and my body's reaction to his breath in my ear. I felt my face grow warm. There was nothing between us but an agreement. An exchange of money for services. Did he say that to remind me of that fact? *You're such an idiot, Elle. Keep it professional.*

Straightening my back, I scooted to the right a bit on my chair, putting more distance between us. Just an inch. But still, it helped that I could no longer feel his body heat.

A server put down a round of Caesar salad in front of us all. I concentrated on crunching the lettuce to keep my humiliation at bay. Luckily, the MC started calling out some ticket numbers and giving out door prizes, otherwise the silence at our table would've been awkward.

By the time our respective chicken, fish or vegetarian dinners came, Devon had expertly maneuvered himself into a friendly conversation with Zebina. I wondered how long she would be smiling at him if she knew he was the PI who'd spilled the beans about her affair with Robert to Celeste. Glancing over at Hope, I noticed her and Ira were watching the exchange with interest, also.

'Next time you go, you must try Chez Casimir. They simply

have the best cheese plate in Paris. Right, darling?' Zebina turned to Robert.

Robert nodded, seemingly timid about joining the conversation. He wasn't the only one. Any talk of traveling the world made me feel inadequate and envious. The furthest out of Clearwater I'd ever been was right here on Moon Key.

'I'm Devon, by the way.' He lifted out of his seat a bit to offer his hand.

'Zebina.' Her dark eyes narrowed. 'Where do I know you from? You look very familiar.'

'It's a small island, Zebina. I'm sure we've been in the same place at one time or another. Lovely name, by the way. Greek?'

I hid a smile behind my napkin and made a mental note of his expert dodge for when I was looking for a straight answer from him.

'Yes. Oh, I'm being rude.' She flicked her dark hair behind a bare shoulder and rested a hand on Robert's arm. 'This is my fiancé, Robert Green.'

The two men nodded over the span of the table and then Devon said, 'Green? Any relation to that woman, Celeste Green, who died at the Pampered Pup Resort?'

I watched as Robert stiffened and glanced at Ira. Zebina's gaze fell to stare at her still full plate.

Robert's voice was thin and strained when he answered. 'Yes. She was my ex-wife.'

'So sorry for your loss.' Devon suddenly looked very focused on the couple, all sense of light conversation gone. 'Even though you weren't married any longer, there's still history and love there, I'm sure.'

Robert nodded. 'Of course. Yes, it was very tragic.'

Devon raised his beer bottle. 'To Celeste, then.' Everyone lifted their glasses except Zebina. This seemed to amuse Devon. 'May she have eternal life in the hearts of those who loved her.'

'Amen.' I clinked my wine glass with Devon's bottle and then reached across to clink Ira's. Ira's eyes were glassy and his mouth turned up a little into a sad smile. My heart sank even further.

When everyone went back to finishing their dinners, I leaned over to Devon. 'We should tell Ira about the Botox bottle I ran over in the parking garage.'

He nodded. 'We will.' Then he slipped his arm around the back of my chair and leaned into my ear. My pulse did something that felt dangerous to my health. 'Zebina is weary of me now. She keeps glancing at me. I think she may be trying to place where she's seen me before, so we need to make sure she believes we're here on a date.'

I faked a laugh and pushed him away so I could breathe for real. Handing him my empty glass I said louder than I normally would, 'Would you get me a refill please, darling?'

Taking my glass, his eyes sparkled as he held my gaze and lifted my hand. Gently brushing his lips against my skin he answered, 'Anything you wish.'

I took a shuddering breath in as he left the table. That's it. The man is evil. He knows exactly what he's doing to me and enjoying every second of it. We had to figure out who killed Celeste quickly before his charm sent me into cardiac arrest.

I made the mistake of glancing at Zebina, who was grinning at me like we shared a secret. I managed a smile and shoved a forkful of broccoli into my mouth.

After dinner a band took over, giving everyone ample time to bid on the silent auction items now that we'd all been plied with delicious food and, more importantly, alcohol.

'We're going to take off, Elle.' Hope's face was pale and she was scratching her left forearm, something she always did when she was upset. 'Ira didn't realize people would actually believe he had something to do with Celeste's death. He's pretty upset. I think more so about that than the possibility of being arrested.'

'I understand, Hope. I'm so sorry.' I gave her a hug. 'Is he going to let Devon help him?'

She glanced over at Ira waiting by the exit for her. 'I don't think so.'

'Hang on.' I motioned for Devon. When he approached, I whispered, 'We have to tell Ira about the bottle now. Before they leave.' He nodded his agreement. I turned to Hope. 'I think we have some information that may change his mind.'

We all approached Ira and walked with him into the less crowded lobby. I turned my back to the front doors so I didn't accidentally catch Alex's eye.

'Ira, I know you don't like the idea of hiring a private investigator to help you, but I found something in the parking garage at the Pampered Pup I think really needs investigating. Something I think will prove you didn't have anything to do with Celeste's death, especially in light of the fact that Botox is what killed her.'

'What's that?' Ira asked, loosening his bow tie.

'Something that had rolled under my tire the day she was killed . . . a bottle of Botox.'

Ira and Hope were both staring back and forth from me to Devon, their expressions part confusion, part expectation. Hope asked, 'What does that mean?'

'Well, Celeste had a parking space just a little ways down from mine. What it could mean is someone attacked her with Botox, stabbing her in the neck *after* she left Ira's office. Maybe attacked her in the parking garage and then dropped the bottle and couldn't find it? Had to leave in a hurry? I don't know. It's just a theory right now.'

Devon rocked back on his heels. 'It would've had to be someone who knew Celeste's schedule. Knew she'd be coming from your office and having that specific procedure done. Someone who wanted to frame you for her death.'

'That sounds unlikely, even to me,' Ira said, frowning.

Devon turned to me. 'Are there cameras in the parking garage?'

I shook my head no. 'You have to get in with a gate card so I guess they didn't see any need for cameras.'

'Isn't this something that should be turned over to the police then?' Ira asked, sounding exhausted.

'Sure,' Devon answered. 'And it will be. But you have to know it'll sit in evidence for months on end, waiting for forensic tests to be done in underfunded, overburdened labs. That is, if they even think it's worth investigating when they already have a suspect they know did, in fact, give her a Botox injection to the neck.' He looked pointedly at Ira.

'Right,' Ira said, blowing out a deep breath. He exchanged

a glance with Hope and then rubbed the back of his neck.
'OK. Mr Burke, you're hired. I'll have Hope call you tomorrow
with a credit card number for billing. Do whatever you need
to do. Money's not an issue. Time is.'
  'I understand.' Devon shook Ira's hand. 'Better get back to
it then.' He disappeared back into the ballroom.
  I gave Ira a hug, feeling a little guilty at my relief that he
was now footing the bill for the investigation. 'We'll figure
this out, don't worry.'
  'Elle, if someone did attack Celeste in the parking garage
. . . please be careful. Don't go getting yourself hurt on my
account.'
  'Yes, Elle,' Hope said sternly. 'Ira's right. If there's a
murderer lurking around the Pampered Pup, you need to be
careful.'
  I smiled gratefully at my friends. I wasn't worried, but I
appreciated their concern. I really felt Celeste was killed for
personal reasons, that it wasn't just a random act of violence.
Still, they didn't need anything else to worry about. 'I'll be
careful, I promise.'
  I walked around the auction tables, viewing and bidding
on some items just for the fun of it. There was a particularly
beautiful silver yin-yang symbol necklace I really fell in
love with. I scribbled a number on the sheet, knowing my
meager offering would be outbid. But, maybe it was too
small a bauble for these ladies to care about. A girl can
dream. That was becoming my motto in life since working
on Moon Key.
  Speaking of dreaming. A strong arm suddenly slid around
my middle, pulling me into a solid chest. Devon's husky voice
was once again sending very strong messages through my
body as he pressed his cheek against my hair.
  'You need to get into the conversation Zebina's having right
now and get yourself invited to that party.'
  I wanted to ask him what party, but I couldn't catch my
breath in time. His departure left me more aware of the empty
space around me than I had ever been. I shook it off and went
to search out my mission.
  'Oh sorry,' I said, bumping into Zebina from behind. 'So

sorry, I'm not used to these heels, and I'm really feeling the wine.'

'No problem, Elle,' Zebina laughed, pulling me into her circle. 'Ladies, I'd like you to meet my doga instructor, Elle Pressley. Max just loves her classes.'

I greeted the glassy-eyed, rosy-cheeked women and then I remembered something. 'Oh, Zebina. Do you know what happened to little Princess?'

'Yes,' Zebina said, looking very pleased with herself. 'Celeste's good friend, Billie Olsen offered to take her. Good thing, too. That dog was so spoiled, it would have never survived in a shelter.'

They were going to put Princess in a shelter? My blood boiled. I bit my tongue. And then took a swig of the bottled water I had switched to, to wash down the blood.

Then seeing my reaction, Zebina chuckled. 'Just kidding, Elle. Of course, we wouldn't do that to Princess.'

'I'm so glad we could do something tonight to help those poor shelter animals,' said a woman with flawless mocha skin and short-cropped gray hair. 'So tragic to have so many animals without proper homes.'

'Yes, well. Speaking of helping, I've got my eye on a diamond and emerald bracelet that I simply must have,' said a tall, sleek woman in a silver gown who resembled a strand of tinsel. 'Going to go check the bid. Zebina, I'll see you at the party next Saturday.'

As she left the group, I put on my best excited smile. 'Party? Are you having a party, Zebina?'

'Oh, yes, it's a Botox party.' She let her eyes roam over my face with an assessing gaze. 'You should come, Elle. It's going to be a fun girls' night.'

My smile froze for a split second and then melted in confusion. 'Botox party? Are you serious?'

'Well, I know it seems insensitive,' she laughed. 'Considering Celeste's death and all, but we can't all walk around wrinkled because of one person's tragedy.'

'I wasn't really thinking insensitive.' I gaped at her. 'More like unsafe.'

'Oh, it's perfectly safe, dear,' the woman who'd been

introduced to me as Helen chimed in. 'We just do our crow's feet and forehead. Nothing along the—' she motioned with blood red nails along her neck, her yellow-tinged eyes widening – 'you know.'

'Oh,' I said, nodding with fake understanding. 'I see. Sure then, I'd love to come.'

TEN

At the end of a long evening, Devon and I climbed back into his Jeep. The air was thick with a promised storm as thunder rumbled in the distance.

'Please tell me you're as exhausted as I am,' I sighed.

'Knackered. But it was a very productive evening.' Devon eased the Jeep away from the curb, following the steady flow of expensive cars leaving the resort.

I toed off my heels, wiggling my aching toes and rolled my head on the leather headrest to look at him. 'Yeah? How so?'

He removed his bow tie with one hand and tossed it in the console. 'Well, for one we learned from Zebina's reaction to my mentioning Celeste that she feels guilty about somethin'. Whether that guilt comes from her murdering Celeste or just running off with the woman's husband remains to be seen.' He steered the Jeep smoothly around a curve and then accelerated again. I closed my eyes. They felt like sandpaper and my lashes were sticking together.

He went on. 'We also learned a lot of people do believe Ira had something to do with Celeste's death . . . Bonnie and Robert being the most vocal.'

My eyes flew open. 'Robert said that to you? That's what everyone thinks? But we know Ira didn't in fact have anything to do with her death, right?'

Devon threw me a smirk. 'Right, Elle. Don't worry. Unless Ira is a sociopath, a person can't fake the emotional pain he was going through tonight.'

'Thank you,' I said, truly relieved that he believed in Ira's innocence.

'Unless it was accidental,' he added grimly.

I shook my head. 'No, Ira's an excellent plastic surgeon. He wouldn't make a fatal mistake like that.' I didn't know anything about the procedure Celeste had been given, but I knew Ira. He was meticulous and careful to a fault. 'It's much more likely the Botox bottle I found had something to do with her death.' I knew I sounded defensive but I couldn't help it. I wanted him to believe in Ira's innocence as much as I did.

Devon was silent for a few minutes and then he added, 'Well, you've got yourself an invitation to a Botox party next weekend. That's a huge opportunity to learn more about how easy it would be for Zebina, or anyone in fact, to get their hands on a bottle of the toxin.'

I moaned at the thought of the party. 'I'm so thrilled. So that's what you want me to go for?'

He nodded. 'That and anything that may tell us who else would want to harm Celeste. Listen carefully to any gossip. Also, I'm assuming the party'll be at Robert's house since they're living together now. He may have been given some of Celeste's belongings after her death, since she hadn't taken him out of her will yet as far as I know. Anything electronic like her computer or cell phone would be useful to find.'

'You want me to take them if I find them?'

'No. He'd realize they were gone. Just see if you can look through her emails or current phone calls. If there's a password, try "Princess". That's what she used with our correspondence. Can you do that?'

'I guess.' *Could I? I'd have to.* 'But, wouldn't the police have done that already?'

'Not yet. They'll open an investigation now that they know the cause of death. But, we have some time before they'll get around to locating her belongings. That's the advantage we have over the police . . . we don't have to worry about warrants and such, so we can work faster.'

'What if Robert catches me snooping around his house?'

Devon frowned and raised an eyebrow at me. 'Don't get caught.'

He steered the Jeep around the large fountain in front of the Pampered Pup and pulled up to the front doors. The guard, George, and I exchanged a wave.

Devon threw the Jeep in park and turned to me, curiosity dancing in his blue eyes. 'So, are you staying here then?'

I let my eyes fall. 'Yes, for now. I'm kind of in between places.'

He must have noticed my embarrassment. 'Well, I'd say a girl could do worse than stay here. It's one of my favorite hotels, architectural-wise.'

'Is it?' I asked suspiciously.

Devon nodded. 'Sure. Its style is a mix of Moorish Revival and Spanish Baroque. Very rare.' His finger traced the air around the horseshoe-shaped arches that jutted out intermittently along the length of the outside stucco walls. 'Those would be your Moorish Revival influence. The towers on the corners and balconies with that intricate ironwork, that's the Baroque features. Very charmin' together.'

I studied the sizeable, four-story building in a new light. It was quite beautiful. 'A photographer and private investigator who knows about architecture?' I studied him in a new light, too. A very, very alluring one.

'Well—' the dimple appeared as he smiled self-consciously – 'I do appreciate beauty in the world . . . man-made or otherwise.' He hopped out and came around to open my door while I plucked my shoes off the floorboard. There was no way those torture devices were going back on my swollen feet tonight.

The pavers were warm and rough on my bare soles. I spread my toes in an automatic reflex, pressing each toe pad evenly on the ground, enjoying the feel of being barefoot. 'Not to change the subject to something so morbid, but is there a day this week I can show you where Celeste died? Maybe Monday?' I blushed. We did need to move fast to clear Ira, but my reaction suggested an underlying motive.

He ran a hand through his dark waves and thought for a moment. As if echoing my thoughts, he sighed. 'Monday would be better, we do need to work fast on this. But, unfortunately, I'll be off island until Wednesday. Until then, you can still do some askin' around at the spa. See if anyone saw anything suspicious that morning.'

I pushed aside my disappointment at not seeing him for four more days, not willing to examine whether it was because that was four days we weren't working together on clearing Ira or because of my growing attraction toward him. 'Wednesday, around noon?' My morning class would be over by then.

He stared down at me, his top teeth teasing his bottom lip. He looked unsure about something.

'What's wrong?' I searched his face. 'Noon not good?'

'Noon is fine.' His voice had that husky quality again. 'Turn around and close your eyes.'

OK, this was strange. I threw him one more questioning glance and then turned away from him as he'd asked, closing my eyes. My heart began to thump in my chest as I became more aware of his scent and presence behind me.

Suddenly I felt a feather-light touch above my cleavage and his warm hands at the nape of my neck. He cleared his throat. 'You can open your eyes now.'

I did and glanced down at my chest. There, nestled perfectly was the black-and-white diamond yin-yang pendant I had placed a losing bid on.

'Oh . . .' My words were lost in surprise as I fingered the pendant. I whirled around, feeling the prickling of tears in my eyes. 'Devon . . . I don't know what to say. You bid on this? For me? Thank you. How . . . how did you know?'

He looked pleased but a little embarrassed. 'I saw your name on the bidding sheet. I wanted to make sure you won it.'

'But . . . why?' A tear slipped down my cheek. He reached up and wiped it with his thumb, cupping my cheek as he did. 'You really shouldn't have.' I pushed the words past the lump in my throat. 'No one's ever done something so nice for me before.'

He smiled sadly and caressed my face. 'Well, that's a shame.' He took a deep breath and, closing his eyes for a moment, his jaw tightened. 'I'll see you Wednesday. Good night, Elle.' Moving quickly back around the Jeep, I barely had time to wave as he took off.

Did this mean it was a date? 'You are a strange man, Devon Burke,' I whispered after him.

ELEVEN

Wednesday after doga class finished, I walked Buddha out front to find Devon already waiting for us. I approached his Jeep, trying to ignore the little dance my pulse was doing.

He removed his dark sunglasses and smiled at me. 'So what's the plan?'

I helped Buddha into the back then I hopped in the front. 'Well, I've got my parking pass so let's start with the parking garage.'

'Good plan.' Devon reached behind him and gave Buddha a scratch under the chin. Which, my dog repaid with a long string of drool on Devon's bare arm.

I grimaced as Devon wiped it off on his jeans. 'Sorry about that.'

Devon laughed. 'I've had worse slung on me in my travels.'

'I really hope that's not true,' I said, laughing with him. 'All right, let's go. I'll show you where Celeste used to park and where I ran over the bottle of Botox.'

Devon nodded silently and circled the fountain to head back to the parking garage.

'Second deck,' I instructed as he eased over a speed bump. His Jeep seemed to handle those darned things with much more grace than my Beetle. Certainly a lot less complaining. I led him to my space. 'You can park here.'

He shut off the Jeep and we all hopped out.

'OK, this is where I was backing out when I ran over the bottle.' I walked him the short distance, with Buddha in tow, to the parking space. It still had a reserved sign on the metal pole for Celeste. 'And this is where Celeste would have parked.'

Devon eyed the parking space and then turned slightly to stare at his Jeep. 'It is possible. The garage does slope that way. The bottle could've rolled.' He hiked up his jeans and squatted to investigate Celeste's parking space more closely.

After a few minutes, he stood. 'I don't see anything that would indicate a struggle but that doesn't mean much. If Celeste was attacked here, she probably knew her attacker, considering you need a card just to get in.' He motioned to the elevator. 'Easy getaway. Any cameras in there?'

I shook my head. 'No, though I heard Rita, the manager, has convinced the owners to have cameras installed now.'

We moved into the elevator, and the door slid smoothly closed. In this close proximity, I became acutely aware of Devon's physical presence. I glanced up at him. His eyes flicked to the necklace he had given me on Saturday night and then met mine briefly. I watched the corner of his mouth twitch slightly and then the doors opened.

'Here we are then.' He cleared his throat and motioned for me to exit in front of him.

I pointed down the hall to our right. 'The mudbath room is right there. If you go left and down the hall, my studio is the French doors on the left and down a bit further opens up into the lobby.'

Devon thought for a moment. 'So, if Celeste was attacked in the garage, the mudbath room would've been the closest place to go to for help.'

I shrugged. 'But her dog, Princess, was scheduled for a mudbath treatment in there around that time. So, that's what everyone thinks she was doing in the room.' I had a horrible thought. 'Maybe that is why. Maybe she knew she was dying and wanted to see her dog one last time.'

Devon nodded. 'Possibly. All right then, let's have a look.'

After I showed him the mudbath room – which I still had a hard time entering without picturing Celeste lying there on the floor – I walked him down to my studio and then out into the lobby.

Bonnie came around the corner, spotted us and then hurried across the lobby. 'There you are, Elle. I wanted to give you this. Hello.' She nodded to Devon, then turned her attention back to the object she was handing me. 'I thought maybe you could hang it in the studio, in remembrance of Celeste.'

'Sure,' I whispered, studying the framed photo. Celeste was grinning, her face pressed against little Princess, who had a tiara perched atop her tiny head. She looked so alive. So happy. I felt the threat of tears and moved my attention back to Bonnie. 'I'd be happy to.'

'Thank you.' Bonnie glanced down at the photo, a soft, sad smile on her lips. 'She wanted me to take that picture of Princess modeling that particular tiara because it was a replica of Princess Diana's.' She cleared her throat and gave me one last smile of gratitude before turning quickly away.

'They had become friends,' I explained to Devon after her abrupt departure. 'She's taking Celeste's death hard.'

'There is nothing easy about death.' Devon sighed. 'All right. Just one more thing.' He turned to me as we walked back to the elevator. 'Let's see how long it would have taken Celeste to go from Dr Craft's office to the parking garage.'

'OK.' I nodded. 'Won't be long. It's only two buildings over.'

Turned out it took us six minutes to walk to the Jeep from outside the front door of Ira's office and into Celeste's parking space. We both sat there silently, and I wondered if Devon was thinking the same thing as I was.

It was such a short amount of time. It would still be feasible to the police that the lethal dose of Botox came from Ira.

TWELVE

Ringing the doorbell, I suddenly felt nervous. What if I actually had to participate in the shooting of toxin into my forehead? And how in the world was I going to snoop around the house without someone noticing? I adjusted my bag on my shoulder and prayed to the universe there was alcohol here. It would help greatly if most of the guests were too tipsy to notice my snooping.

Zebina's face suddenly replaced the door. 'Elle!' She air-kissed both my cheeks. 'So glad you could make it. Come in.' She led me into an elaborately decorated living room large enough to house twenty elephants. At least a dozen women were milling about, chatting with champagne glasses in their hand. Bending down to give Max a scratch, I silently thanked the universe for champagne. Especially after I realized with horror how underdressed I was in my sundress and flip-flops.

'Elle!' Bonnie marched over in her perfectly tailored black cocktail dress and matching heels and gave me a one-armed hug. 'You haven't been in to visit me this week.' She leaned in and whispered to me with her champagne-sweetened breath. 'I hope that means no panic attacks?'

I smiled and accepted my own glass of bubbly from Zebina, thanking her. 'Yes. It's been a very quiet week.'

'That's good.' She moved her hand to her chest, worry creeping into her eyes. 'We haven't got a chance to really talk since the auction. I've been worried that you're angry with me for what I said to Ira. I know he's your friend, Elle, but you know I'm not one to keep my thoughts to myself. I do apologize for that.'

'It's OK,' I assured her. 'Everyone's entitled to their own opinion. We'll just have to trust that the police will uncover the truth.'

'That we will.' Relieved, she put her arm around my shoulder and led me into the middle of the group to make sure I knew everyone.

Feeling like an impostor, I mostly kept quiet and tried to listen to the conversations going on around me, to see if there was any gossip about Celeste. So far, all the talk revolved around investments, beauty treatments and health issues with some hardy doses of gossip thrown in. Not about anyone I knew, though.

I was trying to nurse my champagne to keep a clear head so my mouth was dry as cotton. I made my way into the kitchen to find a glass of water. The kitchen was incredible; modern stainless steel appliances mingled with an earthy clay-tiled backsplash and center island. A petite, older oriental woman in a black dress was humming as she pulled trays out of the fridge.

'Excuse me?'

She slid a tray on to the counter and turned to me with a smile. 'Yes?'

'Could I bother you for a glass of water?'

She nodded. 'Certainly.' As she dug in the cupboard for a glass and pulled a filtered water pitcher from the fridge, I walked around trying to figure out what my first move should be. There were two doors off the kitchen.

'Thank you,' I said, accepting the glass. 'Is that the restroom?' I pointed to a door on my right.

'No, Mr Robert's office.' She pointed to the other door. 'Restroom there.'

'Thank you.' I smiled, returning to the living room for now. If Robert did have Celeste's things, he would probably keep them in his office or the garage. Florida homes didn't have basements, no matter how rich you were, and I doubted Zebina would allow Celeste's belongings to be stored in the bedroom. Since I didn't have any reason to be in the garage, I would search the office first.

Unfortunately, Zebina came around the corner before I had a chance to make my move.

'Jiao, can you bring some fresh fruit out, please?' She spotted me with my glass of water. 'Elle,' she laughed, 'you're not hiding out in the kitchen, are you?' Putting her arm around me, she led me back into the living room. 'There's nothing to be concerned about. Feels just like a little mosquito bite. Here, watch Rita have it done.'

Her heels clicked on the tile and then were silenced by the Persian rug as she led me over to where Rita was situating herself on a fold-out table covered with a white sheet. A striking woman with her blonde hair pulled back in a severe bun stood behind her with gloved hands, pushing a needle into a Botox bottle that looked just like the crushed one in my glove box.

'Elle, this is Mandy, my dermatologist's assistant. She'll be preforming the injections today.'

'Hello.' I gave her a fluttering wave, moving one hand protectively to my neck. She smiled in return.

'Elle!' Rita adjusted herself on the table and closed her eyes. 'How's the house hunting coming?'

House hunting? Right. The thing I was supposed to be doing but haven't. I'm glad she had her eyes closed. I could feel my face warm. 'I'm looking at a few prospects.' *Liar. I really needed to start looking for a place.* 'Thanks again for letting Buddha and I stay at the spa.'

She waved her hand. 'Happy to help, Elle.'

Mandy nodded to a clipboard behind her. 'Just sign the waiver and you can go next.'

'Great. Thanks.'

'You'll do fine.' Zebina squeezed my shoulder and left me standing there with thoughts of bolting out the door. I let the thoughts go instead. I had something important to do and by stars, I was going to do it.

I watched as Mandy started pushing the needle between Rita's brows and wiping away the drops of blood with a cotton square. Feeling my stomach cramp, I turned away to sign the waiver. That's when I noticed the open box with a half dozen glass bottles and syringes in plastic. With a surreptitious glance behind me to make sure no one was paying attention, I swiped a bottle and syringe, shoving them quickly into my bag. With a trembling hand, I signed the waiver and stepped away from the table.

'Remember it will take about ten days to start seeing results, and they'll last for about three to four months,' Mandy said.

I stared at Rita's face for any sign of discomfort, but she wasn't flinching. I could do this. For Ira and Hope. When she sat up, I stared at the angry red bumps between her eyebrows and on her forehead. 'How long before the redness goes away?' I asked.

'Usually a few hours at the most,' Mandy chirped. 'Ready?'

'You'll be fine.' Rita patted my arm as she climbed off the table. 'The earlier you learn to suffer for beauty, the longer you'll stay beautiful.' The ladies around us chuckled at her remark.

I lay down awkwardly on the table, clutching my bag to my stomach and squeezed my eyes closed. 'Ready.'

'Just relax,' Mandy cooed. I could smell the mint on her breath and then a tiny prick by my brow. A few more pricks and it was over. I sat up slowly and took in a lungful of air.

Mandy laughed. 'I don't think I've had anyone hold their breath all the way through before.'

'First time.' I shrugged. 'Thanks.'

After an excruciating long hour of conversation with our tribe of red-welted women eating fruit and downing champagne, I finally got a chance to sneak back into the kitchen. Jiao was nowhere to be found so I snuck over to the office door and turned the handle. Unlocked. Slipping inside, I clicked it quietly closed behind me then glanced around. The blinds were closed but enough light seeped through from an outside lamp to allow me to snoop. There was a large, dark oak desk in the middle, matching bookshelves, and bingo . . . boxes stacked against the left wall.

I hurried over and read the white labels. 'Celeste's belongings.' Jackpot. Throwing my bag down, I unfolded the top box and peered in. Shoes. Sliding it off the pile and glancing at the door, I opened the next box. Files and folders. Flipping through them and not knowing what I was looking for, I put that box to the side, also.

The next one had jewel-studded collars and harnesses, small dog clothes, a photo album . . . even a tiny jeweled crown in a glass case. Almost like the one Princess wore in the photo now hanging in my studio. *Princess.* My heart cramped. I wondered how she was doing without Celeste.

I opened five or six more boxes, shoving them aside before I found what I was looking for. A laptop. Sitting on the floor with my prize, I was becoming aware of how long I'd been gone from the party. Time was becoming a physical pressure in my chest. Hopefully no one noticed and came looking for me. *Don't think about it.*
I powered up the laptop and typed 'Princess' in the password box. *Please please please. Yes! It worked.* Clinking on the email icon, I scrolled through. I had no idea what I was looking for and didn't see anything overtly weird or threatening. I opened a couple of emails and scanned them. Investments, sales, appointments. *Boring boring boring. Wait . . . what's this?* I clicked on an email with the subject heading: 'I have to confess . . .'
It was from Billie Olsen, the woman who was looking after Princess. I began to read:

> My dearest Celeste,
> Now that your divorce has gone through, I feel like it's the right time to tell you how I feel . . . how I've always felt. I'm in love with you. I want us to spend the rest of our life together. If you don't feel the same, I understand and please don't end our friendship over this. If you could possibly feel the same way though, let's talk. We've always been so close. I would just like to be closer.

Whoa. I clicked over to Celeste's outbox. There didn't seem to be a reply. Was Celeste upset by this? Maybe not. But, if she was . . . a spurned love? That's a motive for murder. Feeling pleased with myself for finding a clue, I powered off the computer and shoved it back in the box. Time to go. I had most of the boxes stacked back in place when the office light suddenly clicked on. I whirled around and Robert Green and I stood staring at each other in surprise.
Devon's words 'don't get caught' suddenly echoed in my head.

THIRTEEN

'Elle?' Robert pushed the door closed behind him and eyed me suspiciously. 'What are you doing in here?'

'What am I doing in here?' *Having a massive panic attack.* 'I . . .' I glanced down into the box in my arms. 'Well.' *Stay calm. Don't act suspicious.* 'I'm so sorry.' I dropped the box at my feet and gave him my best innocent smile. 'I know I should've asked you. I just didn't know how to bring up the subject without upsetting you.'

He inched closer to me, folding his arms. 'What subject is that?'

'Celeste.'

I saw his body tense. I had to get out of there. 'You see, I was looking for the restroom and ended up in here, and then I saw her boxes and I remembered I'm going to visit Princess to take her some of the treats Celeste used to buy her from the Pampered Pup, and I thought about all the accessories that Celeste bought her and thought if they were here, I could take them with me to give them to Billie Olsen.' Rambling . . . something I was good at when nervous. Breathing . . . not so much.

Robert walked over and looked into the box at my feet, then with a sigh, he nodded. 'Fine. The sooner I can get her stuff out of here, the sooner there will be peace in my house. I'll have Jiao put the box in your car.'

I blinked. *Did that actually work?*

'Something else?' he asked.

'No! Great. It's the VW convertible. Thank you.' I stepped over the box and around Robert. 'I better get back to the party.'

A half an hour later, I finally made it out the door and was headed back to my temporary home with the bottle of contraband Botox in my bag and Princess's things in the back seat.

I shook my head, feeling my shoulders finally begin to relax as the warm, night air unthawed me. God, they kept their airconditioning low. Something I still wasn't used to. I was lucky if I got to use a fan in the summer growing up. *What was I doing?* What if I hadn't been holding the box with Princess's stuff when Robert walked in? What if he would've walked in while I was on her laptop? There would have been no way to talk my way out of that. I had to be more careful.

Sunday afternoon the sky was beginning to swell with heavy, charcoal clouds to the south. I flicked the Frisbee once more for Buddha and watched him lumber across the span of sand toward its general landing area. True to form, he got distracted by the possibility of a snack in a pile of seaweed and abandoned the toy. Shaking my head as an excited terrier claimed it, I walked into the warm water up to my knees, enjoying the gentle rocking of the tide against my bare legs.

There were never waves here, just soft white caps that peaked like meringue and dissolved as gently. I let my gaze wonder up to the wooden ramp that marked the entrance of the dog beach. Though I'd never been self-conscious in a bathing suit before – I practically grew up in one – I was reluctant to pull off my cover-up knowing Devon would be here any moment. Instead, I dipped down and cupped some sea water to wet my arms and sticky-with-sweat neck.

A bright yellow jet ski came roaring into view from the distance. I watched in fascination as Devon, with Petey balanced on the seat in front of him, maneuvered the jet ski into the shallower water beside me. Devon shot me a grin as he removed Petey's life vest, tossed it on to the beach and let him jump down. Buddha butt-wiggled his way over to greet his new friend and the two dogs sniffed and play bowed to each other.

'I can see by the suspicious look you're giving me, you've never been on a jet ski,' Devon teased as I waded closer to him.

'That would be a safe assumption.' I crossed my arms, feeling exceptionally vulnerable. The man was dangerous enough without being perched atop a loud, fast machine.

Devon scooted forward, then reached up, grabbed my hand and, before I knew it, I was seated on the contraption behind him. 'Time to change that.'

'Wait!' Terrified, though of what I had no idea, I scrambled
to find any excuse to stop this madness. 'I don't want my
cover-up to get wet.'

He turned his head so I had an up-close-and-personal view
of that dimple when he smiled. 'Then take it off.' His feet dug
in the sand as he began to push us out into the deeper water.
With a growl of frustration, I ripped the thing off over my
head and tossed it toward the shore, barely making it past the
wet sand. His back was warm and my traitorous body happily
pressed against it.

'What about the dogs?' I screeched, feeling the anxiety of
being out of control grip my lungs like a fist.

'They'll be fine. We'll stay close to shore.' At that, he had
apparently had enough talking and gunned the jet ski, sending
it bouncing and flying through the water at what I thought
was a reckless speed.

I pressed myself against Devon's back, my heart pounding,
my arms wrapped around his waist, and my face buried in his
shoulder. The wind was ripping at my ponytail, whipping it
around my face as the sea spray soaked my whole body. Too
terrified to scream, I held my whole being in a clenched ball
and silently pleaded for it to be over.

After a few harrowing minutes of planning my own funeral,
I peeked over Devon's shoulder and gasped. Fresh sea air
rushed into my lungs. *Whoa!* Wondrous, endless ocean flew
up to meet us, disappearing beneath us just as quickly. It was
. . . exhilarating. I was alive. I felt myself smiling and loosened
my death grip just a bit. And then suddenly, I was laughing.
Laughing as Devon did a sliding turn and laughing as he went
against our own wake, jumping and landing roughly and
turning a circle to do it again. As he tore through the water
back toward the dogs, I lifted a fist in the air and yelled,
'Wahoo!' I felt Devon's stomach contract with laughter under
my hand.

I watched Petey bark and splash into the water to greet our
return. Buddha waded up to his belly and stared at me curiously as Devon maneuvered the jet ski back to shore. With a
start, I realized I had my bikini-clad body pressed up against
this solid specimen of man. It was a good time to practice

being in the moment. I moved my attention to the warmth of the place where our skin touched, feeling his muscles move under my skin. I breathed in the faint minty scent of his damp hair, felt the rumble of his words in my own chest as he greeted the dogs. When he let his hand fall to my thigh and squeezed gently, I nearly moaned aloud.

Instead, I dismounted on trembling legs, pushing aside all the emotions going with him on that crazy ride had stirred within me. Retrieving my cover-up from the sand, I floated back to where I'd thrown my towels.

'So, what'd you think?' Devon had plopped down in the sand and was grinning up at me.

I spread out my favorite, well-worn dolphin print beach towel and sat down next to him, not caring any more that I was in a bikini in front of him. What I just did was way more vulnerable an act than being half naked.

What did I think? I think you somehow understand my needs more than I do. 'It was fun.'

'Fun.' Devon squinted at me curiously. 'Yeah, that, too.' Thunder rumbled in the distance. He looked up at the gathering clouds now moving quickly in on us. 'It's about to bucket down. So, let's get to it then. How'd the party go?'

'Awful . . . but productive.' I released my hair from the ponytail to let the intensifying wind dry it out as I talked. I noted Devon's attention as he watched it tumble over my shoulder and a tiny feeling of power surged through me. 'First of all, I had to actually get stuck with a needle. In my forehead. More than once. Though, I did manage to steal a bottle of Botox, so that goes to show how accessible it is.'

'Naughty girl,' Devon said, taking the found Frisbee from Petey and tossing it down the beach. The contraction of his bare, muscular arm did not go unnoticed by me. Power, it seemed, was a two-way street.

I ignored his muscles and his teasing. 'And then, I found Celeste's belongings in boxes in Robert's office. You were right, he had her laptop and "Princess" worked as the password to gain access. There was an email there from a few days before she died, from her friend, Billie Olsen, the lady who took Princess. It was basically a confession. Apparently she's been in love with Celeste all along and she hoped Celeste could feel the same way about her since her divorce was final.'

Thunder rumbled again, this time louder as Devon stared out at the ocean. He lifted his gaze to me. I blushed. I still wasn't used to how blue his eyes were, especially in the outdoor lighting, and how much they affected me.

'Good work. Rejection is definitely a motive for murder, if in fact she was rejected. We need to find out if that was the case. And if so, did this Billie Olsen person go to a Botox party recently or have any other way of getting her hands on some?'

I suddenly sat up, gasping as I remembered something. 'Oh my god . . . BO . . .' I smacked myself in the forehead. 'I can't believe I forgot to tell you this when I showed you the mudbath room. When Celeste died, she had written "BO" in the mud. I assumed she was trying to write "Botox" but what if it was initials? What if she was naming her killer and wrote BO for Billie Olsen?'

'Huh.' Devon stared at me for a moment. 'That's interesting. Yeah, I suppose that's a possibility. All right. We need to talk to this woman ASAP.'

The wind picked up and the dogs came over to lay down by us. I noticed the few people who had been on the beach were hurrying to gather their things. I hated to have Devon disappointed in me, but he needed to know everything that happened at the party. 'Devon, there's one more thing.'

His eyes glittered as he watched me. 'There always is.'

'Robert kind of walked in on me while I was going through the boxes in his office.' I held up my hand as I saw the concern harden his features. 'I think I dealt with any suspicion he had. I simply told him I was looking for Princess's things to take with me when I visited Billie, and I didn't want to bother him. It didn't hurt I was holding the actual box with Princess's things when he walked in.'

'What did he say?'

'He said he'd have the box put in my car. Which he did. That's all. No other drama.'

The wind was whipping the towels around now, and the first fat drops of rain were landing around us. He stood and held his hand out to me. I took it and let him pull me up.

'Try to get a visit set up with Billie Olsen for Wednesday evening if possible. I won't be back on the island until then.' I felt my heart sink at that news. Again, I questioned my disappointment. It had been a week and a half since Celeste was killed. We should be working every day to clear Ira. But, even as that thought congealed, I knew I was lying to myself. I wanted to spend more time with Devon. Some friend I was.

He held eye contact but let go of my hand. 'You did good, Elle.' With a parting smile, he ran toward the jet ski. Petey was at his heels as the sky opened up, dumping cold rain on us all.

FOURTEEN

Wednesday morning I checked my phone after class. *Oh no.* There were about twenty missed calls from Hope. She was in panic mode. Something had happened. I closed the studio doors and called her back.

'Oh my god, Elle, it's happened. They've arrested Ira for Celeste's death. They came right into his office! His secretary, Anna, she called and told me. They took him out right in front of his patients. Can you imagine? He's probably so devastated right now. What am I going to do?'

I plopped down on the wood floor and began to rub Buddha's warm belly to calm myself so I could be strong for her. 'First, you're going to take a deep breath. Have you called your lawyer?'

'Yes, he was going to the Clearwater police station immediately. He said they're charging Ira with involuntary manslaughter, so he'll probably have to spend the night in jail for a few days until he has a bail hearing! Elle, Ira in jail . . . it's just too horrible to think about. He doesn't belong there.' She was sobbing quietly now. I could just picture her hiding her face in a towel like she always did when she was trying not to let anyone hear her cry.

'I know.' I fought back my own tears. I couldn't stand it when she was upset. 'OK, listen. Devon and I have come up with a lead on someone. We're going to talk to this person of interest tonight so I want you to stay strong, OK? We both know Ira is innocent and we're going to prove it. As far as being in jail, you'll probably have to put up a pretty high sum for bail, but then he can go home and wait until this is all figured out from there.'

'But he won't be able to practice. What if everyone believes he did this? They'll be afraid of going to him, and his practice will be ruined. He loves his work, Elle. I know he won't be happy doing anything else.'

I felt her panicking, even over the phone. 'Let's not get ahead of ourselves, OK. Once the real killer is found, no one will be afraid to go to him.'

Hope took a shuddering breath. 'Do you believe Devon can find out who really killed Celeste?'

Did I? Yes, I did. I wholeheartedly believed in Devon Burke. 'Absolutely.'

Hope sniffed. 'And not just because he's hot, right?'

A small laugh escaped me and I swiped at my eyes with the back of my hand. 'There's the Hope I love. No, not just because he's hot.'

She sighed. 'I love you, too, Elle. Thank you for talking me down. Keep me updated with what Devon finds out, OK?'

I had a sudden thought. Since Ira was paying for Devon's services maybe he should be talking with them. 'Do you want me to have him call you directly?'

'No, I'm a mess right now. I can't even think straight. You just keep us updated, and I'll do the same.'

Billie Olsen lived in Seaspray, which were stunning two-story Mediterranean villas situated on the south-west corner of the island and bordered on both sides by mansions. The whole middle of Moon Key was a first-rate golf course with condos, villas, homes and businesses built between the golf course and the shoreline. Being between the Gulf and golf, I silently mused. It was a rich man's *ménage à trois*.

'Elle Pressley to see Billie Olsen,' Devon said to the gate guard. He had picked me and Buddha up and, once again, he was going to play the part of my boyfriend so we didn't raise suspicion. I wasn't complaining.

'Have a great day, Mr Pressley.' The guard buzzed us in after checking his log.

'Don't even,' Devon said, throwing me an unamused glance at the guard's mistake.

After I stopped laughing I asked, 'Does it ever strike you as funny that every place you go here is gated and guarded? I mean, just to get on the island requires a first-born child, so who exactly are they protecting themselves from? Each other?'

Devon chuckled and then his expression sobered. 'One thing

I learned from my da, Elle, is money comes with a certain amount of necessary paranoia.'

I frowned. I wasn't sure money was worth having if you had to spend your whole time worrying about who was going to take it away. Oh well. 'She said to follow the loop around to the second set of villas.'

Devon followed my directions. He had been quiet this whole ride, and I began to wonder if something was bothering him. I wanted to ask him about his trip this week off island but didn't feel like we knew each other well enough for that.

'You can park here.'

I helped Buddha down from the back seat as Devon grabbed the box of Princess's things.

'Come on in.' Billie was a wiry, petite woman who exuded inner strength. She greeted us with a sad smile and opened the door wide so Devon could get the box through. My heart squeezed at the sight of Princess, who sniffed Buddha with exuberance. We exchanged greetings and Billie bent down to give Buddha a pat. 'What a beautiful dog. What is he?'

'The vet seems to think he's an American bulldog mix. I hope you don't mind me bringing him. I thought it might help Princess to see a familiar face.'

'Not at all. It's very thoughtful of you to visit and bring Princess her things. Come sit down. Can I get you some fresh iced tea? Coffee?'

With mounting trepidation, I glanced around at the spotless, white-themed living room. The furniture was white, bleached coral and white seashells adorned every flat surface, and if I had to hazard a guess at the paint color on the walls, it would be 'White Elephant in a Snowstorm White'. 'Sure, tea would be great.'

'Perfect. Be right back, make yourselves at home.'

Moving a pearled silk pillow out of the way, I took a seat tentatively on her white suede sofa and picked a dog hair off my pants. I'd never felt so unclean.

Devon placed the box on the floor and sat down so close to me our thighs were touching. He put his arm around the back of the sofa behind me. I shot him an annoyed look, but he didn't notice. He was studying the room. His gaze stopped on a photo of Billie and Celeste resting on the fireplace mantle. They were on some sugar-sand beach, their arms thrown around each other, smiling with fruity umbrella drinks in their hands.

I felt Buddha's full weight as he leaned up against my leg. Princess had apparently tired of sniffing him and made one graceful leap into my lap.

'Hey there, girl.' I scratched under her tiny ears and let her give me a couple of wet chin kisses. She smelled like she'd just gotten a bath. 'How're you holding up?'

'Should I be jealous?' Devon was staring at me with that sexy half-smile of his.

'I don't think pretend boyfriends are allowed to get jealous.' I planted a kiss between Princess's eyes for good measure and then sat her on the floor so I could dig the Pampered Pup gourmet treats out of my bag. I gave one to each dog and placed the rest of the bag of treats on the glass coffee table . . . next to a sculpture of a white mermaid.

'She seems to be settling in here.' Billie emerged from the kitchen with a tray of glasses, placing them on the other side of the mermaid. 'At first she cried a lot, especially at night and seemed to be searching the house for Celeste.'

I heard the catch in Billie's throat at saying her name. She really did care about Celeste. Picking up a glass of tea I motioned to the photo. 'And how are you holding up? Looks like you and Celeste were close.'

She stared off in the distance, her hand absent-mindedly clutching a gold rope chain at her neck. Her hand was noticeably quaking, which surprised me. 'We've been best friends for twenty years. Honestly, I still can't believe she's gone. I still go to call her and then remember . . .'

'I'm so sorry for your loss. I can't even imagine losing my best friend,' I said and meant it.

Devon's hand dropped to my shoulder, and he pulled me closer to him. 'I couldn't either. Especially one I loved so much.'

I indulged myself and leaned into his solid chest, taking a sip of the iced tea to cool off as Billie smiled warmly at us. 'Yes. I suppose now that there's nothing to lose, I can admit it out loud. She was the love of my life. I'm lucky in a way. I did get to tell her that before she died.'

'And did she share your feelings?' Devon's voice was full of empathy. Was he faking it to get her to talk? Somehow I didn't think so. He wanted her to talk, but the empathy was real.

Billie sighed and stroked Princess, who had curled up into a ball beside her on the love seat. 'No.' A tear rolled down her cheek. She didn't bother to wipe it away. 'She didn't.'

'That must have been hard,' Devon offered. His thumb was gently rubbing my arm and giving me chills. I wondered if he was even conscious of what he was doing.

'Honestly, it broke my heart. But, I was willing to settle for friendship.'

'So, it didn't change your friendship then?'

She forced a smile through the tears. 'Well, she did stop taking my calls for a few days but I know she just had to sort through her feelings and needed time. That's just the way she handled things. We would have been fine. Had she lived.'

'Do you believe what the news is saying? That Dr Craft is responsible for her death?' Devon slid his thumb under the sleeve of my shirt and a jolt of electricity shot through my body. I shivered and felt my skin flush. Leaning forward to place my glass on the table, I used the motion to scoot out of his reach. How did he expect me to concentrate when he was touching me like that? Pretend boyfriend or not.

She shook her head sadly. 'If I had to guess, I'd say it was negligence. Just a doctor getting reckless with a procedure that was basically shooting toxin into her throat. I think people forget how risky these plastic surgery procedures actually are. I kept trying to tell her that, but she was obsessed with staying young.'

'So, you've never tried it? Botox? Those Botox parties seem to be really popular,' I probed.

'No.' She rubbed her wrinkled neck. 'I've never used it, and it shows, I'm sure. But I don't care. The important thing in life is love. Finding that special someone to share your life with.' She smiled knowingly at us.

Devon took my hand and brought it to his lips. The warmth of his mouth on my skin made my breath catch in my throat. 'You're absolutely right,' he said, grinning at me.

I started coughing and slipped my hand from his to grab my iced tea, nearly toppling it in the process. After a long drink, I stood up. Buddha pushed himself off the floor, staring at me expectantly. 'Well, I think we've taken up enough of your time. Thank you so much for letting us visit Princess. It makes me feel so much better she's with someone who will love her as much as Celeste did.'

Billie stood quickly. She may have a few wrinkles but she obviously took good care of herself. There was no sign that stiffness had settled in with age. 'Oh, you're very welcome.' She peered into the box on the floor. 'Thank you for bringing her things.' Reaching down, she lifted the tiny crown in the glass case from the box. 'The money she spent on Princess.' She sighed. 'I guess true love knows no bounds. She really did love that little creature. Is it wrong to be jealous of a dog?' She laughed, but her eyes sprouted tears. Time to go and let this woman grieve in peace.

On the ride back to the Pampered Pup, Devon was quiet again. I glanced at his hand gripped tight on the steering wheel. Closing my eyes, I recalled the feel of that hand on my arm. Sighing, I leaned my head back and stared up at the stars. Pretend boyfriends sucked.

'So, Botox is not in Billie's toolbox. Do you think she's even capable of murder?' I asked.

'Anyone is capable of a crime of passion,' he answered, still distracted by his own thoughts.

'A crime of passion? What does that even mean?' It was a rhetorical question, but he answered it anyway.

'When your brain shuts down and your emotions take over making you do something incredibly stupid and out of character.'

Yeah, I could relate to that. Especially around Devon. I reached up and rubbed the yin-yang pendant between my forefinger and thumb. I still couldn't believe he'd bought it for me.

'Humans are so complicated. I don't know. She seemed pretty stable to me. She wasn't angry about Celeste's rejection, just sad. Sad isn't really an emotion that makes you want to stab someone with a toxin. Sad just makes you want to curl up in a ball and hide from the world.'

I felt Devon glance sharply at me. 'Sounds like you've had a lot of experience with sad.'

I shrugged. 'Not any more than everyone else, I'm sure.' I turned in my seat to face him. 'How is the investigation into your parent's death going? Do you have any leads?'

He rubbed his jaw, which was sporting a very sexy five o'clock shadow. 'Some. I have a friend coming in from Ireland soon who may have something for me. We'll see.'

'A *girl* friend?' I tried to keep my inquiry light-hearted.

He laughed. 'No. No girlfriend.' Then he glanced over at me. 'What about you? Any boyfriends?'

I smiled. 'No. I swore off boys in my twenties.' And that is all I was going to say about he-who-we-don't-speak-of.

He pulled up in front of the Pampered Pup, threw his Jeep into park and turned to me with curiosity making his eyes sparkle. 'Why?'

'You first,' I said, feeling brave. 'Why no girlfriend?'

'What woman would have me?' he laughed. I folded my arms. We both knew that wasn't the issue. 'Well, unlike you, I didn't swear off half of the human species.' He smirked slightly. 'I just traveled a lot with my job and knew it wouldn't be fair to anyone to try and commit to a relationship. And since I've been on Moon Key, I've dated some but mostly I've been concentrating on finding my parents' killer. Your turn.'

I nodded. 'Fair enough.' I reached up and stroked Buddha's head to appease him. He had shoved it between the seats and was panting at me, ready to get to his comfy bed upstairs. I needed to find a place soon. He was getting spoiled. 'Growing up, it was always just me and my mom . . . and about twenty different guys she brought in and out of our lives. Each time she would say, "This is the one, Elle," and give up her entire being to make him happy so he would stay. Of course, it never worked out. There never was a man who changed her life like he promised. And they all promised that. She just became this lost soul who is now a miserable person addicted to beer and Twinkies.' I wiped at my eyes, surprised at the emotion this was bringing up in me.

Devon was silent for a moment. 'So your mum is still around though?'

I glanced up at him, realizing how ungrateful I must sound considering his mom wasn't around any longer. 'Yeah. She's in Clearwater. Though, she's not speaking to me at the moment.'

'That's a shame.' His brow was creased, and his eyes held oceans of empathy. Again, no judgment. Just acceptance and compassion.

I let myself open up a little bit more. 'Yeah, it is. Anyway, I decided I was never going to count on a man or lose myself for anyone. I would make my own happiness and . . . I have.' That wasn't a lie. That was part of it, just not all of it.

Devon sat there, gazing into my eyes for a long time, then a sad smile appeared. 'You have.' He took a deep breath, and I could almost feel him pull away, though he didn't physically move. I suddenly realized he may've taken my stand on men as a personal rebuke. Before I could explain, he hopped out of the Jeep and came around to open my door.

I climbed down, feeling like I should explain that I wasn't saying I wouldn't ever date again. Feeling a bit anxious and scared of the distance I now felt between us, I struggled to find the right words, but they never came.

Devon gently helped Buddha from the back seat. 'Good night, Elle.'

'Night.' I waved as he took off. *Great, Elle. Just great. Way to repel the only guy you would've bent the rules for in a decade.* 'Come on, Buddha.' Dejected, I said goodnight to the guard, George, and headed up to our room.

By Friday evening, I had decided it was a good thing I had unintentionally pushed Devon away. Bend the rules for a man who was going to leave eventually? That was just inviting heartbreak. Besides, my life was stable now. I was happy . . . well, besides my best friend's husband being accused of involuntary manslaughter. And being basically homeless. And not being on speaking terms with my mother. I threw my yoga bag over my shoulder and flipped off the studio lights. I should really go check on my mother since she wasn't answering my calls. At least it would alleviate some of the guilt I was feeling. 'Come on, Buddha.' Might as well get it over with.

The parking garage had already emptied out. It was stuffy and silent as usual. As I opened the passenger door for Buddha, I noticed there was a note tucked under the windshield wiper. Absent-mindedly, I tossed my yoga bag in the back seat then went around to the driver's side and plucked the note from the windshield. I unfolded it. My body began to tremble immediately as I read the one, very short and pointed line:

Stop looking into Celeste's death or you're next.

FIFTEEN

I felt the rumble beneath me. The smell of gas replaced the smell of ocean water as Devon started the Jeep and we disembarked the ferry behind a handful of Mercedes and Jaguars. We were headed for the Clearwater police station. At nine in the morning, the sun was already blazing, and I was feeling nauseous from the stress. It was, after all, my first death threat, and it was surprisingly effective.

I placed a palm against my stomach to try and soothe it. 'Thanks for taking me, Devon.'

Devon kept throwing furtive glances my way as he drove over Memorial Causeway. 'Are you well? Cause you're lookin' a bit pale.'

I offered him a weak smile. 'Yeah, I'll be fine.'

Tentatively, he reached a hand over and lay it on top of mine. 'Elle, I'm really sorry. I should've never let you get involved. This is my fault.'

I glanced down at his hand and then over at him. His jaw was set tight. The warmth and weight of his hand did bring me comfort. I hadn't realized he was taking this threat against me so personally. 'I appreciate your concern, Devon, but I'm the one that got you involved, remember?'

He folded my hand up in his and tightened his grip. 'Yes, but I'm trained. I can protect myself and know the risks. You're . . .' He glanced at me, and I saw fear flash in his eyes. 'You're vulnerable.'

His fear hopped into my head like a contagion. I broke out in a cold sweat. *Was I vulnerable?* Yes, but so was every other human being who cared about something or someone. Being vulnerable didn't mean I had the right to fall apart or hide under a rock when my friends needed me. Hope and Ira needed me. Needed me to be strong. The complete opposite of what I felt.

Readjusting the seat belt, I straightened my spine. Then I

pulled my hand out from the protection of his and rolled my shoulders back. 'I'll be OK, really. It was just a shock.'

We got caught in the stop-and-go morning traffic, which didn't seem to improve his mood. I snuck glances at him from behind my sunglasses. His expression kept shifting, like he was fighting some kind of internal war. His mood settled into a somber silence and neither one of us broke that silence the rest of the way. Finally, he made a left and pulled into a parking garage.

'So, you know this detective we'll be talking to?' I tried to keep up with Devon's stride as we crossed the street. Anger apparently makes people walk like there are hot coals under their feet.

He glanced at me. 'Yeah. I . . . I do know her. She's been very decent about helping me out with my parents' case. Even though the investigation has been officially closed, she knows I haven't given up and supports me. She's not the lead detective on Celeste Green's death but she is part of the investigation. And much more pleasant to deal with than Farnsworth.'

A *female* homicide detective? That surprised me and made me feel a little more at ease. At least I wouldn't be talking to Detective Farnsworth again. I'm pretty sure I didn't make a good impression on him at our last meeting.

We gave up our driver's licenses to a lady behind a bullet-proof window and then waited in the lobby while she let Detective Vargas know we were there.

After a few minutes of reading the wanted posters in the lobby, a petite woman strode through the doors toward us. She was clad in a black business suit, her dark hair rolled up in a loose bun and she looked fairly serious until she made eye contact with Devon.

'Devon.' She approached us, smiling warmly at him and eyeing me curiously.

Devon motioned between us. 'Salma this is Elle Pressley. Elle . . . Detective Salma Vargas.' We shook hands and exchanged greetings. Her hand was small but dry and held mine like a vice grip. I felt like she was sizing me up. I tried not to take it personally, after all, that's what detectives are trained to do, right? 'Elle works at the Pampered Pup where

Celeste Green was found. She came to me for help because she's a friend of Ira Craft's. I'm working for Ira now, trying to prove his innocence.'

'Oh, you are?' Detective Vargas crossed her arms and then turned her deep brown, laser-like gaze on me. She eyed me in a new way . . . one that looked an awful lot like suspicion. 'I see,' she quipped.

'We have some information for you,' Devon said.

Her eyebrows rose slowly as she moved her attention back to Devon. 'You do know Detective Farnsworth is the lead on that case?'

'Yeah,' Devon smiled, 'but you're much easier to work with.'

She shook her head but the warm smile was back. 'Come on then.' She spun on her heels and motioned for the front desk to unlock the doors. After a buzz indicated the doors had been unlocked, we followed her through them and into what looked like a break room, complete with a microwave and fridge. It smelled like someone had just nuked bacon. My stomach twisted in protest. Devon and I took a seat at a large round table.

'Coffee?' she asked as she went to pour herself some.

'Please,' Devon answered.

'No thank you,' I said. My stomach wasn't feeling good enough to feed it caffeine.

She brought over two Styrofoam cups and sat one in front of Devon. I noticed she had given his to him black, without asking. I guess she would know that about him, though, since they spent time together on his parents' case.

She clutched her cup in front of her. 'So, what do you have for me?'

Devon nodded toward me. 'Elle, show her.'

I pulled the baggie out of my purse which held the typed note and slid it over to the detective. 'I found this on the windshield of my car last night.'

She read it, then her eyes blazed as she stared at Devon. 'Why would someone threaten *her* to stop investigating?'

Devon looked appropriately chastised. 'I know. I shouldn't have let her get involved.'

Detective Vargas rubbed her forehead. 'Start from the beginning. How involved is she, and who knows you're working for Ira Craft?'

Devon sat back in his chair; his dark, broody mood getting even darker. 'The only thing Elle's done so far is attend a Botox party at Robert Green's house to see how easy it was to get a hold of a bottle of the stuff. Because . . .' He pulled the crushed bottle from his pocket. He had placed that in a baggie also. 'Elle ran over this in the parking garage where Celeste had a parking space just a few feet away.'

Detective Vargas accepted the baggie. 'When did you find this, Elle?'

Oops. I glanced at Devon cautiously. He pursed his lips and then nodded. I turned back to the detective. 'The night Celeste was killed.'

She shot Devon another angry look. 'And we're just getting this now? Over two weeks later?'

He kept silent but met her stare.

She shook her head. 'So, you're thinking someone else could have administered the Botox in the parking garage?'

'Yes.' Devon sipped his coffee.

'Pretty thin. Why would someone do that? To frame Dr Craft?' She sighed and seemed to soften. From fatigue or empathy, I couldn't tell. 'Well, that's one thing I know Detective Farnsworth is concentrating on right now, the timeline. And to be perfectly frank with you, the detective isn't convinced this was negligence, considering the reputation Dr Craft has as an excellent plastic surgeon. He thinks he has something to prove intent. Do you know what that means?'

I shook my head no, but it couldn't be good.

'It means if he has found a solid motive, the charges will be upgraded from involuntary manslaughter to murder. And Florida does have the death penalty.' Her eyebrows rose to punctuate the seriousness of Ira's situation.

I felt my face drain and tried not to think about the lawsuit Celeste had planned against him. 'But, he didn't do anything wrong!'

Detective Vargas ignored my outburst and instead stared thoughtfully into her coffee cup before sliding her gaze back to me. 'Elle, I don't mean this to be disrespectful, but what exactly is your relationship with Dr Craft?'

It dawned on me that she may think I was romantically involved with Ira. 'Oh, his wife, Hope, is like a sister to me. Since eighth grade,' I added quickly. 'I was maid of honor at their wedding. Ira is a sweet guy, detail orientated and cautious to a fault. I know he didn't do this.' I pushed down the frustration and tears that came all too easily these days.

'So, you would do *anything* to help prove he didn't kill Celeste Green?'

'Yes.' My eyes widened when I realized what she may be implying. 'I mean no . . . not *anything*. I certainly wouldn't make up a story about running over that bottle.' I motioned to the baggie in her hand. I could see the calculating going on behind her eyes and realized her petite frame and easy smile probably came in handy when she wanted people to underestimate her. 'Besides, the note proves someone is afraid of us finding out the truth, and Ira couldn't have put it there since he's been arrested and is in jail.'

'Ira was released on bail yesterday afternoon.'

Her words hit me like a horse kick to the chest. 'What?' *Why didn't Hope call me?*

'Salma,' Devon's voice held a warning. 'Elle did not fabricate evidence.'

The detective shifted her attention to Devon. 'From my point of view, you've brought me two things, which could've very easily been fabricated, from the friend of our suspect. I'm sorry, Devon—' she turned to me – 'and Ms Pressley, but I can't see either item helping Dr Craft be cleared of charges.' She leaned back in her chair. 'I do, however, want to treat the note as a threat to be on the safe side. Please tell me who would know you've been investigating.'

I sighed, suddenly very tired. 'When I was at the Botox party, Robert Green sort of caught me going through some of Celeste's boxes. So, he may have figured it out. Then, of course, he could have mentioned it to his fiancé and Celeste's arch enemy, Zebina. We also just talked to Billie Olsen, Celeste's best friend. Billie was actually in love with Celeste and was rejected by her shortly before Celeste was killed. So,

I suppose she could have suspected we were digging for information, if she were guilty. She seemed genuinely upset about Celeste's death but Devon seems to think anyone is capable of a crime of passion.' I shot him a doubtful look. Detective Vargas mumbled something in Spanish under her breath and then rubbed her temples. 'OK. Here's what I'm going to do. I'm going to give these items to our forensic lab to see if we can pull any fingerprints or DNA. Doubtful, but we'll try. And I'm going to fill Detective Farnsworth in on this conversation. And if anything happens to this young woman—' she pointed at me while still glaring at Devon – 'it will be on you. *Comprendes?*'

Devon nodded and glanced at me. I caught the guilt before he turned away. Is that what he was brooding about?

'Good.' She sighed and stood up. 'And it goes without saying to be careful. Both of you.'

'Where are we going?' I noticed Devon had turned the opposite way of the ferry.

Silently, he maneuvered the Jeep down a two-lane sandy road lined with pine trees. At my question he slowed and pulled off to the side. He turned to me, his eyes full of an emotion I couldn't interpret. It looked a lot like anger. *Was he mad at me?*

'Let me ask you a question, Elle. Are you going to stop trying to figure out who killed Celeste Green?'

I narrowed my eyes, trying to decide where he was going with this. Probably best to just be honest with him. 'No. I'm not.'

'Even though you now know your life is in danger?'

'Well, I mean, I'll be more careful, of course. I won't go into the parking garage alone. I'll make sure I have my phone with me.' I crossed my arms as his expression darkened. I could see the little scar on his upper lip turn white as he pressed his lips together. I dug my heels in. 'Hope has always been there for me, Devon. This is something I have to do for her.'

'That's what I thought,' he growled. 'Stubborn as a bloody mule.' He shook his head. 'You did hear the good detective say that if anything happens to you, it's my arse, right?'

I flushed, not appreciating being treated like a child by him of all people. 'I'm a grown person, and I'll take all the responsibility of my actions. So, consider you and your . . . arse off the hook.'

'Elle.' He took a deep breath and blew it out, meeting my gaze again. His frustration suddenly melted into something softer and warmer as he stared at me, those blue eyes still lit from within by an emotional fire. 'It's not that simple. If . . . if anything were to happen to you, I couldn't live with that. Do you understand?'

'No,' I said. Mainly because I was aggravated that he was trying to tell me what to do, but also because deep down I wanted him to explain why he cared at all what happened to me.

Devon closed his eyes and sat there for a moment. When he opened them, he suddenly reached over, slid his hand behind my head and pulled me to him. He stared into my eyes from mere inches away. I could smell the rich scent of coffee on his breath. My own breath caught in my chest as emotions rushed through me; surprise, fear, excitement. He pulled me even closer, pressing his lips against mine. Gently at first and then so passionately the world around us fell away. His mouth was soft, warm and stirred up things for me that had been buried for a decade.

When he released me, my chest convulsed with ragged breaths. His lips were shining and his blue eyes were heavy with desire. I just stared at him, unable to pull my attention away. He was the most striking, intense man I'd ever met, and I just wanted to get lost in him. Something I suddenly hated myself for.

His voice was low and raw as he said, 'Do you understand now?'

I managed to nod.

'Good then.' He threw the Jeep into drive and resumed following the sand-packed road.

I was still trying to process the kiss and what it meant when we turned right and ended up in a parking lot. A very loud parking lot. My smile faded.

'A gun range?' I gasped, feeling my pulse do its own version of a rapid-fire machine gun. 'I . . . I've never shot a gun before.'

'Time to change that. If you're going to insist on putting yourself in danger, then you need to be able to protect yourself.' He reached across me, unlocked the glove box and pulled out his gun. 'Come on.' He hopped out. I followed him reluctantly into the front office, where he proceeded to greet the guys behind the counter like long-lost relatives.

'Come here much?' Sarcasm was one of my many defense mechanisms. Devon just smirked at me and then gathered the things we'd been given off the counter.

'Here, put these in.' He handed me a pair of tiny orange earplugs as we stepped out on to the range.

'I don't know, Devon. I'm just not a gun type of person.' I shifted back and forth on my feet. 'What if I just watch you?'

Bang! I jumped. *Bang!* Trying to get the squishy earplugs in, I hurried to catch up to him. 'Seriously, this isn't a good idea. I'm a yoga teacher, remember, we practice non-violence!'

He completely ignored me as he led us to the far end of the range and laid the gun, binoculars and box of bullets on a table.

'OK.' He glanced up and a smile twitched at the corner of his mouth. 'You're going to have to get a bit closer to the gun.' *Sarcasm. Fantastic.*

Pouting, I went to stand next to him. The earplugs did muffle the gun shots around us but they also muffled his voice so I had to concentrate on his mouth, which was even more distracting than before he had kissed me. Now that I know how incredible those lips felt . . .

'Elle? Can you hear me?'

'Yes, sort of,' I said, forcing myself to take a deep breath.

He eyed me but chose to ignore my obvious anxiety. 'OK. First I just want you to get comfortable with your stance.' He moved behind me and put his hands on my hips. I forced myself to think about the gun and not his strong grip. 'Your arms are going to point in the direction of your hips, so your hips should always be pointed toward whatever you're shooting at. In this case, it's that target. Got it?'

'Got it.'

'Good.' He released my hips. *Disappointing.* 'Now we're

going to go over a few basics.' He showed me all the parts of the gun, how to turn off the safety and load it. I held the loaded gun, pointed at the target with two hands, my index finger off the trigger until I had the target lined up like he showed me. It was heavier than it looked. 'Now squeeze the trigger slowly and smoothly. Take your time.'

I took a deep breath and held it as I tried to steady my shaking grip. Also my heart was pounding so hard, it was distracting me. Just breathe, Elle. After a few deep inhales and exhales, I held my breath and squeezed smoothly like Devon had instructed. *Bang!*

Beaming like a kid, I squealed, 'How'd I do?'

He pulled his eyes away from the binoculars and, grinning himself, gave me a thumb's up. 'Hit the black a few inches from the bull's eye at two o'clock. You're a natural.'

'Again?' I asked, my adrenalin pumping.

'Go for it.'

And go for it I did. For two hours I practiced, feeling my anxiety fall away and a new confidence take its place. Eventually, I blew out the bull's eye completely. I was sweaty, my arms ached and my trigger finger was numb, but I was happier and calmer than I'd been in a long time.

'Thank you, Devon,' I said as we walked back to the office. 'Thanks for pushing me out of my comfort zone. I can't believe I just did that.' I laughed. 'Hope will never believe it.'

He smiled and put a warm hand on my back. 'We're not done yet.'

Our next stop was a gun shop where I filled out the necessary paperwork for a background check while he picked out a gun light enough for me to handle.

'You can pick 'er up in three days.' The shop owner shook Devon's hand, and we were back on the road.

'You did really good . . . for a girl.' He grinned at me and ducked as I swatted at him. 'Hungry? Want to grab a bite?' he asked.

'Starving.' Then I remembered Buddha. 'Oh, I need to get back though. Buddha's been in the room since this morning. Novia was going to check on him for me, but I don't like to leave him this long.'

'Well,' Devon said, pulling into the ferry lot. 'Why don't we swing by and pick him up. Then we'll go to my place and I'll make everyone dinner?'

'You . . . cook?' I raised an eyebrow playfully at him.

'Don't act surprised, Elle. I have talents you can't even imagine.' He threw me a wicked smile. I felt myself blush. *Yeah, I bet you do.*

SIXTEEN

Two sides of Moon Key were bordered by sandy beaches, the other two were protected from the sea by rock walls; these were the south side, which held most of the elite twenty-million-plus monstrous mansions and the west side, facing the Gulf. The west side, along with a smattering of mansions, held the more reasonable two-million-dollar beach 'bungalows' and the beach dog park. Devon thankfully lived on the west side in a bungalow. Having to deal with my growing feelings for him in a twenty-million-dollar mansion would have been way too intimidating.

The bungalows had been constructed so the back of the home actually faced the street. This way the amazing sunsets over the Gulf were visible from the front of the house. In order to do this, the driveways curved around each side of the house from the street and curled back into the garage at the front. I noted his bungalow was actually just three doors down from the one I dreamed of living in, the one that had the fire. The Spanish-styled homes sat about fifty feet from the beach and were expertly landscaped with tropical plants and bushes, my favorite being the Bird of Paradise, which I admired on the way to the front door.

Petey met us at the door in his usual haven't-seen-you-in-years happiness. He jumped up and put his paws on Devon's chest and barked.

'None of that, boy.' Devon ruffled his ears playfully. 'Behave in front of our guests.' Petey licked his chin and then lowered himself to sniff us. He and Buddha turned a few circles around each other and then took off deeper into the house.

'Guess Buddha's making himself right at home.' I laughed.

'Come on, we'll let the dogs romp around out back.' Devon led me through the Mexican-tiled entranceway into the breezy, open living room.

'I like the minimalist style in here.' I took in the expansive, almost empty space. It had been sparsely furnished with an overstuffed wicker sofa and love seat set and boasted a dark-blue-and-white nautical theme. White cotton curtains hung from each side of the wall of sliding glass doors. We crossed the room and he slid one glass door open to let the dogs out. Out back sat a Mediterranean courtyard complete with a firepit and private Jacuzzi; beyond that a lush, green backyard with an eight-foot wall of perfectly manicured bushes blocked anyone's view from the street. 'Why would you ever leave home?' I sighed.

'I'm not really the hermit kind,' Devon said, taking my hand. 'Come on, full tour.' He led me through the house, which had the Mexican tile throughout just like the other bungalow M.J. Morgan had shown me. He led me through three baths, a media room, office, three bedrooms (where I tried not to stare at the unmade bed in the master bedroom and imagine him in it) and finally the kitchen. I had thought about asking him if we could stop by my mother's house while we were in Clearwater so I could check on her. I was suddenly glad I hadn't. Then I felt guilty for being ashamed of how I grew up. *Ugh. Just enjoy the moment, Elle.*

'Have a seat.' He motioned for me to sit at the kitchen island, which I did, putting my bag on the stool next to me. A huge, rectangular kitchen window offered a postcard view of the ocean. 'We'll feed the dogs when they decide to come in. And for us . . . do you care for seafood?'

'I do.'

'Brilliant. I just got a hold of some wild salmon. Payment for a break-in case, actually.' Devon uncorked a bottle and poured us some white wine. He handed me a glass and held out the other in a toast. Staring at me for a moment, his gaze held more seriousness than I thought the moment called for. 'To getting out of our comfort zone then. The both of us.'

We clinked glasses. 'Cheers.' I eyed him over the glass as I took a sip and wondered, *What comfort zone was he getting out of?* The dry fruity liquid hit my tongue and exploded. 'Mm. Wow. This is delicious.'

Devon turned away and went to pull out a skillet. He placed it on the stove top, his back to me. I could still hear the emotion in his voice, however, when he finally spoke. 'It was Ma's favorite.'

Oh. Ouch. 'She had good taste.' I eyed the kitchen solemnly with its earthy-toned tile backsplash, marble countertops and decorative copper range hood. 'So, this was your parents' place?'

'No.' Devon unwrapped the fish, shook some spices over it and transferred it to the skillet. 'They had a home over on the south side. I sold it and bought this place. I could see no sense in havin' a place that large.'

I took a longer drink of wine as the implications of that information hit me. Having enough money to stay on Moon Key was one thing. Having enough money to own a mansion on Moon Key was a whole different ballpark kind of rich. He could probably have his own yacht and plane. What would that kind of freedom feel like? I couldn't imagine. No, that's not true. Seeing how people live on Moon Key, I was starting to. 'Guess you're set for life then.'

Devon seemed to sense my reaction and turned to look at me. 'In the financial department sure, but there's much more to sort out in life than that.'

I shook my head. 'Yeah, but doesn't everything else sort itself out once you have that kind of money?' And then I frowned. 'Wait a minute. You could afford any car you wanted. Why do you drive a Jeep?'

He popped a lid on the fish and turned the oven on. Coming over to stand in front of me, he crossed his arms. 'First you insult my dog and now my car?'

I laughed, I couldn't help it. 'Sorry. It's a nice Jeep.'

'Thank you.' Grinning, he picked up his wine glass and took a sip, holding eye contact with me. After he swallowed, his mood turned thoughtful. 'Because I grew up with money, I guess making it was never a priority for me. Enjoying life, spending it doing something I was passionate about, that was and is my priority. Don't get me wrong, there was a battle. My da really wanted me to follow family tradition and attend Trinity College.' The corner of his mouth twitched as his attention moved inward, presumably recalling that argument. He shook his head. 'Luckily, Ma was my advocate, and so

I got to set out into the world on fairly good terms with my da.

'Though, good terms meant I had to pay for my own plane tickets and hotels by doing some things I wasn't passionate about. But, I had some amazing adventures and met some really grand people. Eventually I learned enough to start making money with my photography and got comfortable with that. This—' he motioned around the room – 'is all unnecessary for my happiness and a bit embarrassin' if I tell the truth about it.'

I stared at him thoughtfully. 'I'm sure your parents are glad you're enjoying the fruit of their labors though. If I had a son, I'd want him to have no barriers in life. Money does take away a lot of barriers, you have to admit.'

He nodded in agreement. 'It does. But, I would exchange it all in a heartbeat to have them alive.'

Luckily, the dogs came sauntering in through the open glass door at that moment and changed the somber mood that had fallen over him. They were both panting and looking very pleased with themselves. 'And what have you two been up to?'

'Probably smelled dinner.' The scent of cinnamon was beginning to fill the house from the cooking fish. 'It's even making *my* mouth water.'

'I like the sound of that.' Devon clapped. 'OK boys, dinner time.'

While Devon gave the dogs food and water, I slid off the stool and went to explore his refrigerator. You could tell a lot about a person by this simple act. *Impressive.* It was clean and boasted a fair amount of healthy foods, besides the bottom shelf full of Guinness. I opened the vegetable drawer. 'Do you mind if I throw together a salad?'

'Knock yourself out.'

We worked side by side in the kitchen, talking and laughing as we shared a second bottle of wine. By the time the sweet potatoes were baked, so were we. I found myself thinking more than once that I didn't want this day to end.

Devon pulled some plates out of the cupboard. 'I'll light the tiki torches and we can eat out back.'

Startled, I glanced over at the window. 'Is it dark already?'
'Soon.'

I walked over to the kitchen window. The sun was setting,
and the sky was streaked with bands of brilliant oranges and
golds over the sparkling Gulf waters, like strokes from a giant,
iridescent paintbrush. I would never get tired of sunsets over
the Gulf. They were magical. 'Now that is beautiful.' I sighed.
I saw Devon move into my peripheral vision. 'That it is.'
Click. Click.

'Devon!' I threw my hand in front of my face to block his
camera. 'Stop that.'

Laughing, he said, 'All right.'

But as soon as I took my hand away and glanced at him,
he snapped another photo. Suddenly remembering how grungy
I was after the gun range, I lunged toward him and put my
hand over the lens. Then I remembered I shouldn't be standing
so close to him. I probably smelled as bad as I looked. 'Devon,'
I growled.

He held up his hand. 'OK. Sorry.' Then he stroked my cheek
with the back of his hand. 'I couldn't resist. It's just the warm
lighting and that expression of pure joy on your face. . . . It
was true beauty. You're beautiful.'

His eyes blazed with that same intensity they had right
before he kissed me the first time. My heart raced and I felt
dizzy. 'I really need to check in with Hope. I'll . . . meet you
out back.'

'Elle . . .' Devon tried, but I was already walking away. As
quickly as my wobbling legs would carry me, I went to the
closest bathroom and locked myself in.

What are you doing? That was the thing. I had no idea. I
was so far out of my comfort zone with trying to find a killer
on an island I didn't belong on in the first place, riding jet
skis and shooting guns . . . and being with a man that has
traveled the world and looks like a god. And will leave eventually. *What the hell was I doing?* Whatever I was doing, it
was so far out of my comfort zone, I'm not even sure the
place I was in had gravity.

My chest began to tighten. *No. No. No.* I went to the marble
and gold sink and splashed water on my face. *You are not*

going to let him see you fall apart. I pulled my hair up into a knot and tied it, then leaned into the counter and closed my eyes. Taking three deep, cleansing breaths I felt the anxiety begin to subside. Opening my eyes, I stared at my reflection. Surprisingly, he was right. I did look happy. My cheeks were flushed from the wine, and my green eyes sparkled with some joy he had released in me like an uncorked bottle. *OK. You're good. Just enjoy the moment. No hopes for the future means no heartbreak.*

'Hope!' Holding the phone to my ear, I peeked outside to see Devon arranging the food on the table. 'What's going on? Why didn't you call me when Ira got out of jail yesterday? How is he holding up?'

'I'm so sorry I didn't call, Elle.' Hope sounded exhausted. 'I don't even know what I'm doing right now. Ira is so devastated. He kept himself locked up in his office all night and met with Reed Black, our attorney, today. Reed says despite letting him out on bail, the police have discovered Celeste Green was planning a lawsuit against Ira and are considering that motive. Which means they could upgrade the charges to murder! Oh god, Elle . . .' Her words dissolved into sobs.

Wow, Detective Farnsworth was working faster than Devon thought he would. I fought back my own tears and padded to the kitchen to grab a glass of water. Time for some tough love. 'Listen, falling apart isn't going to help Ira. You've got to stay strong for him, do you hear me?' Hope blew her nose. I'd take that as a yes. 'We're working on a few leads that may clear him. In the meantime, you can help by having Ira think of anyone who might want to frame him for this.'

'Frame him? Everyone loves Ira. What kind of leads?' Hope blew her nose again.

'Well, I found out it's really easy to get a hold of Botox. Especially on Moon Key, these women have Botox parties instead of Tupperware parties. So, we're working the angle that someone else attacked her with Botox when she arrived at the Pampered Pup, after her appointment with Ira. Also, Celeste's best friend, Billie Olsen, was actually in love with her, and Celeste rejected her right before her death. Devon

and I went and spoke with Billie and confirmed this. So, see
. . . there are things in the works.'

Hope sniffed and then sighed. 'OK but . . . please tell me
something else is going on between you and that hunk of Irish
man other than investigating. I need some good news right
now to take my mind off this nightmare.'

I took a sip of water and checked to make sure Devon was
still at the table. 'Yeah. He kissed me.'

'Whoa, now that's what I'm talking about. And?'

'And it was incredible. I mean, I've never felt this way about
anybody. Not even you-know-who. That was a childish crush
compared to how I feel around Devon. But . . .'

'But, you don't want to lose yourself, I know. But, Elle,
that's part of falling in love. You don't have to give up who
you are, though. Yes, you do go crazy for a little while and
eat and breathe each other. Ira and I would fall asleep with
the phone to our ear for months because we couldn't bear to
be apart. But that temporary insanity lets you go eventually.
And then the love is different, deeper and softer and more
sane. And as for the other reason you're afraid to fall in love
. . . you guys were too young, you need to just let that go.
Just let it happen with Devon, Elle. You deserve it.'

I don't know why her words brought up tears, but I was
suddenly blinking at the ceiling with a lump in my throat.
'Well, I should go. I'm at his house and dinner's ready.'

'He cooked you dinner? Elle, I'm going to kick your butt
if you don't let this happen. I mean it. And . . .' She took a
deep breath. 'Thank you for giving me something else to think
about for a minute and for all you're doing for Ira.'

'Ditto. Now go give that man of yours a hug and let him
in on our progress so far.'

'Everything all right?' Devon asked when I sat down.

'Yeah.' I unfolded my napkin and put it on my lap, glancing
around at the simple but elegant table of food he had set.
Everything he did was so thoughtful. 'Yeah. Fine. I just had
a quick conversation with Hope. She said the police have
discovered Celeste's plan to sue Ira so that motive Detective
Vargas talked about . . .' I shook my head.

Devon winced. 'And with motive comes the murder charge.'

'It's all so unbelievable.' Sighing, I took a tentative bite of salmon and closed my eyes as it melted in my mouth. 'That is just delicious.' I made a bowing motion. 'I stand corrected for doubting you.'

'Thank you.' Looking pleased, he took his own bite and chewed slowly. 'OK. I'm thinking since this is a time-sensitive investigation, we need to push the suspects a bit. So, next I need to have a chat with Robert Green. Lay out our suspicions to him and see how he reacts. See if he gets defensive. Or better yet . . . violent.'

I glanced up at Devon. 'I agree we need to step up the pace but . . . you want him to get violent?'

'Sure.' He shrugged. 'We don't want him to stay cool, in control. He'll never let anything slip that way.'

I cut my sweet potato in half and fed half to the dogs lying patiently at our feet. They each swallowed their piece without chewing and licked their chops, looking up at me for more.

'You don't chew either, Petey?' Chuckling, I lifted my water glass and then looked at Devon. 'If he even has anything to hide. What about Zebina? I know for a fact she wanted Celeste out of their life. How far would she go to make that happen? And wait . . . what do you mean *you* need to have a talk with Robert? Don't you mean *we*?'

Devon mumbled something as he shoved a forkful of salad in his mouth. I kept the pressure on with my glare. 'I already told you, I'm not staying out of this. Especially now that the death penalty could be on the table. I even agreed to the gun to make you feel better about it.'

He shook his head and swallowed. 'Fine. You can go with me to talk to Robert, but you're not to do any investigating on your own. I mean it, Elle,' he added when he saw my look of defiance hadn't wavered.

I thought about the kiss and my shoulders fell. 'Fine. But, no leaving me out of it either.'

'Fine.' He took a swig of his water and grinned at me. 'Are you sure you're not Irish?'

I laughed. 'What are you trying to say? That I'm hard headed? Isn't that the kettle calling the pot black? And honestly, I have no idea. Knowing our family history wasn't a priority in our house. My father was just a name on a birth certificate. He got my mother pregnant when she was eighteen and skipped town when she told him. He was older. I think in his thirties. Probably married, who knows. She won't talk about him at all.'

'Seems like you turned out OK.' He smiled at me around a mouthful of food.

'That's debatable.' I chuckled. 'So tell me about Ireland. About how you grew up. What was it like?'

He set his fork down and leaned back in his chair with a mischievous grin. 'Well, for starters, while you have Disneyland here in Florida, Dublin has the Guinness brewery.'

I laughed, thoroughly enjoying his company and excited I was about to learn more about him. 'Oh really? Go on.'

We sat there for hours under the stars, sharing stories about our childhood, the dumb things we did as teenagers, our dreams and fears. Wiping my eyes from a hilarious story he told about getting food poisoning in Shanghai, Devon shook his head as he continued. 'Did you know they had a case of exploding watermelons there because of some chemical the farmers were spraying on the plants to get them to grow faster?'

I stared at him in horror. 'Ah. No.'

He held a hand over his heart. 'Truth.' Then he sat back and crossed him arms. 'All right. I just totally humiliated myself for your entertainment. Your turn.' His eyes sparkled in the moonlight.

I groaned and looked to the dogs for help. They were both sacked out on the pavers, oblivious to my plight. Taking one more glance at his expectant grin, I suddenly knew I could refuse him nothing.

'Fine.' I covered my face with both hands for a second. Then I sighed at him, feeling my face flush. I knew it was only the liquid courage from the wine allowing me to admit this at all, and I'd probably regret it. 'My mother is the biggest Elvis Presley fan in the world. So . . .' I closed my eyes, deciding to just get it over with. 'Having Pressley as a last name, she apparently just couldn't resist. She named me after him.'

Peering between my fingers again, I watched Devon put it together. Suddenly, he threw himself back in the chair and burst out laughing.

I tossed my napkin at him. 'It's not that funny!' *But, yeah, I knew it was.*

'Elle . . . Elle is short for Elvis?!' he roared, disturbing the dogs, who lifted their heads just long enough to make sure their crazy humans weren't in serious trouble. The more he tried to stop laughing, the more he laughed and the more I glared at him. Finally, he got up from his chair and came to kneel in front of me. 'Sorry.' He shook his head, but trying to calm down only made him lay his head on my knee and shake with a fresh round of laughter. 'I'm truly sorry, I'm not laughing at you . . .' He lifted his head. 'Elvis!' That just did him in. His laughter was out of his control.

I pushed him to the ground where he lay in convulsive fits. 'It's really not that funny.' But, his laughter was contagious, and I found myself in the clutches of giggling as well.

He pushed himself up, grabbed my hand and pulled me to the ground beside him. Staring down at me, he wiped his eyes and cleared his throat. 'Forgive me?'

'Hmmm.' I pursed my lips, trying to hide my own smile. 'Why should I?'

'Because—' he lowered his mouth to mine, placing a soft kiss on my lips – 'I'm very very—' another soft kiss – 'very sorry.'

I watched the change in his eyes as they darkened and felt his breath grow shallow against my side. His mouth lowered to mine again and this time, he deepened the kiss, letting me feel his hunger for me. When he finally broke contact and met my eyes, I would have forgiven him anything.

'It's getting late, Devon. I should go.' OK, even I was shocked that's what came out of my mouth. Obviously I had intimacy issues even I wasn't aware of.

Devon lowered his forehead to mine and whispered, 'Stay. Please.'

I let myself run my fingers through his thick hair. God it was soft, like fine silk. 'Maybe next time.'

I felt the groan rumble deep in his chest. 'OK. Come on

then.' He helped me off the ground, but before he released me he slid his arm around my waist and pulled me to him. With one hand behind my head, he gave me the sweetest, gentlest kiss . . . I nearly melted right there on the spot. 'You sure?'

I could only nod. I didn't trust myself to speak.

He kissed the tip of my nose and then released me. The emptiness I felt when he walked away was almost unbearable. And that's what scared me.

With shaky hands and a raging storm of emotion going on inside, I helped him clean up the dishes and put the leftovers in the fridge. Then Buddha and I climbed into his Jeep for the ride back to the Pampered Pup.

Devon was quiet during the short ride, and I was a mess inside. There was something seriously wrong with me. *How could I be walking away from this when it's what I desperately wanted?* I didn't need Hope to kick my butt. I was doing a bang up job of it myself.

SEVENTEEN

We were meeting Robert at the Moon Key Country Club on Monday between doga classes. I stared out at the water from a table we chose between the tiki bar and beach. There wasn't a cloud in the sky, just pure blue and raging sunshine. As picturesque as the view was, we would've been miserable outdoors if it wasn't for the whirling fans hanging from the thatched roof above us. I had thrown on a sundress, as coming to an elite country club in fur-covered yoga clothes didn't seem respectful. I was, however, wearing my standard footwear of flip-flops, so the breeze felt nice on my bare toes.

'Remember to be careful, Devon,' I said for the millionth time since our drive over. 'Robert and Ira are golf buddies . . . or used to be. If I'm just being completely naive and wrong and Ira were somehow involved – though I'm not – it could be because Robert used Ira to get rid of his ex-wife. He could have blackmailed him or threatened him. I don't know what kind of man we're dealing with here. So, I don't think pushing him to act violently is a good idea.'

Devon nodded his understanding as the waiter brought our sparkling water. 'Kid gloves. Got it.'

Robert arrived a short time after that. He kissed my hand. 'Elle, so good to see you, dear.' And then shook Devon's hand. 'Mr Burke nice to see you again as well.'

'Devon, please.'

The man definitely oozed charm, but cold-blooded killers could be charming. Look at Ted Bundy. I eyed him as he took a seat and ordered a Scotch on the rocks, trying to assess him in a new light. Probably in his mid-sixties, even dressed down in a buttery yellow polo shirt and golf shorts, he exuded confidence as if he had the world by the tail and knew it. I had noted this since working on Moon Key – money came with a large dose of confidence. I was hoping some of it would rub off on me.

Robert also kept himself in top shape physically. His gray eyes were slightly bloodshot but sparkled with intelligence beneath neatly trimmed gray brows. Devon had done some digging and learned he was a retired defense attorney and successful in the stock market. He certainly was a little intimidating. Could he have threatened Ira into helping him kill Celeste? No. As much as I tried to keep an open mind about all the possibilities, I still couldn't believe Ira would have had any part in that. Then could Robert have hired someone to attack Celeste in the parking garage, thereby framing Ira? That was certainly a more plausible possibility.

'Do you golf, Devon?' Robert asked.

Devon smiled easily. 'Not very well, I'm afraid. But, I do try now and again so I can drive around on the beautiful green.'

Robert chuckled. 'It is one of the finest courses in Florida. Where are you from?'

'Dublin.'

'Ah. I've had the pleasure of playing at the Portmarnock course there. Now that was an unforgettable day.' He took a sip of his Scotch when the waiter brought it. 'So, Elle, you said there was something important you needed to discuss with me.'

Right down to business then. 'Yes.' I wrapped my hands around my chilled glass to keep them from shaking. 'I actually have a confession to make. Robert . . . Devon is a private investigator, and he's helping me look into Celeste's death.'

Robert sat back in his seat and glanced at Devon. 'I see.'

I decided not to tell Robert about Devon's part in Celeste finding out about his affair with Zebina. We needed Robert's trust. 'I'm involved because of Ira. He's a really good friend of mine, as you know, and I'm positive he didn't kill Celeste. But, he is being charged with her death. Manslaughter as of right now. That may be elevated to homicide.'

'Yes, I know. The police contacted me when he was arrested.' His demeanor changed from defensive to open. 'Elle, I know Ira is your friend. And I would have considered him a friend, as well. But, he did treat her with Botox right before she died . . . from Botox.'

'So, you think he's guilty?' I maintained eye contact, though

I wanted to look away. I wasn't used to staring down powerful men.

'I don't think he killed her on purpose, no. But, even professionals get careless. Make mistakes. And they have to be held accountable for those mistakes. Especially when they take a life.'

I flicked my gaze toward Devon. He nodded almost imperceptibly. For some reason, he was letting me take the lead on this. 'What if I told you I found a bottle of Botox in the parking garage at the Pampered Pup, near Celeste's parking space?'

Robert's brow rose and he held his expression carefully neutral. 'Really? When?'

'The night she was killed. Someone could have attacked her with it in the parking garage, after her appointment with Ira.'

'Well, that would certainly be something to give to the police. But, that would also suggest someone killed her on purpose. I'll admit she could be a feisty little thing, but I can't imagine her angering someone to the degree of murder.'

Not even the woman who stole you away from her? 'Did you know she was planning on suing Ira? The police think this is a plausible motive.'

He waved his hand dismissively. 'Celeste sued people for sport.'

'What about your fiancé?' Devon finally chimed in. 'Elle witnessed more than one fight between Zebina and Celeste. In fact, she had to ask Celeste to come to a different class to avoid them being in the same room.'

Robert shook his head. 'Celeste was harassing Zebina, yes. She was bitter about the divorce.' *And the affair,* I thought but didn't say it. 'But, trust me, Zebina isn't capable of killing someone. Besides, she was with me the morning Celeste died.'

Devon and I exchanged a glance. 'So, you and Zebina are each other's alibis,' Devon stated with a smirk.

Robert folded his hands on his lap and smiled. 'Neither one of us killed my ex-wife. Elle, Ira is your friend, but the simplest possibility usually prevails. I'm sorry, but a careless plastic surgery procedure wins in my book over conspiracy of murder.'

Devon took a long pull of his water. Then his line of questioning changed. 'How well do you know Billie Olsen?'
Robert took a sip of his Scotch and his shoulders fell as he relaxed. 'Very well. She and Celeste have . . . had been friends for decades. She was Celeste's travel companion.'
'Did you know Billie was in love with your ex-wife?' Devon asked.
Robert's expression suggested amusement. 'In love? What do you mean?'
Devon looked to me to answer that.
I leaned forward so I didn't have to speak too loudly. 'When we took Princess's things over to Billie, we had a chance to talk with her. She admitted she'd been in love with Celeste and had confessed this to her a short time before her death.'
Robert's eyebrows twitched and his gaze shifted to the calm Gulf waters. I watched as he seemed to be putting some pieces of a mental puzzle together and then he looked back at me. 'Did she say whether Celeste returned her feelings?'
'She said Celeste had stopped speaking to her.' I watched as this seemed to bring him some relief. 'Something else, Robert. I don't know if the police told you this detail, but Celeste had started to write in the mud when she lay there in the spa mudroom dying. She wrote the letters "BO". So, do you think Billie Olsen is capable of killing Celeste over being rejected?'
'I . . . honestly don't know.' He suddenly seemed deflated. 'Being a criminal defense attorney for over thirty years, I've learned people can surprise you . . . and not in a good way. But, Billie was always so kind and thoughtful. Even offering to take Princess. That was just typical of her thoughtfulness.' The frown lines around his mouth deepened. 'Of course, now I know why.'
'Is there anyone else you can think of who may've wanted to harm your ex-wife? Anything else Celeste was involved in that may help us?' Devon was leaning on the table now, staring hard at Robert.
'Robert, we really need your help,' I pleaded.
Straightening his back and regaining his confidence, he nodded. 'Of course. The truth about Celeste's death should

be known. Sure we were divorced, but I'll always care about her. And I wouldn't want Ira to pay for something he didn't do. All right, listen, I'll go through Celeste's things and see if I can come up with anything that might help.'

'Thank you,' I said, feeling good about his offer to help. He was the closest person to her, besides Billie. 'You have my number if you find anything.'

Devon nodded. 'Shall we order then? I'm starvin'.'

'What do you think?' I asked as Devon drove me back for my afternoon class. Laying a hand on my full belly, I realized I'd have to take it easy after the two huge fish tacos I just scarfed down. One of the perks of this island was the fresh seafood and top chefs. A girl could get spoiled here.

'We'll see if he comes up with anything. I don't like the fact he and Zebina are each other's alibi. They could've decided together to get Celeste out of the picture. I'm sure Robert was paying Celeste a hefty alimony check. Money and jealousy? Pretty good motives.'

I sighed, feeling frustrated suddenly. This investigating business was taking too long. 'You know Celeste could've tried to write "Bob" in the mud, too. That's what she called him.'

Devon stopped at a red light and removed his sunglasses. 'Look, Elle, there's something else you need to realize. We're going as fast as we can here, but sometimes murders take months, even years to solve. If they even do in fact get solved. You understand?'

I thought about how long he'd been working on his parents' deaths. 'Yes.' I tried to give him a reassuring smile but it fell flat. We didn't have months and definitely not years. An innocent man, my best friend's husband, could be tried for murder. It was inconceivable. Unjust. The world just couldn't work like that. I refused to accept it.

Devon pulled around the fountain and stopped in front of the Pampered Pup. 'Here, I picked this up for you this morning.' Reaching over, he popped open the glove box and pulled out my gun. He showed me it wasn't loaded. 'Safety's on. For now keep it in your glove box, bullets in the trunk. I've got the paperwork ordered for your concealed carry permit and

got you set up for another lesson at the range this Sunday.'
He suddenly looked sheepish. 'If that's OK with you?'

'Yeah, I can do that. Thank you for picking it up.' Shaking
my head, I placed the gun and bullets in my bag for now. 'I'm
probably the only yogini in the world packing heat, you know,'
I teased him.

'I doubt it.' He shot me that sexy smile I was growing so
fond of. 'But, you are one of a kind, Elle.'

EIGHTEEN

'Start to wiggle your toes, your fingers. Bring your awareness back into your body.' Tuesday morning's class seemed especially scattered and high energy so I kept them in *savasana* for an extra five minutes. From the look of the relaxed bodies – both human and canine – strewn about the studio floor, it had the desired effect. 'Give yourself a full body stretch and then roll gently to one side. Push yourself up slowly to a seated position.' Leaving the lights dim, I moved back to sit in front of the mirrors as everyone began to stir. Seeing their content, relaxed faces as they sat up was my favorite part of teaching.

Shakespeare shook himself off and came up front to say hi to Buddha. I gave him an ear scratch. 'Let's share the sound of om three times.' I closed my eyes and began the chant. '*Aaaauuuumm . . .*'

Everyone joined in and I stifled a smile when Ghost began to howl along. When we were finished, I pressed my palms together and held them in front of my heart. '*Namaste.*'

The ladies followed suit and then slowly began to gather their things. I smiled with contentment seeing that the frantic energy they had upon arrival was now a serene, calm one. I decided against breaking out the dog toy box today since they were all in a calm state.

Beth Anne came up front to gather Shakespeare. 'Thanks, Elle. Great class. I feel so refreshed.' She scooped up the shih-tzu and adjusted the blue-checkered bandanna around his neck, which matched the one in her own hair.

Whitley approached us. 'Hey, Beth Anne, is Shakespeare going to be in the fashion show this year?'

'Of course he is!' Beth Anne cupped Shakespeare's face and gave him a kiss on the nose. 'Brandy's designing him a tux as we speak.'

'Great. I'll see you at rehearsal tonight then.' She adjusted her glasses, looking uncharacteristically excited. 'I think everyone is going all out this year.'

'Moon Key has a pet fashion show? And designers?' I asked, amused.

'Are you talking about the fashion show?' Zebina practically squealed. 'This year is going to be amazing. Elle, you have to experience it to understand. The theme this year is royalty so Max is going to model a white tailcoat with real gold buttons. He's going to look so handsome! Won't you, Maxie.' Zebina scratched lovingly under Max's chin. 'My prince in a tux.'

More like a sausage roll in a tux. A dog fashion show? Oh, I had to see this. 'So, how do you get tickets for this shindig?'

'I can get you one. Not a problem,' Violet interjected. 'Or should I say two?' She grinned at me.

I felt myself blushing. I knew they couldn't resist giving me a hard time about Devon eventually. 'Two would be great. Thanks.'

'That man sure is a handsome devil,' Violet said. 'How is he in the sack?'

'Violet!' Beth Anne interjected. 'That's none of our business.'

Everyone stared at Beth Anne. We were all thinking the same thing. We loved her, but she was one of the biggest busybodies on Moon Key. She thought everything was everyone's business.

'You feeling all right?' Violet smirked.

'I'm fine.' She winked at me as I blushed furiously. 'I'm just starving. Who wants to join me in the café?'

'We'll go,' Violet said, checking her watch. 'I've got an hour before tee time.'

'I'm in,' Zebina said, putting Max down and clipping on his leash.

'Maddox and I will come.' Whitley also clipped a leash on her dog.

'Elle, you should come with us,' Violet said.

'Me?' I'd never been invited into their circle outside class before, which was fine with me. In the studio I was comfortable, but outside, in their world of money and prestige? That made me nervous. I stood frozen for a moment. Then the seed of bravery Devon had planted in me took root. What the heck. If I could shoot a gun, surely I could handle lunch with the Moon Key elite. 'Sure, why not?'

Café Belle, named after one of Priscilla Moon's Yorkies, was not as simple as its name suggested. Whitley, who owns a design business specializing in hotels, actually helped them revamp the restaurant two years ago, including making it more 'environmentally sustainable'.

I glanced over at her as we approached the hostess. Her normally calm gray eyes were shining with approval behind thin designer glasses as she took in her creation. I smiled and joined her in appreciating the view.

Even without the decor, the cavernous room was a beautiful space. Being situated at the back of the hotel, the wall of glass windows afforded diners a spectacular view of the Gulf and the city of Clearwater. It was especially breathtaking after dark, when the city came alive, outlined with sparkling lights beyond the black waters. I'd only eaten here once at night, with Hope and Ira to celebrate when I first got the job, but it was a memorable night – for Buddha, too, I suspected. They sure didn't leave out their patrons' pets when it came to pampering.

Handblown glass balls from a local artist hung above our heads in various sizes and lengths as we were led to a table by the window. Both the ceiling and floor were a dark bamboo, a stunning contrast to the light decor. The café was relatively empty today, but that would change soon when season started.

The five of us took seats around an oversized, round table while our pooches settled on to the pillows placed next to each chair. They knew the drill. Find a comfortable spot, sit back and wait for the magic to happen . . . usually in the form of gourmet beef or lamb kibbles. Buddha settled on his pillow after a few turns with a content sigh.

A waiter came by promptly with an organic chew for each dog. Luckily they were complimentary because just having a small salad in this place was going to be a splurge for me. He poured water for us and then recited the menu of the day. Because the café serves mostly local and seasonal foods, their

menu was constantly changing. By the time he finished, my
stomach gurgled in anticipation. That's it, I was having soup,
too. I just wouldn't eat dinner tonight.

'That baked goat cheese salad sounds delicious,' Whitley
purred.

'No salad for me today. I'm starving,' Violet said.

'Yes, I suppose you have to keep up your energy for your
nightly activities.' Whitley grinned at her over the top of her
glasses.

One glance at Violet's smirk told me she took the comment
as it was intended – good-humored ribbing between friends.

'Why do you think she moved to the privacy of Moon Key?'
Beth Anne interjected. 'So one of her men can't come knocking
while she's entertaining another.'

Violet raised her water glass with a salute. 'The girl does
not lie.'

This caused a round of laughter and clicking glasses at the
table. I noticed the waiter was waiting patiently, professionally
ignoring our conversation.

'Oh.' Beth Anne sat up straighter, her gossip radar going
off as she pointed to the hostess station. 'Look who it is with
Bonnie.'

We all turned to stare at the large, well-dressed man at
Bonnie's side. 'Who is it?' I asked. A celebrity? Actor?
Producer? Had to be somebody famous the way they were all
staring.

'Jamie Boccelli,' Zebina cooed. 'Only the premier jewelry
designer for pets.'

My brow rose. 'You're kidding?' You would think things
like this would stop surprising me by now.

They all ignored me as Bonnie and the pet jewelry royalty
approached our table.

'Bonnie! Jamie!' Zebina waved. Her excitement seemed a
bit over the top, but what did I know. Maybe this guy was
worthy of such adoration.

'Ladies.' Bonnie smiled down at us, in better spirits than
I'd seen her lately.

Jamie chose to check his phone rather than consort with us
peasants. Nope. Just as I thought, not worthy.

Zebina was scooting her chair closer to me and motioning for them to sit down. 'Join us, please.'

'Oh, I don't know. Jamie and I have some business to discuss. We were just going to get something to go,' Bonnie said, looking a bit distracted.

'Business will wait,' Zebina said, not taking no for an answer. 'You have to eat, and your digestion will thank you for not talking business over lunch.'

'You know you're a pain in my rear, Zebina,' Bonnie chuckled. 'But you're right. Take a seat, Jamie,' she said, motioning to the empty chair next to me. 'Chef Raul made the best clam chowder last week. I wonder if they've got any left.' She waved her hand between me and Jamie. 'Jamie, that's Elle, she's the doga instructor here. I think you've met everyone else.'

'Nice to meet you, Elle,' Jamie said half-heartedly and then went back to his cell phone.

Being ignored in lieu of a cell phone rubbed me the wrong way and threatened my confidence, which stood on shaky, newborn colt legs as it was. I wanted to poke him with a fork. Instead I said, 'So, the ladies tell me you're a jewelry designer for pets. Are you designing anything for the big fashion show coming up?'

'Of course.' Not even eye contact. What a rude man. I picked up my fork.

Bonnie jumped into the conversation. 'We've just added some beautiful pieces to the shop collection. Including a new, breathtaking ruby and diamond tiara. God, your creations make me want to get a dog. Wish I had time for one right now.'

'Real rubies and diamonds? Whoa, how much does something like that go for?' It dropped out of my mouth before I remembered where I was and who I was sitting with.

'Honey, if you have to ask, you can't afford it,' Violet said good-naturedly.

That was the truth. *Who would even buy . . . oh wait!* 'I noticed a tiara in Princess's things when I took them over to Billie Olsen. Was that one of your designs, Jamie?'

'The one Celeste Green bought? Yes,' Jamie answered. 'That was one of my best work. The delicate scrollwork, the diamond teardrops fastened so they appeared to be floating.' He made a disgusted noise in his throat. 'A shame it won't be worn in the show now.'

'A shame about Celeste's death, too,' I said with narrowed eyes. I did not like this man.

Jamie glanced up at me, making eye contact for the first time. His dark brown eyes seemed to be void of light. I shivered. 'Of course.' He went back to his phone.

'She bought that a few months ago. She was very excited about this year's show.' Bonnie's mood had noticeably fallen.

Luckily at that moment, the waiter came back to take our order.

After we ordered for ourselves and the dogs, Bonnie said, 'Speaking of jewelry, that's a lovely necklace, Elle. Is that new?'

'Oh.' I reached up and caressed the diamond yin-yang symbol. 'Thank you. Yes, it is.'

Zebina leaned over and nodded. 'Did you get that from the auction? I think I bid on that one.' Smiling, she tugged on a silver chain and a diamond and sapphire pendant the size of a robin's egg popped out of her shirt. My eyes widened. *Holy crap, she wore that to doga?* 'Robert won me this one, though. Diamonds are definitely a girl's best friend.' Giggling, she leaned over and scratched the top of Max's head. 'Sorry, Maxie.'

'That's real pretty, Zebina,' Beth Anne cooed. 'I just love sapphires.'

'Did your sexy Irishman win that for you, Elle?' Zebina teased.

Blushing, I wasn't sure if I should be offended. Did she mean because I could never afford it? I just nodded.

'See that look, ladies?' Violet pointed at me. 'Our little Elle is a goner.'

Everyone laughed, as they agreed. I couldn't argue and thank heavens my phone chose that moment to ring.

'Excuse me,' I said, checking the number. I didn't recognize it. Turning slightly from the table, I said, 'Hello?'

'Elle, it's me, Robert.'

'Oh . . . I didn't expect to hear from you so soon. Did you find something?'

'I did. But I prefer to show you in person. Can you meet me at my office tonight around seven? It's in the Lake Building, suite 207.'

The hairs went up on the back of my neck. I didn't like the idea of meeting one of our suspects alone. Then again, I didn't get any murder vibes off Robert. Still, I'd better ask Devon to go with me. I did promise him I wouldn't do any investigating alone. 'Sure. Your office, seven o'clock. Got it. Thank you, Robert.'

NINETEEN

I t should've still been light out around seven, but a wicked storm had sprung up, as they had a tendency to do in the summer evenings. Angry black clouds had rolled in and the pounding rain made the visibility nearly zero as I pushed my Beetle towards Robert's office. Amazing how quickly the roads flood when you're at sea level. At some point I believed I was actually floating not driving. But I made it, just a few minutes late. Pulling into the parking lot on the side of the building, I readjusted the beach towels draped over the passenger seat. They were already soaked from the leak in my canvas top. I really needed to get that fixed but its priority level right now was way below not being homeless.

One. Two. Three. I pushed open the door, shoved the umbrella into the downpour and popped it open. My clothes were immediately soaked but at least the top of my head stayed dry. I was about to make a run for the front door when I recognized Robert's red BMW a few spots away. The driver's side door sat ajar and the inside light was on. Was he waiting for me in the car? Probably because I was late. I splashed through the deluge of water in the parking lot as the storm assaulted my umbrella, threatening to rip it from my hand.

'Robert?' I called over the cracking thunder. Through the window, I could see his head down. 'Robert?' Grabbing the handle, I pulled open the door. My heart stopped. His face was purple and a needle was sticking out of the front of his throat. 'Oh my god, Robert!' Grabbing his wrist I checked for a pulse. His hand was still warm but there was no pulse. My chest squeezed the breath out of me. Panic was quickly setting in. Someone *just* did this to him. Killed him! Was it Botox again? Oh god! Who should I call? Devon hadn't answered his phone when I tried to reach him to come here with me. The police would take at least twenty minutes to get on the island. Moon Key Security it was. I reached over Robert's body to grab his cell phone out of the console, exposing my backside to the rain. Shivering and trying to suck in enough air to speak, I dialed security. 'Lake . . . Building . . . hurry!' The sky lit up bright blue and thunder rumbled angrily around us.

As I tossed his phone back in the console, I heard a sharp bark. Glancing at the passenger seat, I saw Angel materialize for a split second, and then she was gone. A folder lay on the seat. My body shook with adrenalin. Did Angel want me to see something in that folder? Leaning over a dead body was about the last place I wanted to be, but I couldn't bring the folder out of the car, it would be soaked in seconds. With shaking hands, and trying unsuccessfully to keep my stomach from touching Robert's legs, I bent over his body and flipped open the folder. Inside was a stack of papers stapled together. I read the top of the first page. 'Jewelry appraisal forms'. Then I quickly flipped through the first few pages. Reports on four-karat diamond earrings, a six-karat diamond cocktail ring, a black diamond necklace. What did this have to do with Celeste's murder? Maybe this wasn't what Robert wanted to show me. I'd have to search the car.

Suddenly, the passenger door flew open, and I was hit with a spray of rain. Before I could even glance up, I was smacked again, viciously . . . with something hard. The jolt from the impact threw my head against the seat and then there was only darkness.

TWENTY

A faint beeping sound came to my awareness first. My body felt heavy and confined. I forced my eyelids open and the hospital room came into view. Angel was there. At the bottom of my tucked-in feet, just like the first time she had appeared to me. At that time I was nine, and I'd gotten caught in a riptide and nearly drowned. She lifted her head and gave me a soft bark and then she was gone.

Devon appeared, taking my hand and staring down at me with a mixture of relief and fear. Purple half-moons had formed beneath his eyes and his jaw was scruffy with dark, unshaven whiskers.

'You don't look so good,' I whispered. My mouth felt like the desert.

I was rewarded with a smile as Devon collapsed on the narrow bed beside me. 'Jaysis, Elle.' He brought my hand to his mouth and pressed his lips against my knuckles, closing his eyes. 'You sure know how to scare the life out of a guy.' Shaking his head, he poured me some water from the plastic pitcher and adjusted my bed so I was sitting up more. 'What the bloody hell were you thinking talking to Robert Green? You promised me no investigating on your own.'

I took a sip of the water he held up for me and forced my foggy brain to recall how I got here. It was hard to push past the dull ache behind my eyes. *Oh yeah.* 'Robert's dead. Someone hit me on the head.' I lifted my right arm and stared at the IV. 'How long have I been here?'

'Twenty-four hours. It's Wednesday evening.'

My heart leaped. 'Buddha?'

Devon held up his hand. 'He's taken care of. I picked him up last night from the Pampered Pup, and he's having a good old time with Petey.'

Relief and gratitude flooded me. 'Thank you.' My focus shifted to the dozens of huge flower arrangements situated around the small room for the first time. 'Wow, those are lovely. Who are they all from?'

Devon walked over and started reading the cards. 'Prayers for a speedy recovery from Rita. Get well from the doga gang.' His eyebrows shot up. 'Speedy recovery and see you soon. Love, Alex.' He smirked as I visibly cringed. 'And this monstrosity . . .' He plucked a card from the biggest bouquet in the room. 'Says, "Get well soon or else. We love you, Hope and Ira.".' I smiled as he continued to read a few cards and then pulled the one from the smallest bouquet, a grouping of carnations, and handed it to me.

Confused, I took it and read, 'Sorry, Elvis. Call me. Love, Mom.'

Two things were making my head ache as I tried to make sense of them. First, my mom thought buying something that would eventually die was just ridiculous. She didn't do it. Ever. And then, 'How did she know I was in the hospital?'

Devon sat back down on the bed and intertwined our fingers. 'I called her. Well, I called a half a dozen Pressleys in Clearwater, but I finally got the right lady. She sounded really worried. I said I'd keep her updated on your progress.'

I stared at Devon, feeling too groggy to process what him taking the time to contact my mom meant. All I knew at the moment was it warmed up my insides like I had swallowed the sun.

Someone knocked lightly on the door and then a nurse entered. 'Ah, she's awake. That's a good sign.'

Devon slid off the bed as the nurse came over to check all the machines around me.

'I'm Lauren, and I'll be your nurse this evening. How are we feeling?'

'Good enough to go home,' I tried.

She laughed. 'Well, we'll let the doctor decide that. I'll let him know you're awake, and he should be in to speak with you later this evening. Hungry? You missed dinner, but I can grab you some soup or Jell-O.'

I shook my head no. 'What's wrong with me?'

She wrapped a blood pressure cuff around my arm. 'You've got a concussion, some swelling and bruising and a pretty nasty cut that required stitches. The doctor can tell you more from your MRI, but I can tell you with a few days of quiet recovery, you should be feeling much better.'

'I told you she was hard-headed,' Devon said, sounding grumpy.

The nurse chuckled and winked at me. 'And I'm sure she'll remember you said that.'

I closed my eyes and sighed, feeling the pull of sleep. 'I'm really tired.'

I was suddenly back in the car with Robert, his dead eyes staring helplessly at me. My body jerked involuntarily, and I opened my eyes again. *Whoa.*

'The tiredness could be the morphine or the trauma. But, either way, you need rest.' The nurse was staring at me with concern. 'You OK?'

'Yeah.' But, it suddenly sank in that Robert's murderer was probably the same person who knocked me out. *Oh god. They could have finished me off, too. My life could have been over.* I stared at my own mortality in horror, feeling more vulnerable than I've ever felt . . . but also more alive. It was an overwhelming feeling.

'Elle?' The nurse came over and started rubbing my arm. 'Your heartbeat just went through the roof. Why don't you try to get some rest?'

My stomach heaved as acid flooded it. 'Actually, I think I would like to try some soup.'

She nodded. 'All right then. Be right back.'

After she left, Devon pulled the chair up beside me and leaned his elbows on the bed. 'Detective Farnsworth is going to want to speak to you. Can you tell me what happened?'

I squeezed my eyes shut against the throbbing, trying to push through my brain fog. 'Robert called and said he had something to show me and asked if I could meet him at his office around seven. I tried to call you to go with me—'

Devon groaned. 'I'm so sorry, Elle. I was with a client and didn't get your message until it was too late.'

'Don't beat yourself up, Devon. You can't babysit me twenty-four hours a day. And besides, it was just Robert, we knew him . . . it was a public place.'

'What could go wrong, right?' Devon frowned. 'So, when you got there, he was already dead?'

'Yeah. But just. He was still warm.' I shivered.

Devon pulled the blanket higher on my body and his voice was strained as he said, 'So the killer was probably still there.'

'Yeah. Oh!' I cringed as a pain shot through my skull. *Ouch.* 'There was a folder full of jewelry appraisals Celeste had requested. Can you find out if the police have them? We need to have a better look through them. I think that's what Robert wanted to show me.'

'Sure. I'll give Salma a call in the morning.' He leaned forward and planted a gentle kiss on my cheek.

I heard the door open and someone cleared their throat. 'Am I interrupting?'

I peered around Devon and smiled at Hope. Devon gave my hand one more squeeze. 'I'll see you in the morning. Get some rest.'

'OK.' I smiled. 'Thanks for . . . everything. Give Buddha some extra cuddles for me, and tell him I'll see him soon.'

'I will.' Devon stood and nodded to Hope. 'She's all yours.' Then he left.

'Somehow I doubt that.' Hope forced a smile and hugged me gently and then took Devon's place in the chair. She had no make-up on and her eyes were bloodshot. It was so unlike her to not be completely put together, it made my heart ache. Her brows were scrunched with worry. 'Did this attack have something to do with investigating for Ira?'

I didn't really want to answer her because I could see the guilt already causing her more pain. She grabbed my hand. 'Elle, tell me.'

I sighed. 'Yes, but—'

'Oh my god, Elle.' The tears came then. 'You almost got killed. Because of us! That's it. You have to stop. We'll figure something else out.'

'Like what?' I held her stare until she dropped her gaze.

'I don't know.'

'Exactly.' I squeezed her hand. 'Hey, we have to concentrate on the fact I wasn't killed, OK? I'm still here, and I'm not going anywhere. But, this person needs to be put away. I know what the risks are now, and I know to be more careful.'

Hope shook her head. 'I don't know, Elle. What if Ira ends up in prison? I can't lose you, too. I'd go crazy.'

My head was really beginning to pound now. 'Neither one of those things are going to happen.'

She shook her head and pushed her palms into her eyes. When she dropped her hands she said, 'The police came by our house last night. They wanted to know where Ira was around the time of Robert's death. I said he was home with me. But then they asked if I was physically with him at that time. And I had to say no because he was in his office all evening. As you know, his office has a door to the outside, so when they asked if he could've left without my knowledge I had to say yes.' A pained groan escaped her. 'I'm so scared, Elle.'

'I know. And that's exactly why we can't stop investigating.'

Someone knocked and a young girl in pink scrubs came in. 'Hi, I've got some chicken noodle soup for you.'

Hope pulled some Kleenex from her purse and blew her nose as the girl moved a tray in front of me and arranged the soup and a can of Sprite for me. 'There you go.'

'Thank you,' I said, feeling my stomach churn.

'When do you get sprung from this joint?' Hope asked after the girl left.

'I don't know. The doctor is supposed to come in and talk to me this evening. The sooner, the better.'

'Well, Devon said you've got concussion. And a pretty nasty cut under that bandage, so you stay here as long as you need to.'

I glanced at her in surprise. 'Devon called you, too?'

She nodded slowly, a genuine smile bringing some life back to her eyes. 'Mmmhmm. Anything you want to tell me? Have we moved on from just a kiss?'

I smiled, despite the increasing intensity of the ache in my skull. 'Honestly, I have no idea where this is going. I know we like each other, and I know I love being around him. But, I also know he's not sticking around Moon Key forever.'

'Unless he has a reason to.'

I poured the Sprite into the plastic cup of ice, my arm shaking with the effort. It had been years since I'd allowed myself a soda, but right now I didn't care. If a girl couldn't have a soda after being knocked unconscious by a killer, then when could she have one? 'Kind of hard to compete with the need to travel and explore the world. If I had a chance to do that, I wouldn't give it up for anyone.'

Hope's smile softened. 'You'd be surprised what love will make you do.' Then she stood up. 'I'm going to let you eat and get some rest now. I'll come by tomorrow. And Elle—' her expression turned to fear – 'if you ever scare me like this again—'

'I know. You'll kick my butt.'

'You know it.' With one last careful hug, she left.

I had finished my soup and was just falling into the clutches of sleep when someone knocked again.

Forcing my eyes open, I watched as a tall figure tentatively entered the room.

'Zebina?' I croaked.

'Hi, Elle.' She slid into the chair next to the bed. I rolled my head toward her. She wore a black suit and her hair was pulled back in a sleek ponytail. I was feeling too drowsy to understand why she was here. Then it hit me like a sledge-hammer. *Robert.*

'I'm so sorry, Zebina,' I managed through my foggy brain.

'Thank you. I can't believe he's—' her breath hitched – 'gone.' A cry broke free and she muffled it with a handkerchief. 'Oh, god, Elle. Who would do this? Why?' She broke then, the sobs shaking her shoulders. I didn't know what to say, so I just let her cry it out.

Eventually, she calmed down enough to talk. 'The police said it looks like someone killed him with Botox, just like Celeste. And you were there. You were the last person to see him.'

Was that an accusation? I tried to shake my head but stopped when bowling balls started rolling around, bashing the inside of my skull. 'He was already . . . gone when I arrived.'

'Why were you there? Were you meeting with him?'

'Yeah. He called and said he had something for me.

Something of Celeste's.' I didn't want to explain why I was there. Zebina was still a suspect in my mind.

'Did he give you something?'

That was a strange question. I studied her through the filter of my drugged brain. Did she seem nervous? She was clutching her Louis Vuitton purse with white-knuckled strength. She was also pale and shaking, but that could be from grief. 'No, he didn't.'

Her shoulders fell. *Was that relief?* I eyed the giant diamond engagement ring on her hand, sparkling even in the dim hospital room. My mind kept returning to the jewelry appraisals, but it was still too hard to link thoughts together.

'OK.' She stood and ran her hand down the front of her dark blazer. 'I thought maybe you got to speak to him before he . . . died. I have some arrangements to make, so I should leave you to rest.' She placed a hand on my arm. 'Speedy recovery.'

And then she was gone, leaving me alone with my questions and nightmares.

TWENTY-ONE

Monday morning I fished a pair of yoga pants from my suitcase and sat on the edge of the bed to pull them on. I was still feeling a bit weak but at least the dizziness and headaches had subsided. Today I was going back to teaching for the first time since I was released from the hospital. Devon wasn't happy with the decision. He thought I needed more than the weekend to recover, but I was going stir crazy just lying around his house.

I'd given in when he'd insisted Buddha and I stay with him until I recovered. I knew it was so he could keep an eye on me. *Was it simply out of guilt?* Either way, I'll admit it was nice being solely in his presence as he nursed me back to health these past few days. He was the most attentive person I'd ever met, though given the mother I'd grown up with that may not be saying much. All I knew was, as he tucked me into the guest bed every night, I wanted so badly to ask him to stay, to know what it was like to fall asleep in his arms. But, Tommy Mathers had stopped me. I finally sat down and allowed myself to think about my first love for the first time in years.

Tommy had stolen my heart after high school. We had an algebra class together at St Pete College. I'd had no idea what I wanted to do with my life, so I just enrolled in the basic first-year classes. Tommy was this tall, blond-haired, blue-eyed creature with a poet's soul who met my stare as he waltzed into the room the first day of class and took a seat right beside me. There was an instant chemistry between us, and for two years we were inseparable. But, Tommy *did* know what he wanted to do with his life. He wanted to be a professional surfer. He was in college to appease his parents so they would fund his trips until he could get sponsors. His heart belonged to the ocean.

His surfing trips took him all over the world . . . and away from me. I never minded, though. Absence really does make the heart grow fonder, and we were closer than ever when he returned. Until the end of the second year of our relationship when a completed associate degree and an offer from a sponsor to fund travel took him away from Florida . . . and me. For good. My panic attacks had kept me from even considering going with him. He never looked back. I was beyond heartbroken. I was devastated.

After the appropriate mourning period for losing the love of your life, I hung a 'closed for business' sign on my heart and began the journey to heal myself through yoga. Hope and I also made a pact never to speak his name again. I had done a pretty good job of never giving him a second thought over the years. Until now. Now someone else had ripped that sign on my heart down and blown the door wide open. And it was terrifying. I didn't think I could survive another heartbreak like that.

Sighing, I finished getting dressed, pulled my wet hair up into a loose bun, grabbed my yoga bag and made my way into the kitchen. Devon was there, shoving kale into the Vitamix.

'Morning,' I said, coming up behind him.

He whirled around and, searching my face, folded his arms. 'Good mornin' yourself. You sure you're up to this?'

I shrugged. My yoga bag already felt heavy on my weak shoulder. 'Won't know until I try.' Besides, I had already told Rita to call the ladies and let them know classes would resume today. Too late to back out now. I smiled up into his worried eyes. 'I'll take it easy, I promise. I can teach the class from a seated position if I need to.'

He nodded. 'All right then. But any signs of dizziness you come back and rest.' Kissing the tip of my nose, he turned his attention back to peeling a banana and tossing it into the Vitamix. 'Breakfast is almost ready.'

I did end up teaching most of the class from a seated position but nobody seemed to mind. The ladies just all seemed grateful that I was back, which I accepted with just a touch of suspicion. They did seem sincere though. They even hugged me carefully, cringing at the stitches above my brow, and fawned

over Buddha. He loved the attention. Even the usually sarcastic
Violet got choked up as she told me how worried they all were
when they'd heard I'd been attacked. It was really touching
and for the first time in my life I felt like I was a part of
something important.

I knew some people didn't understand what I do and may
even think it's frivolous, but I suddenly realized just how much
more the ladies got from these classes. It wasn't just about
relaxing and stretching. It was about being a part of a commu-
nity with other women. We may have all come from different
backgrounds and have different lifestyles, but we all shared a
love of our pets. And this hour we spent together with our
beloved dogs was a safe space, where we could let ourselves
be vulnerable for a while in a world where that, more often
than not, would get you hurt.

After class, Violet came up to me grinning and handed me
two tickets. 'Two tickets, front row.'

'Oh, thank you! I forgot all about the fashion show. Front
row, huh?' I raised a brow playfully at her and then cringed
at the pain that movement brought with it.

'Yes and please don't ask me who I had to kill to get those.'

My expression must have given away my shock because
she suddenly burst out laughing. I shook my head, joining in
the laughter. It felt good, even though I felt a pinch of guilt.

'If we can't laugh in the face of tragedy, Elle, we're letting
it win.' She winked at me.

'Well, thank you,' I said, clearing my throat and feeling
lighter. 'For the tickets, too. It gives me something to look
forward to.'

'You're welcome.'

'Hey, how's Zebina holding up?' I'd noticed her absence in
class.

Violet shook her head. 'I haven't heard from her since
Robert's memorial in Tampa on Friday. I think she just needs
some time to grieve.'

I nodded. 'Of course.' I hated that I missed Robert's memorial and a chance to say a proper goodbye to him. It would be
hard not to remember him the way I saw him last. An involuntary tremor ran through me. Shaking off the image, I called

to Buddha and flicked off the studio lights behind the last client.

I tried to help out around the spa as much as I could, but before my four o'clock class, I had to give in and rest in a suite. With Buddha snoring happily beside me on the bed, I set the alarm on my phone and fell into a deep sleep.

Images of Celeste rising out of the mud, pointing her finger and screaming at me that it was my fault Robert was dead, haunted my dreams. Then Robert came to me, and he was trying to tell me something but no sound was coming from his mouth. I was trying so hard to read his lips. Then he began to turn purple, clutching at his neck.

I awoke with a jolt. Buddha lifted his head and stared at me, his ears alert. I sat up, trying to calm my jagged breathing. *That was so real.* Buddha pushed himself up, his paws sinking in the luxurious mattress as he trudged over to lie against me. I slid my arm around his wide girth and buried my face in his fur. The comfort was immediate. 'Thank you, boy.'

After class, I decided to go pay Hope a visit. She wasn't answering her phone or returning my calls, which was worrying me.

I wrestled my Beetle's convertible top into place, a rather tedious manual process which I usually avoided by leaving the top down in the parking garage, but the attack made me see the gravity of my situation. I needed to be more cautious. A good knock on the head will do that, I suppose, though I was trying not to let it make me a paranoid freak. I didn't need another phobia.

Suddenly I caught something out of the corner of my eye. A shadow behind one of the cars. A cream Mercedes three parking spaces down was one of a half dozen cars left on this level and yep, there was definitely a shadow moving behind it. *Was someone crouched there?* The hairs stood up on my arms and adrenalin rushed through my body. Trying to breathe quietly, I leaned into the passenger seat, opened the glove box and pulled out the gun. 'Stay, Buddha.' No time to grab the bullets from the trunk, but I didn't actually want to shoot anyone anyway, just let them know they couldn't mess with me.

Abandoning my flip-flops so I could tiptoe quietly toward the back of the Mercedes, I clutched the gun in both hands, finger off the trigger like Devon had drilled into me, and snuck up on the shadow. As I got closer, I could hear a scraping sound. And breathing. My legs trembled with adrenalin but I managed to stay upright. Almost there.

Closing my eyes and taking a deep breath, I jumped out from behind the car and yelled, 'Freeze!'

'Aaaaa!' A scream and then I was pelted in the face with what felt like a handful of pebbles. Mrs Obermeyer had fallen back on the ground in her cream pants suite. Staring up at me, she clutched her pearls to her heart with one hand and held herself upright with the other. I stood above her with the gun still pointed at her. Our round, terrified eyes were locked.

'Oh, my god!' I breathed, finally dropping the gun to my side and reaching down to help her up. 'Mrs Obermeyer, I'm so sorry!'

Her Pomeranian poked its tiny head up inside the car and began yipping at me through the driver's side window. Mrs Obermeyer took my offered hand reluctantly, still eyeing me and my gun with suspicion. Her complexion was whiter than her hair.

'Elle?' She leaned against her car to catch her breath. 'What in heaven's name are you doing sneaking up on me . . . with a gun? Is that thing real?'

Closing my eyes in utter mortification, I pressed my lips together and nodded. 'It's . . . it's not loaded. I'm so . . . *so* sorry.' Opening my eyes I tried to explain my utter paranoia, the same paranoia I'd just convinced myself moments ago I'd successfully avoided. 'I saw the shadow and thought you were someone hiding behind the car, waiting to . . . you know, attack me.'

She was still staring at me with wide eyes behind thick glasses. 'Attack you? No,' she said, her voice noticeably shaky. She held up her hand. In it she clutched a tin mint can. 'Just dropped my mints. Was trying to clean them up.'

Nodding, I dropped my head. Then plucked a mint from where it had lodged itself in the top of my tank top. Not pebbles then. 'Mints. Right.' I was an idiot. 'Please tell me how I can make this up to you,' I pleaded. I knew the woman was in her mid-eighties. I could have given the poor thing a heart attack.

She reached behind her and opened the car door. It dinged as the light came on, and she struggled into the soft caramel leather seat, nudging her still yipping dog to the other seat. Waving a shaking hand at me, she said, 'Not necessary. Just—' she glanced once more at the gun in my hand – 'maybe get that head injury checked out, dear.'

She shut the door, and I jumped out of the way as she punched the gas and squealed the tires trying to get away. From me. I just scared the living hell out of an eighty-year-old woman. *Way to go, Elle.*

Tossing the gun back into the glove box, I plopped into the driver's seat and leaned my head against the worn vinyl. Buddha licked my hand. I stroked his head and groaned. OK, shake off the humiliation. It was time to check on Hope.

TWENTY-TWO

Hope answered the door in a stained T-shirt; her hair matted down like it hadn't been washed for a week, and the only color to her face was the red rimming her eyelids.

'Hope,' I gasped, pulling her into a hug. Her naturally thin frame now felt like sharp, pokey angles as I held her. 'Oh, Hope.' I closed the door behind me, let Buddha off his leash and pulled her deeper into the house and up the spiral staircase. 'No. You're not going to do this to yourself.'

A mix of sorrow and anger fueled my actions as I deposited her on her bed and then went to run her a hot bath. My tears fell into the bubbles as I leaned over to turn off the water. *Get a grip, Elle. She needs a strong friend right now.* Taking a few deep breaths, I concentrated on what needed to be done at the moment.

'Come on.' I pulled Hope from the edge of the bed, where she had sat and stared at the pile of laundry on the floor since I had put her there. 'You're going to take a hot bath while I make you something to eat.' As I helped her into the tub, her expression finally cracked, and she broke into sobs.

'Oh, Elle, I'm so scared. Ira has himself locked up in his office just waiting for them to arrest him on new murder charges. Reed Black said when this happens, there will be no bail. He'll have to stay in jail until the trial. But the worst thing is Ira's not talking to me. He's never done that. We've always said we can handle anything as long as we do it together, so why is he pushing me away?'

'I'm sure he's just scared and doesn't want you to see him like that. This is such a nightmare, Hope. But, we're going to get through it.' *I prayed to the universe that was true.* 'You may just have to give him some space right now. I mean, the prospect of being rearrested on murder charges is terrifying him, I'm sure.'

She swiped at her nose with a hand covered in bubbles and met my gaze with swollen eyes. 'No, you don't understand. When I say he won't talk to me . . . I mean he's never shut me out before and I feel like . . .' Her mouth twisted in agony as she whispered, 'I feel like he's hiding something from me.'

'Like what? Hope, you don't believe he got careless and made a mistake, do you? Because we've talked about this. Ira is the best at what he does—'

'No.' She shook her head. 'I still believe your theory that someone tried to frame him by killing Celeste after she left his office. But, I just feel so guilty because I'm letting my imagination run wild. I mean, just because he's shutting me out and acting secretive shouldn't make me suspicious of the man I love. I know this. I just . . . need him to talk to me!'

As she sat there in the bathwater, sobbing and letting out all the grief that she'd been holding in, I gently washed her hair, massaging her scalp to release the tension. 'Oh, Hope. Just think about that trip to Greece. It will happen as planned so imagine being there, sharing a great meal, holding hands and having all this mess behind you.'

I ran some warm, fresh water to rinse her hair. 'Tell you what. Why don't we drag him out of that office and have a sit down heart-to-heart with him. You can tell him what you just told me, and I'll be right there beside you for support.'

'No!' Her eyes widened. She looked so much like that scared little new girl, who'd moved to my neighborhood twenty-some years ago, it almost broke me. 'I don't want him to think I have any doubts about him at all.'

'OK then. I'll ask. It'll come from me.' I poured clear water over her hair and watched her shoulders fall.

'OK.'

'OK. Now, I'm going to go make you something to eat and then we're going to have a conversation with Ira. Get all this out on the table.'

Leaning back in the tub with a sigh and sinking into the water, she nodded. 'Thanks, Elle.'

Rummaging through her fridge, I could tell food hadn't been a priority for them lately. Buddha followed, sniffing at the spot in the kitchen where they used to keep Jelly-Belly's bowls, then plopped himself on the cool tile, looking up at me with sad eyes. 'I know. I miss him, too.' I pulled out some wilted spinach, mushrooms and eggs. Omelet it was.

As the eggs cooked, I cleaned up around the kitchen. It looked like the maid hadn't been here for a while, either. What was that about? Hetti would never let the place look like this.

As I finished loading mostly coffee mugs into the dishwasher and turned it on, Hope came into the kitchen in a bathrobe, her wet hair slicked away from her pale face.

'You don't have to do that, Elle.' Sliding into a chair at the table, she scratched at her forearm. 'I haven't found a new maid yet. Hetti quit. Said she couldn't work in a house that had such bad karma.'

Whirling around, I stared at her. 'Seriously?'

'Yep.'

Chuckling, I cut the huge omelet in half and transferred it to two plates. 'Well, look on the bright side,' I said, putting the plates on the table and sitting down. 'You'll get a chance to hire someone who won't steal your sugar and flour.'

Hope shrugged and then shot me an annoyed look as I stopped her from scratching at her already raw skin. 'I never really minded that. Figured if she needed it that badly, more power to her.' Obediently she chewed and swallowed. I doubted she tasted it. 'That's the hardest thing about all this though . . . well, besides Ira having to close his practice doors. It's everybody assuming he's guilty. People who've been in our lives and should know him better. Makes me wonder if we had any real friends at all.'

'Hey!' I held out my hands. 'What am I? Chopped liver?'

Hope's eyes crinkled at the corners as she finally let herself smile. It was nice to see. 'More like chopped organic kale. When did you get to be such a hippy?'

I laughed, more in relief at her feeling up to making a joke. 'I'm not a hippy. I'm just trying to keep all my parts and pieces together. It's hard work. Especially after thirty.'

Hope raised a sparse brow. 'Tell me about it.'

We finished eating and after muttering, 'Here goes nothing,' Hope went to fetch Ira from his office with the excuse that I needed to update him on Devon's investigation. Which wasn't a lie but wasn't our motive for getting him out of his self-induced isolation, either.

I made myself comfortable on their leather living room sofa, which threatened to swallow me whole, as I tried to figure out exactly what to say to Ira. Too soon, Hope was back with Ira straggling in behind her. I tried not to react to his appearance. He looked as bad as Hope had with his disheveled, wrinkled clothes and thin, pale face. I should have made an extra omelet.

'Hello, Ira.' I stood and gave him a hug, instinctively being careful, though it wasn't his physical frailty that concerned me as much as his mental.

Releasing me quickly, as if afraid of human touch, he reached down and scratched Buddha behind the ear. He tried to smile but failed miserably. 'Good to see you up and about, Elle. We were extremely worried about you.' Finally making eye contact, he looked sternly at me. 'Hope told me the person who attacked you was probably the one who murdered Robert Green. I would've hoped you'd distanced yourself from this investigation by now.'

It was my turn to force a smile. 'I definitely learned my lesson.' Well, I had. I knew I had to be way more careful now. I may have been naive before about exactly how much danger I was in, but I was a fast learner and apparently really good at being paranoid. I mentally cringed at the image of me pointing a gun at Mrs Obermeyer.

Shaking his head, he went to the bar and poured himself a drink of amber liquid. 'Ladies? Care to join me? It's the best cognac on the market.'

'Sure,' Hope answered. Her glance told me she was looking for some liquid courage.

Not a bad idea. I accepted his offer, also.

He handed us each a glass and then took a seat in the over-stuffed leather chair across from us. I swallowed a swig of the smooth, amber fluid and let it warm my insides.

'So, Hope says you have news?'

'Yes. As you know, the night Robert was killed, I was meeting him because he said he had something to show me he felt was related to Celeste's death. What you don't know is when I got there, there was a folder of jewelry appraisals sitting on his passenger seat. I have no idea what it means, but Devon is hoping the police will let him take a look at them for any clues. But the main point here is, I hope you'll see the silver lining in this. Robert believed there may have been a reason Celeste was killed, and it didn't have anything to do with you. I've explained this to Detective Farnsworth. This, along with the Botox bottle I found in the parking garage, and the fact that Robert was also killed with Botox, should give them enough doubt about you to start looking in a different direction.' I was explaining this as much for Hope's benefit as for Ira's. She needed to hear the facts laid out to assuage any seeds of doubt she had about her husband's innocence.

Ira was very still, chewing on the inside of his lip. Finally, he nodded. 'Unless they try to pin Robert's murder on me, too. Since no one can vouch for me being in my office at the time.' He glanced apologetically at Hope.

'Right. There's that.' I took a swig of the cognac. Well, I did my best to address a murder charge, but there was still the existing manslaughter charge. Despite the fact that neither Hope nor I were willing to entertain the idea that Ira could've screwed up that royally, the fact remained that the police did believe it was possible. And no matter what Hope said she believed, obviously this whole situation was making her beliefs unstable. I couldn't blame her.

Here goes nothing. Like ripping off a Band-Aid. 'Ira, I know what an excellent surgeon you are, so please don't take this as me doubting you in the least. But, why in the world do the police think they have a manslaughter case against you? I mean, doesn't Botox work immediately? Wouldn't Celeste have had difficulty breathing before she even left your office?' I waited for Ira to answer, but he just dropped his head, so I continued, making sure to convey patience and understanding. 'Devon and I figured out it would've taken Celeste about five or six minutes to get to the parking garage from your office and down to the mudbath room, where she collapsed. Doesn't that prove she didn't receive the fatal injection in your office?'

Ira rolled his head back and forth and then lifted it with

effort. After a few uncomfortable glances between me and Hope, he rubbed the back of his neck.

'Unfortunately, no. We know Botox does spread to the brain and nearby muscle and tissue. That's why it's so important to get the dosage and targeted muscles right.' He looked pained suddenly and the look he gave Hope made my heart ache. 'So, it isn't out of the realm of possibility that the toxin spread to her larynx. I give conservative doses but it only takes seventy-five nanograms to kill a person.'

Stunned, I leaned over to dig my fingers into Buddha's fur around his neck, something akin to a baby grabbing the corner of his blankie. He angled his head to look up at me, and I gleaned comfort from his wide, smiling mouth and melted-chocolate eyes. 'So, you're saying it's not out of the realm of possibility that . . . you may have killed her . . . accidentally?' I was speechless. Both Hope and I had brushed this possibility aside from the beginning. I still couldn't believe it.

Ira nodded once, dropping his head again.

Hope placed her glass on the coffee table with a loud clink and flew off the couch, landing in his lap. 'Oh, Ira.' Hope grabbed his chin and made him look at her. 'Why didn't you tell me? You've had to have been worried sick!'

'I was. I am.' He took her hands in his and pressed them against his face. 'I didn't want to worry you.'

'So this is why you've been avoiding me?' Hope let her head fall on to his shoulder.

I placed my own glass on the coffee table, my free hand still resting on Buddha. 'But, Ira, you know that's not what happened, right? I mean, if that's all it was – just an accident – then somebody would've had no reason to kill Robert. Someone killed him to keep us from finding out why Celeste died.'

'Yes.' Ira sighed, kissing the top of Hope's head. 'Of course, you're right. I've just been so wrapped up in guilt. Just going over and over her procedure in my head to see if there was any way I could have . . . I haven't been thinking straight.' He let a brief smile flitter over his lips as he looked into his wife's eyes. 'I haven't handled this well at all. Forgive me?'

'Nothing to forgive,' she whispered, wrapping her arms around his neck.

And that was my cue to leave. They had a lot to talk about. 'Come on, Buddha. Our work here is done.' Now, to figure out who did kill Celeste Green.

TWENTY-THREE

By the time I reached Devon's bungalow, my head was pounding and my legs were so heavy it felt like someone had replaced my flesh and bone with cement. Petey greeted Buddha and me at the door like we'd been gone for months, which actually it felt like we had been. Then the scent of fresh garlic hit me and nothing mattered but my stomach.

''Ello,' Devon said, coming to greet us.

'That smells just a little amazing,' I said after he planted a kiss on my lips.

'*That* is fresh garden vegetables over spaghetti squash. Don't think I haven't noticed your affinity for all things vegetable.' He closed the door behind me and grabbed my hand. 'Come on. You look exhausted.'

'Who are you?' I laughed as he pulled me out the sliding doors to the table already set for two, complete with lit candles. I noticed the hot tub was also bubbling away.

'I'll feed the dogs, stay right here.'

Where would I go? I should move back to the suite at the Pampered Pup. I was healed enough and working again. It was time, but I didn't want this fairy tale to end. Letting my head fall back to gaze at the span of sky dripping with stars, I felt an overwhelming sense of gratitude and peace. There was nowhere I'd rather be right now. And that thought caused fear to bubble up, slinging me back to reality. This couldn't last and when Devon left, he would take my heart with him. No, I couldn't let that happen . . . again.

Devon returned with two steaming plates. He set them down and then tilted my chin up with his index finger. 'What's wrong?'

Why did he have to be so observant? Attentive? Gorgeous? And a great cook? It was maddening. Before I could stop it, a tear slipped down my cheek. I wiped it away.

'Just a long day.' *Think of something, Elle, or he's going to keep pressing for a real answer.* 'I stopped by and saw Hope and Ira. Hope looked terrible. I'm really worried about her.'

Devon kissed the top of my head, accepting my answer. 'I know. She means a lot to you.' Sighing, he moved to his chair. 'I have some good news and some bad news.'

Twirling the soft spaghetti squash on my fork, I said, 'Let's have the bad news first.'

'I talked with Salma today.'

I studied his expression. Why did he always talk to Detective Vargas and not the lead detective on the case? And why did he call her Salma? Had they gotten that close? He looked tired, too. 'And?'

'She said the jewelry appraisals were not recovered at the crime scene.'

I sank back into the chair. 'That is really bad news.'

He held up his hand. 'Now the good news. Because you remembered the business name, A Cut Above, they're going to get a warrant and get a copy of the appraisal given to Celeste.'

My heart fluttered with hope. 'How long will that take?'

'A few days.'

'OK.' I nodded slowly. 'OK. That's something. At least they're willing to look somewhere besides at Ira.' I slid a forkful of the dinner into my mouth and the flavor burst on my tongue: fresh tomatoes, garlic, onion, peppers. An involuntary moan escaped me.

Devon chuckled. 'I'll take that as a compliment.'

I shook my head, enjoying the way the moonlight animated his eyes and accentuated the planes of his cheekbones. 'You are a dangerous man, Devon Burke.'

'You've got your own weapons, Elle.' His tone was teasing, but even by moonlight I could see his eyes were dead serious.

I knew that look. Time to change the subject. 'So, did Detective Vargas give you any other ideas about what they found at the crime scene?'

'No, she wasn't feeling very generous. She was furious that you were hurt after she warned you to stay away from the investigation.' His brow rose as he pointed his fork at me. 'And I don't blame her.'

Swallowing and patting my mouth with the napkin, I nodded. 'I know. I screwed up. Won't happen again.'

Devon shook his head. 'I'll believe that when I see it.'

I ignored his anger. 'So, nothing useful?'

'They do know it was Botox used to kill Robert. Probably just a few minutes before you arrived.'

I felt guilt flare up, hot and stifling. 'If I would've just been on time. It was storming so badly, I could barely see to drive.'

'Hey—' Devon reached across the table and slid his hand over mine – 'Robert's death was not your fault, and I won't allow you to take any blame. There's a killer out there, Elle. That's who's to blame. You were lucky to come out of the whole thing alive yourself,' he growled. Sighing, he pulled his hand back, and we ate in silence.

The dogs strolled outside, licking their jowls and sniffing around the table for any handouts. 'Go lay down, Buddha.' I pointed to the ground. With a big, silly grin he obeyed, plopping belly-first on to the pavers. Petey turned some circles and lay beside him.

'He's very obedient. Maybe you could give me some pointers for Petey.'

'Well, we worked hard on that, didn't we, big guy?' I smiled fondly over at Buddha. His ear twitched. 'The first time I saw him, he was almost my new hood ornament.' I shook my head. I could still remember the screeching tires, his terrified eyes in my headlights. 'He had darted across the road in front of me one night about five years ago, then ran two blocks to hide under a rusted car up on blocks on the side of a house. I followed him to see if he had a collar or tags, because you know . . . that's what a sane girl does in a bad neighborhood.' I cringed, thinking about how that decision could have altered my life. That particular street was the location of a gang shooting death two weeks before, which I didn't know until much later. 'I think it was just the adrenalin because normally I would not be walking around that part of the neighborhood after dark. Anyway, I had shined my cell phone light under the car and could see his eyes glowing. I tried to coax him out but he wasn't budging. He didn't growl at me, though, so I decided to come back the next morning with food and see

if he was still there.' I shook my head. 'I got a little obsessed
with rescuing him. It took two weeks of bringing him food
and leaving it before he would come close enough to let me
touch him. He was a mess. Skin and bones, half his fur missing.
Once he trusted me, though, I got him in the car and straight
to the vet.

'He had all the lovely stuff living on the streets gives a dog:
mange, malnutrition, parasites. But luckily he was heartworm
negative and such a sweet little guy once I earned his trust. I
don't know. There was just something about his eyes. I was
smitten. And I think I needed him as much as he needed me.'
I chuckled. 'Of course the poor thing had no idea how to be
a pet, wasn't even potty trained, though the vet estimated him
to be around a year old. Which just gave my mom fits. I had to
convince her every day to let him stay. I spent a lot of my
time checking out dog training books from the library and
watching training videos online. In fact that was pretty much
my life, temp jobs, training Buddha and yoga.' I paused to
take a bite and see if I was boring Devon. His patient smile
encouraged me to go on.

'Anyway, I was having a life crisis. One day Hope and I
were at the dog beach, and I was talking about how the office
jobs were killing my soul and complaining about my mom
giving me a hard time every time I left for a job, refusing to
even take Buddha out to the bathroom. I was also telling her
about how I was thinking of getting my yoga teaching certificate, since yoga was pretty much the only thing keeping me
sane. Well, as I was talking, I had Buddha lying in front of
me stretching out his legs like I did at home when he'd curl
up on my mat with me. Suddenly Hope jumped up and started
yelling, "Oh my God! It's kismet! Oh my God!".' I laughed
as I remembered her jumping around on the beach that day.
'So, she is rambling about how the manager of Pampered Pup
was just telling her she had this big studio space at the spa
she was trying to find some use for. And she pulls out her
phone and starts showing me these videos of women in yoga
classes with their dogs. And she says, "Doga!" And I looked
at her, completely dumbfounded and said, "That's a thing?"
And she plopped back down with a huge grin and said, "Yep.

And you're going to teach it at the Pampered Pup. It's perfect. Buddha can come to work with you every day." And the rest is history.' I grinned at Buddha and then Devon. 'So you see, he saved me just as much as I saved him.' Devon glanced at Petey and smiled, though it didn't reach his eyes. 'They tend to do that, don't they?'

I waited a beat and then asked quietly, 'Petey saved you, too?'

'He did. When I first arrived here, I was a bit lost. My parents' house was so empty and quiet. I wasn't used to all the silence. Anyway, I was working on tracing their last week, where they had spent their time. My ma, she was a huge dog lover. Horses and dogs were her passion. I found out she'd volunteered at this shelter in Tampa a few days before she died. I wasn't really expecting to find anything, I don't think. It was more just about feeling a connection with her. Walkin' in the places she walked in her final days.' He cleared his throat. 'So, they have these long rows of kennels, and I'm walkin' down the aisles with the dogs barking, making a huge racket, really trying to get someone's attention. Such a sad place. So, I suddenly stop at Petey's cage because he was just lyin' there, this huge grin on his face, his tail swishing back and forth. Just the happiest dog I'd ever seen, especially considering his incarceration. It was just so strange and really touched me.' He shrugged. 'I figured he could teach me a thing or two about being happy with the hand that life deals you. And I could give him a home. So, I did just that . . . brought him home.' His expression lightened as he chuckled. 'The big house was not so quiet after that.'

I laughed too. 'I can imagine.'

We finished dinner and Devon took our plates to the kitchen. I picked up our glasses and followed him. He turned from the sink and rested his hands lightly on my hips. 'Up for some hot tub time?' Bending down, he pressed a soft kiss on my lips.

I pulled my head back and looked into his eyes. They were sparkling with mischief. He was clearly in a playful mood. 'And by hot tub time, you mean . . .?'

His grip on my hips tightened and he pulled me flush against

him. 'Two adults sharing some really, really, really hot . . .'
His mouth came down on mine and made me suck in a breath.
That only encouraged him to deepen the kiss. When we came
up for air, my lips felt swollen and my head and heart were
floating. 'Water.'

*Water, right. How was I going to say no? I had to. If I let
this go to the next level, I was done for. There would be no
escaping heartbreak.*

He must have seen the struggle on my face because he
backed off. 'Come on.' Taking my hand he led me to the guest
room. 'Put on your suit and meet me outside. It'll be good
for your sore muscles. And—' he released my hand – 'I'll
behave like a gentleman, I promise.'

The rejection was reflected in his demeanor, and it killed
me that I was responsible for it. Especially because I wanted
nothing more than to show him how much he already meant
to me. I choked back the frustration and nodded.

As I changed, I tried to think logically about the situation.
Was I wrong to avoid heartbreak? Would it be worth it just
for a short time with Devon? It took me years to recover from
my last heartbreak. No, obviously I was still screwed up from
it. And the way I already felt about Devon, it would be a
million times more painful.

Thank heavens Devon was already submerged in the steaming,
bubbling water when I walked out. I don't think I could have
held my position if I had to see him half-naked. I tossed my
towel to the side and slipped into the water beside him, cringing
at first and then sighing with pleasure as the heat sunk into
my bones. 'Wow, that feels amazing.'

Devon had his head resting against the tiled ledge. He rolled
it toward me as I settled in beside him, letting my body sink
in up to my shoulders. The steam rose around us. I noticed
he was eyeing the stitches in my forehead. The swelling had
receded but the skin around the stitches had turned an ugly
shade of mustard yellow. I suddenly realized how comfortable
I was around him. How did that happen in such a short amount
of time? Some Irish magic, I bet.

'So, you were leaning over Robert's body, the killer opens
the car door and whacks you with something hard enough to

knock you out. When the door opened, do you remember seeing anything? Trousers maybe? Or shoes?'

I pursed my lips and tried to think. 'No. Sorry. It was raining so hard, when the door flew open, I got pelted in the face so I closed my eyes.'

He went back to staring at the immense span of darkness and stars above us for a moment. Then, he suddenly turned back to me. 'When you talked to Robert on the phone, was there anyone around you?'

I thought back to lunch when I took his call. 'Yeah. I was at Café Belle with Beth Anne, Whitley, Violet and . . . Zebina. Oh, then Bonnie joined us with a guy named Jamie Boccelli. Apparently, he's some fancy shmancy dog jewelry designer. A real pompous jerk.' I stared at Devon. 'Why, what are you thinking?'

'I'm thinking someone might have overheard your conversation about meeting Robert.'

I narrowed my eyes. 'Or the killer could have heard it on Robert's end.'

'True. Except one of our main suspects was with you.'

I ran my hand through the bubbles. Adjusting my position so my back was against the massaging jet stream, I thought about where everyone was when I took the call. 'I did mention out loud where I was meeting him. But, while I can see Zebina killing Celeste, I can't see her being Robert's killer. I think she truly loved him.'

'Probably loves not going to prison more, though. If she knew he had evidence of a motive for her killing Celeste, she could have offed him to protect herself.'

'I don't know.' I bit my lip in concentration. 'What would Celeste's jewelry appraisals have to do with Zebina?'

Devon ran a hand through his wet hair, pushing it off his forehead. 'That would be the million dollar question.'

We were both lost in our own thoughts for a bit. I was starting to feel sweat around my hairline and a bit light-headed when Devon's leg brushed up against mine. We both turned and our eyes met.

'Elle,' Devon whispered, 'you're not your mother. And I'm not one of those men coming through the revolving door.'

His expression was so imploring and sincere. I opened my mouth and closed it again. *Was it time to tell him about my extreme anxiety?* I had worked hard to be comfortable leaving my safe zone and traveling to Moon Key every day. But to travel anywhere else? My heart was palpitating just thinking about it, and I wasn't ready to confess being so weak to him. I didn't want him to think less of me. The sincerity in his eyes almost made me blurt out a full confession, but I stopped halfway like the chicken I was.

'Devon, I can't do a "let's just have fun together" kind of thing. And you once told me you knew it wasn't fair to get into a relationship when you traveled so much.'

'But—'

'And,' I cut him off, 'you also told me Moon Key is temporary for you. You miss traveling. It's in your blood.' I tried to keep my tone soft. The last thing I wanted to do was sound resentful about who he was. I didn't want him changing for anything. Especially me.

He opened his mouth to answer me when suddenly there was a loud noise out front. The dogs scrambled up and ran into the house, barking like crazy.

'Stay here.'

My heart pounded as I watched him leap from the hot tub, slip on the wet tile pavers and slide through the opened glass doors. I climbed out of the hot tub after him and grabbed a towel, my heart racing. The dogs made a beeline for the front door. Devon had already found his gun and was twisting the lock. I was right behind him as he pulled the door open and scanned the area, gun at his side. Beyond the sound of the ocean, there was the sound of a car speeding away behind the house. Petey and Buddha scrambled through the door and out to the driveway. We followed them; Devon tense as a coiled spring and me with my heart knocking against my breastbone.

Devon quietly followed the dogs around the back of his Jeep. Then we both stopped and stared at the tiny pebbles of glass glittering in the moonlight beside my Beetle. Someone had smashed the driver's side window. I groaned. Was this covered by insurance?

Petey and Buddha tried to sniff around it but Devon shooed them back into the house so they wouldn't cut up their paws. 'Who would do this?' I felt sick to my stomach. And violated.

'Don't know.' Devon motioned to my towel. 'May I?' I handed it to him and he used it to carefully pull open the door with a whispered expletive and wipe the glass from the front seat. Then he arranged the towel on the seat.

'Should we call island security?'

'No, there's nothing they can do. I'll phone Salma and let her know about this. First, check the car to see if they took anything.'

I sighed. 'On the bright side they didn't slash the roof. That would have been expensive.' It would've forced me to get the leak fixed though. I climbed in and opened the glove box, the only place I had anything worth stealing. Looking up at Devon's expectant face, I told him, 'The gun's gone.'

He ran a hand through his damp hair in frustration. 'They got what they came after then. We'll have to call the Clearwater police now and have them take a report on the missing gun. If it ends up being used in a crime, I don't want that coming back on you.' He held out his hand. 'Come on. Let's get you back inside.'

TWENTY-FOUR

The next few days flew by fairly quickly. I felt stronger each day, and the headaches were less frequent, so I was getting anxious about our progress on the case. Devon and I had argued this morning about me moving back to the Pampered Pup. I thought it was time, but his stubbornness won out in the end, and I promised him one more week. Truth be told, I couldn't have been happier he wanted me with him . . . even if it was for just one more week. And it would make it easier for us to work together to clear Ira. That's what I told myself anyway.

At the end of Thursday's class, as I was leading everyone slowly out of *savasana*, Devon slipped into the room. I offered him a curious smile as he lifted a hand in greeting and then leaned against the wall to wait. Buddha spotted him and, practically wagging his butt off, left my side to go greet him. I couldn't blame him, if I had a tail it would be wagging right now, too.

'Roll to one side and sit up at your own pace.' As the energy in the room shifted and grew livelier, I tried to concentrate but it was impossible. *Why was he here? Did something happen?* I sat in lotus, bringing my palms to touch. The class followed suit. A few of the dogs stood and shook off in anticipation of the special treats their owners gave them at the end of class. I snuck a glance at Devon. He didn't look anxious. '*Namaste.*'

'*Namaste*,' the ladies repeated in unison.

I rolled up my mat as Devon weaved his way through my clients and their dogs, greeting a few of them by name. The knowing grins being thrown my way did not go unnoticed. My skin warmed as he approached.

'What's up?' I kept my head down so he didn't notice my blush. Being with him alone at his bungalow was somehow different than this. There it was private, no one to judge why we were together or make me question myself. Out here in the real world, his presence just made me feel silly, like a little girl believing that fairy tales could come true.

Seemingly oblivious to my inner discomfort, he said, 'Salma called. They've got the jewelry appraisals. Have time to go look at them?'

'Yes!' Finally, good news. I stuffed my mat in the bag and threw it over my shoulder. 'Just let me give Buddha a short walk in the garden and tell one of the girls I'm leaving him in a suite for a bit.'

I was suddenly nervous as we drove off the ferry and toward the police station. The fact that Angel had appeared for a split second right on top of the folder had contributed to my certainty that this list did indeed have something to do with the murders. But now I thought, what if she had just appeared because I was about to be knocked silly?

I sighed out loud. 'What if this doesn't lead us anywhere?'

Devon reached over and took my hand. 'Let's just wait and see, Elle. We'll be there shortly.'

Detective Vargas led us back into the same room as before, though we had to walk fast to keep up with her. She seemed agitated, glancing from me to Devon as she slid the folder across the table toward us. Devon picked it up and opened it calmly, seemingly unaware of Detective Vargas's mood.

My leg was shaking under the table as we scanned the items, our heads just inches apart. The first sheet I remembered: the four-karat diamond earrings, a six-karat diamond cocktail ring, a black diamond necklace worth more than my car. Devon glanced at me and I nodded. He flipped to the second page. We scanned it silently. More earrings, a few diamond and gemstone bracelets, an antique pearl watch. Then the third page.

'The woman sure had a lot of bleedin' jewelry,' he growled under his breath as we moved to page four.

Holding his finger under an item in the middle of the page,

he cocked his head toward me. 'Does that say "canine gem-encrusted tiara" for twelve hundred dollars? For a dog?'

I nodded. 'It was in the box we brought to Billie Olsen, remember? I didn't realize it was worth so much. Bonnie didn't put price tags on anything in her shop.'

'Now we know why.' Devon rubbed a finger over his bottom lip. 'Billie Olsen did ask to take Celeste's dog. Though, I can't imagine she would kill for a twelve hundred dollar dog accessory. She didn't look bad off financially.'

Glancing over, I noted Detective Vargas watching our exchange silently but closely. 'Agreed. Keep going.'

By the end of page eight, we were both frustrated. And I was more than a little bewildered by the amount of money in jewelry Celeste had owned. It was enough to buy a house . . . or two.

'So, nothing?' Detective Vargas finally said, leaning back in her chair. Her demeanor had gone from irritated to almost a quiet acceptance as she looked from me to Devon. I hoped she wasn't giving up. Ira couldn't afford for any of us to give up.

Devon stared at the table, lost in thought, his hands clenched in front of him.

Detective Vargas turned her attention to me. 'You said you gave Billie Olsen the dog tiara listed on there?'

'Yes.' I shrugged. 'But I don't think she killed Celeste to get it. Why would she? She really doesn't need the money. What else would she want it for?'

'Why would *anyone* want a dog tiara? Sentimental value maybe?' She sighed. 'But it's worth interviewing her. I think your instincts are right. Robert Green died because of something in that report.' She folded her hands into a steeple and stared at Devon. 'Any other thoughts?'

Devon lifted his head to meet her gaze. When I looked back at the detective, I saw a flash of admiration in her eyes before she quickly hid it behind a scowl. *Or was it something else? Was that why Devon always called her? Did they have more than a professional relationship?* I stopped that train of thought right in its tracks. Nope. Not getting tangled up in that emotion. I had already learned jealousy was the most dangerous of all emotions for me. It ate at me like a disease, and I wasn't ever going back there.

Devon turned to me. 'Elle, what was that you were telling me about a dog fashion show?'

I felt the insecurities melt away under his gaze. *And I still loved the way he said my name with a little lilt.* 'It's this Saturday at the resort. It's a very big deal. The ladies in my class have all lost their minds preparing for it. They've even hired designers to make dresses and tuxes for their dogs.' I felt myself smiling as I recalled how they all lit up when they talked about it. I held up my hands. 'But it's for a good cause, so I'm not judging.'

Detective Vargas suddenly perked up. 'And along with these dresses and tuxes, will the dogs be wearing tiaras?'

'Yes, they will.' I bit the inside of my cheek as I thought about her question. 'In fact, Princess was supposed to be in the fashion show. That's why Celeste bought the tiara.' *Yeah, something felt like it was falling into place, but what?*

Detective Vargas looked like she had that same feeling. 'All right. Detective Farnsworth and I will interview Billie Olsen and see if we can find any motive around the tiara. I'll also send someone to inventory Zebina's jewelry to see if anything matches up with any items on the list. If this list is the key, then we have to find a way to tie it to the killer.' She stood and addressed Devon. 'I'll call you if and when we find something. Meanwhile—' she raised a brow – 'I assume you two are going to this dog fashion show?'

I smirked at Devon. 'I do have two tickets. Front row.'

Devon suppressed a groan and muttered, 'Grand.'

The detective crossed her arms. 'And I assume, Devon Burke, that you've learned your lesson about keeping Miss Pressley out of danger?'

'Yes, ma'am. Don't plan on lettin' her out of my sight.' He winked at me as he helped me up.

When I stood, I caught the expression Detective Vargas was giving us. She didn't look happy.

She let Devon walk out of the room, but stopped me on the way out. 'You seem like a nice girl, Elle, so let me give you a piece of advice, woman to woman. Devon Burke doesn't do commitment.' She gave me a weary look and then left me standing there.

So, there was something more to their relationship. I felt like I had been punched in the gut.

TWENTY-FIVE

A crowd already buzzed around the resort entrance like a disturbed beehive. I took Devon's hand as he helped me climb out of the Jeep, not an easy task in the heels I had borrowed from Hope. Or the dress. She and Ira had planned on attending the fashion show, but now they didn't feel like being a public spectacle, so she insisted I wear the black sequinned scrap of material she had bought to wear. I felt half naked and, judging from the amused glint in Devon's eye as he raked my body with his gaze, I looked it.

Devon slipped an arm around my waist and whispered in my ear. 'You're going to be the death of me in that dress, Elle.'

My body tingled from his words. I smiled, taking in the scent of him and the comfort of his arm holding me tight. I wanted nothing more than to belong to this man . . . body, mind and soul. Well, I also wanted Ira and Hope to have their lives back. There seemed to be a high price to pay for both.

We followed the surging crowd to the ballroom entrance, where I presented our tickets. We then strolled into the show area where I immediately felt awash with excited energy in the charged atmosphere. A steady hum of voices rose above the music. Glancing around, I decided I'd have to thank Hope for being on top of Moon Key fashion. Almost everyone was dressed in black. For the first time in my life, I felt like I fit in. But, when I really thought about it, it didn't feel as rewarding as I had imagined.

'Row one, seats fourteen and fifteen,' I said.

Devon led the way to our seats, still clutching my hand possessively. I didn't mind his grip or the view. The man looked just as good in a tux from behind. He found our seats. Sure enough, they were front and center of the runway.

'Good evening.' Devon greeted the couple next to us and

we introduced ourselves. Devon tucked the camera he had brought along carefully under his seat.

'Nice to meet you both. Great theme this year, don't you agree?' The woman who had introduced herself as Dottie asked.

'Yes,' I said, leaning up a bit to see around Devon and trying to match her enthusiasm. 'Royalty. Should be a fun show.'

Devon took advantage of my close proximity and placed a kiss on my earlobe. An electric current shot straight to my core. 'I'm having a hard time being a gentleman tonight, Elle,' he whispered, laying a warm hand on my bare knee.

And I was having a hard time breathing now, thank you very much.

'Devon Burke!'

I recognized the sticky sweet voice before I even pulled my attention away from Devon. Sure enough, Georgia Waters had sauntered up. Her black satin dress barely held in her tanned cleavage, which almost had its own wardrobe malfunction moment as she enthusiastically bent over to embrace Devon. *Lovely.*

'Good to see you again, sugar,' she purred, completely ignoring me. I shook my head as Dottie's husband, Darren, made no effort to conceal his fascination with the leggy blonde.

'Yes, lovely to see you as well.' Devon smiled at her, gripping my knee tighter. When she finally let go, he shot me an apologetic look. I put my hand over his and intertwined our fingers to let him know I understood.

'Can you believe who they got to MC tonight?' Georgia asked. 'Vivian Atherton! Crazy, right?'

I smothered a smile as Devon struggled with a response. I knew he had no idea who the popular soap opera star was. 'Beyond crazy,' he finally managed. I had a feeling he wasn't talking about Vivian Atherton.

Georgia finally seemed to notice me as she slid into the chair next to me. Her perfume was the flowery kind and made my eyes water.

'Oh, Elle. Hello.'

I glanced at her and nodded slightly. 'Georgia.'

She forced a smile and then redirected her southern charm

to the man next to her. Poor guy, he wouldn't even know what hit him.

Soon, the seats around the runway filled up and the lights dimmed, the music switching to a soft background piano solo.

'Ladies and gentlemen,' a voice boomed over the speaker system. 'Welcome to the Fourteenth Annual Moon Key Pet Fashion Show!' A round of applause vibrated the room as Vivian Atherton appeared from the back curtain and sauntered down the runway, microphone in hand. Dressed in an elaborate gold gown and tiara, she waved at the crowd.

'How do I look?' She did a turn as whistles erupted from the crowd. Georgia produced a loud, shrill whistle with her fingers to her mouth. My eardrum rattled. I hoped she wouldn't be doing that all night. There weren't enough deep breathing exercises in the world to keep me from breaking her fingers if she did.

'I couldn't let the pooches out-dress me, adorable as they are, right? I do have a reputation to uphold.' Vivian expertly waited out the laughter from the crowd. 'In all seriousness, this event is for a great cause, St Anthony's no-kill shelter, and I am honored to be your MC tonight. But, you didn't come here to hear me babble on this stage, so let's get this party started!'

She sashayed to the back corner of the stage while the music switched once more to an up-tempo beat. A spotlight then appeared and swept dramatically over the stage. 'Without further ado, I'm pleased to introduce our first couple of the evening, Beth Anne Wilkins and Shakespeare.'

A round of clapping ensued as Beth Anne emerged from the curtain in a pink chiffon gown and lavender wig with French twist curls. She was all smiles as Shakespeare trotted beside her in a black-and-white tux ensemble, his tiny tongue hanging out and a king's crown perched on his little black-and-white shih-tzu head.

'Shakespeare is wearing Dogs by Design, courtesy of Brandy Miller,' Vivian announced. More clapping ensued. Devon retrieved his camera and started snapping pictures.

Beth Anne waved as she spotted me in the front row and,

smiling, I gave her a thumb's up. Camera flashes were going off all around the stage, including beside me. Shakespeare really did look cute and Beth Anne never looked happier. It was nice to see in the wake of all the upheaval this little island had experienced lately. I needed to take their lead and let myself enjoy the evening. And I would do that, I decided. Right after the killer was behind bars, and Ira was back at work.

More whistles and clapping ensued as Violet emerged from the curtain next, dressed in a corseted gown fit for medieval royalty. Ghost seemed a bit less sure of himself as he stopped mid-runway and tried to hide behind Violet's hooped skirt. A wave of laughter rolled through the crowd as Violet tried to sort through the material to find him. His sash had fallen down around his feet and he began frantically turning circles trying to get it off.

'Poor Violet. Ghost is such an introvert,' I whispered to Devon, feeling her embarrassment. To her credit though, she recovered nicely and never lost her smile.

After another thirty-minute parade of costumed Moon Key socialites and their dogs, Zebina emerged from the curtain. Devon and I shared a surprised glance. I hadn't seen her since that day in my hospital room. She hadn't shown up to a doga class all week and now here she was, looking like a Disney princess in yellow chiffon, a tiara glittering from her up-do. As she moved down the runway, she soaked in all the attention and applause with a sparkle in her eye and a sway in her walk. No sign of grief. *Interesting.*

Max trotted beside her, panting hard in a royal blue-and-gold velvet suit. A gilded sapphire crown had been affixed atop his head, and it glittered in the spotlight.

'Max is wearing Ruff Draft Creations by Gia and crown by Jamie Boccelli. Aren't they just a stunning couple?' Vivian said, eliciting another round of applause as Zebina did a slow turn at the end of the runway, savoring the attention it seemed. Everyone handles grief differently, I suppose.

I studied the tiny tiara as they strolled back by us. 'Wonder if that's another twelve hundred dollar creation by Mr Boccelli?'

Georgia made a derisive sound beside me. 'Twelve hundred dollars for a Boccelli? You're so . . . cute, Elle.'

I chose to ignore her. I knew passive aggressive mixed with condescension when I heard it. I made myself feel better by concentrating on the hand Devon periodically rested on my knee. Once in a while, his thumb would even rub my bare skin lightly, sending a current up my leg. I leaned closer to him and away from the negative energy on the other side of me.

I recognized a dozen or so of my other clients as the evening progressed. Including a woman I'd grown very fond of, Roxanne, who hadn't been in class for a few weeks. I'd have to find her after the show and make sure everything was all right. Her Irish wolfhound, Ebby, strolled protectively beside her.

Devon leaned into me, his mouth near my ear. 'Now there's a fine lookin' animal.'

I smiled. 'Not biased, are you, Irish?' Though, I had to agree, and apparently so did the crowd as a round of applause – that had grown monotonous – now erupted with enthusiasm. The hundred-pound, charcoal dog eyed the crowd confidently under her princess tiara as if assessing her subjects. She gave a deep *Woof!* at the end of the runway and the crowd went wild. Everyone began to stand, laughing and applauding while the press jockeyed for position and flashes exploded.

Roxanne took a bow, and I caught the slight finger motion she used for Ebby to bow beside her. I had always been impressed with Ebby's intelligence and training. Tonight was no exception.

A parade of dogs and owners filtered through the curtain, filling the stage. We all remained standing as the change in music signaled the show's conclusion. The ladies curtsied, accepting their praise for a show well done, and then filed back behind the curtain.

Vivian moved to the end of the stage. 'And now I give you the designers that made all this fabulousness possible.' She began calling out names, one by one, until a dozen men and women had taken the stage, all looking satisfied and exhausted. I could only imagine the fires they had to put out all evening in the form of wardrobe malfunctions, accidents . . . and possibly models chewing on the wardrobe.

Chuckling to myself, I glanced over at Devon. He had his gaze locked on Jamie Boccelli.

TWENTY-SIX

We mingled after the show and each accepted a glass of champagne from a server while we waited for the press to get done interviewing Jamie. We had a few questions of our own.

'Popular guy,' Devon said, watching the feeding frenzy around Jamie. 'No doubt all the adoration has inflated his ego. High stakes, a large ego. Means he has something to lose. A fall from grace would be a death sentence.'

I watched Devon as he worked out his thoughts, the intensity apparent in his twitching jaw. He raised his camera and snapped a photo of him.

I took a swallow of the champagne, its bubbles nipping at my tongue. 'Jamie Boccelli, the egomaniac. Yeah, that fits.'

'It's well earned,' a voice said beside me. 'His ego.'

My blood pressure spiked as I turned to Georgia. She was like a piece of bubble gum you couldn't shake off your shoe. *You would know all about ego.* 'You're a fan, then?' I said instead.

She eyed Devon openly with a slight smile on her artificially plumped lips. 'I'm a fan of any attractive man who's worth millions.'

Did she just say that out loud? I squelched an urge to grind Hope's high heel into her foot. She did not bring out the best in me. Then, I remembered her reaction to my comment about the price of a Boccelli-designed tiara.

'So he makes millions just from designing pet jewelry?' I hated to show my ignorance to such a creature as Georgia. I'm sure she would use it against me in the future, but I had to know. 'How much exactly would one of his designs go for?'

'Well, it depends on how many gems he's used, of course.' She motioned with her champagne glass. 'For example, the tiara on that little black-and-brown beast right there. That's got rubies, emeralds and about two carats worth of diamonds. That one would be about twenty-five grand.'

I almost swallowed my tongue. 'Twenty-five thousand dollars?'

We suddenly had Devon's attention. 'Twenty-five thousand for what?'

Georgia smiled seductively, moved to stand beside Devon and pointed to the 'beast', which was actually a cute little teacup Yorkie. 'That.'

I could only stand there with my mouth open, trying to wrap my brain around someone spending that amount of money on a dog accessory. And not even a leash or bowl – something you could at least use every day. It was incomprehensible.

'Poor thing looks shellshocked.' Georgia's soft laughter underlined her words as she touched Devon's arm like they'd just shared a secret. Then she swung her condescending sky-blue gaze to me. 'If you haven't noticed, Elle, money is no object on Moon Key. I know it's hard to imagine if you're not used to being around money. It's a different world. Not made for everyone.'

I'd had about enough of this southern-belle, she-devil's cutting remarks. My habit of avoiding conflict seemed to be emboldening her. I downed the rest of my champagne, mostly to keep myself from tossing it in her face. But, also to cool off the flame of anxiety and insecurity she had lit. *Don't go to the dark side, Elle.*

Devon must have felt the shift in my energy, because he moved away from Georgia and slid an arm protectively around my waist. 'Excuse us,' Devon said, tightening his grip around my waist and leading me away. As we made our escape, he chuckled. 'Do you two have a history then?'

'We do now,' I seethed. He obviously didn't understand her claws were coming out because of him. 'Thanks for saving me.' I glanced up, sinking into the calmness he possessed as he led me through the room. 'Were there ever any Irish knights in shining armor?'

He laughed, producing that dimple I'd grown to love. 'Yes. The Knights Templar. A powerful military group during the Crusades.'

'You'll have to tell me that story one day.'

He kissed the top of my head. 'Are you asking me to tell you a bedtime story? Because that is something I am very good at.'

All thoughts of Georgia and her hurtful words left me as my heart melted. With a huge smile on my face, I suddenly spotted Roxanne in the crowd.

'Oh, I have to run over and say hi to a client. I'll meet you in Jamie's line.'

Devon nodded, sliding his arm reluctantly from around my waist. 'Hurry back.'

Roxanne stood in a circle talking to some of the ladies from class. They were all still in the large gowns, though they had thoughtfully removed their dogs' costumes.

Roxanne waved when she saw me approaching. 'Elle! So good to see you here.'

The ladies moved their skirts aside so I could give her a hug and stroke Ebby's large head. She reciprocated with a lick of my wrist.

'Good to see you, too. That was quite a show you two put on, everyone loved it. I've missed you both in class.'

'Yes, we've been traveling, and I just can't seem to get back into my routine. We'll be there soon, promise.' She frowned. 'I heard about Celeste and her husband, though. Just terrible news.' She turned to the ladies. 'Do you all feel safe on the island?'

Some of them shrugged or nodded.

'Maddox would tear someone's throat out if they tried to hurt me.' Whitley peered affectionately down at the greyhound resting on the ground beside her foot.

'Yeah, real killer, that one.' Violet rolled her eyes. 'Oh, there's Vivian, Whitley. Didn't you want to get her autograph?'

'Oh, yes.' She glanced at all of us, a guilty look on her face. 'For my sister, of course. I don't have time to watch trashy daytime TV.'

'Of course.' Violet chuckled as Whitley hurried to catch up to the TV star.

'Hey, Violet.' I moved closer to her. 'I heard some of those tiaras the dogs were wearing can go for twenty-five grand. Is that true?'

She nodded. 'Sure. That and more.' She adjusted the tight waist on her dress, cursing under her breath. 'The most uncomfortable design . . . anyway, haven't you ever wondered why Bonnie keeps those things in a locked glass case in her store?'

'Yeah, but I didn't know they were real gemstones used. That's just . . .' I searched for a word that wouldn't be offensive. 'Surprising.'

Her green eyes met mine. 'Is it?' It seemed it was the first time she'd thought about it. 'Well, I suppose most of us are just getting to the age where we realize we can't take our money with us, so we might as well spend it doing what we love.' Violet shrugged with a grin. 'And we do love pampering our pets, especially while outdoing each other.'

I smiled and shook my head. Then glancing back, I noticed Devon was next in line to speak to Jamie. 'Ladies, I've got to run. Roxanne, hopefully I'll see you two in class soon. You girls enjoy the rest of the evening and wonderful job tonight.'

I wasn't quite sure what Devon was going to say to Jamie, so I just stood quietly beside him as he introduced himself.

'Nice to meet you, Mr Boccelli. Your work is fantastic. I was wondering if you do custom pieces.'

Jamie made no attempt to hide the fact he was assessing Devon's appearance. Probably wondering how much he could charge him for a custom piece. 'I could design something for you, yes. I'd need just a general idea of what you want . . . tiara, collar, charms? I like to be in control of the design, though. If you can trust me, we can work together.'

'Trust you?' Devon folded his arms. 'I suppose. I have no reason not to, do I?'

Jamie's smile faltered. 'What is it you do, Mr Burke?'

The corner of Devon's mouth turned up into a charming grin. His accent was thicker than usual. 'Don't do much. Play golf mostly. Spend too much money on my dog, Petey.'

This seemed to relax Jamie. He laughed. 'Well, I can sure help you do the latter. Tell you what—' he pulled a card from his tux jacket – 'here's my cell number. You give me a call in the next few days while I'm still on Moon Key and we'll have a sit down.'

I scanned the room for Zebina. She was the last item on our agenda, but she had seemed to disappear. Time to go home.

'What did you think about Zebina being in the show?' I asked as we made the short drive back to Devon's bungalow. I had my eyes closed, enjoying the evening breeze. Fatigue seemed to be my constant companion since getting popped on the head.

'Don't know what to make of her.' Devon ran his thumb along my palm. He had kept us physically connected all evening. Going to bed alone tonight was going to be difficult. 'I suppose she could've been just keeping her commitment by being there.'

'She sure was enjoying herself though. Not looking much like a grieving widow.'

'No, that she wasn't.'

'What about Jamie Boccelli?'

'A feckin' idiot but a killer? Don't know. I'll give him a call and set up a meeting on Monday. I'll know more then.'

I noticed he said 'I' and not 'we' but I didn't have the energy to argue.

I opened my eyes and looked over at him. 'Well, I do know one thing. Billie Olsen may not have killed Celeste over a twelve-hundred-dollar tiara. But a twenty-five-thousand-dollar one? That could be motive, right?'

Devon got that far-away look. 'Money is definitely a good bet for a motive.'

I had a feeling he wasn't talking about Celeste any more. He had that same pained look he got every time he talked about his parents.

The dogs were happy to see us. I knelt down and gave Buddha and Petey hugs and scratches before we let them outside, getting a wet face for my trouble. Devon opened the sliding doors and stepped out back. I followed the dogs out.

Devon was staring up at the night sky. When I came to stand beside him, he turned to me.

'Have you ever been to Ireland, Elle? We could go to Dublin. I could take you when this is all over.' He had his hands shoved in his pockets, his gaze locked on me. The intensity in the way he asked the question was not lost on me. Was I willing to let down the wall I had kept between us and take the first step into his world? He was waiting for an answer. 'It's a beautiful place,' he offered. As if I needed a reason other than I'd be with him.

My chest was closing in on my lungs like some medieval torture device as I tried to imagine getting on a plane. I opened my mouth and closed it again. I wanted to be excited, cry, 'Yes of course. That would be wonderful!' I wanted so much to be that girl who could jump on a plane to a magical land with her prince. Instead I was the girl, staring in horror, beginning to gasp for air like a dying fish. ''Scuse me.' I managed to stumble into the house and lock myself in the bathroom.

I slid down to the floor and let the tears fall, unspooling handfuls of toilet paper off the roll to muffle my sobs. *How did I get to be a thirty-five-year-old who runs and hides from an offer like that?* I thought I had come so far, but I was beginning to realize I was still standing on the starting line. A trip back to the therapist was in order.

After a while, a soft knock on the door pulled me out of my self-flogging. 'Elle? You all right?'

I took a shuttering breath and tried to make my voice steady. 'Yes, I'm fine.'

'Come out and speak with me, please.'

Well, I'd have to at some point. I couldn't very well live in his bathroom. I squeezed my eyes shut and pulled myself up to the counter. I glared at myself in the mirror. Swollen, red eyes full of loathing glared back at me. Fear had completely possessed me again, and I hated myself for it.

'I . . . I'll be out in a sec.'

Running the water, I let it get as cold as possible. Then I alternated holding my hands under the stream and pressing my fingers against my eyes until the swelling went down a bit. I was still a hot mess as I gingerly opened the door and peered out.

Devon had taken up a spot on the floor, his back against the wall. His white tux shirt had been pulled from his slacks, and a dog lay on each side of him. He looked exhausted and sad.

'Sorry,' I choked, trying desperately to keep my emotions in check.

He pushed himself up, grabbed my hand and led me to the guestroom I'd been sleeping in. The dogs trailed in behind us.

He transferred my suitcase from the bed to the floor and we sat down facing each other. I kept my eyes lowered, completely at a loss for what to say.

'Elle, look at me.' Devon's voice was gruff with concern. 'What's going on in that head of yours?'

I let my eyes lift to meet his. It was time to come clean about my anxiety. But, once I told him I'd never be able to travel with him, I knew what we had would be over before it began. I wanted just one more night. 'I'm just so . . . exhausted, Devon. Can we talk about it tomorrow?'

He stared at me for a long time, and then he nodded in defeat. 'Sure.' He toed off his shoes and shifted himself up on the bed, patting the pillow beside him. 'Come on then.'

With relief, I crawled up into his arms. He wasn't going to leave me tonight. I didn't even care I was still in the dress. Pulling me close into him, he wrapped his arms around me and snuggled into my neck. I felt his breath on my skin, his heartbeat in my own chest. 'Elle, I'll not push you any more. But, I'd like for you to talk to me about this soon,' he whispered.

I felt the bed shift as Buddha jumped up and lay at our feet. ''Kay,' I said sleepily, already falling into the warm, safe cocoon his presence created. It chased away all my demons. For a little while at least.

I don't think I moved all night but when I woke, the bed was empty beside me. Sliding out of bed, I tiptoed through the house, still clad in Hope's dress. When I got to his bedroom door, I could hear his shower running. And life goes on.

Feeling sad and confused, I decided to take the dogs down to the beach and do a little yoga. I needed to be grounded and have a clear head when the now inevitable discussion occurred.

It wasn't even eight o'clock yet, and the sun was already too cheery and bright, raising the temperature of the air like an oven. As Petey and Buddha explored the beach and splashed in the gentle surf, I spread my toes firmly in the warm sand and raised my arms for my first sun salutation.

I quickly got lost in my breath and the flow of my body, so I hadn't noticed when Devon joined us. I peered at him upside-down from between my ankles as I sank into down dog. He lifted his hand in greeting and then stood, brushing the sand from his jeans. I pushed up, too.

'Mornin'.' He seemed tentative as he approached me.

'Hey, sorry. I didn't realize you were there.'

We didn't move into our easy morning ritual of a kiss and embrace like usual. Our greeting was awkward for the first time, and it was all my fault. I had thrown up an even bigger wall between us by my reaction last night.

'Yeah. I didn't want to disturb you.' His gaze shifted to the shoreline as Petey barked at something in the water. In the sunlight, his eyes shone like sapphires under dark lashes. I could also see the swirling storm of concern in them. 'I have a full schedule today,' he said, bringing his attention back to me. 'Do you mind looking after Petey?'

Petey must have heard his name. He came bounding up to sit in front of Devon, his tail swishing the sand. Devon knelt down and scratched behind his ears, letting Petey give him a lick on the cheek. 'That's a good boy.'

I watched his muscular hands stroke the dog, remembering how that same hand warmed my knee last night at the fashion show. I bit my lip to keep the tears at bay. 'No, of course I don't mind.'

Standing, he nodded. 'I've got to pick my friend up from the airport tonight. He's coming in from Ireland. We'll be coming back after nine but you'll be here?'

'Do you want me to be?' I couldn't blame him if he had tired of my elusiveness.

He moved closer and reached out, resting a hand behind my neck. His smile held regret and sadness. 'I think I've made it perfectly clear what I want, Elle.' Pressing a soft kiss on my forehead, he released me, and I watched him make his way back up to the house.

Perfectly clear? Not really. By his own admission he didn't do relationships. And the warning from Detective Vargas didn't help. He didn't do commitment. Yeah, I knew that because he told me that himself. What did he want then? A one-night stand? A summer fling? Swiping at my eyes with the back of my hand, I walked down to the water, scattering a group of sea gulls along the way and stared out at the ocean. My security blanket. The one familiar thing in my life, and the one thing that would always be there. A swim was in order.

I spent a quiet Sunday with the dogs on the beach, swimming, running, throwing the Frisbee for Petey. And most of all just sitting. Thinking and then practicing letting those thoughts and fears go. By the time we all straggled back into the house at dinner time, sun-drenched and waterlogged, I felt more peaceful than I had in a long time. I fed the dogs and then they crashed on the tile floor, both completely worn out. Then I opened the fridge and started pulling out stuff to make a salad. I'd have to go shopping tomorrow and replace the groceries I'd been using while here. It would be a good time to visit Mom, too. I'd left a message for her when I got out of the hospital to let her know I was all right, but she hadn't called me back. I wouldn't let that build up into resentment between us again. That was one thing in my life I could control. I'd apologize and tell her I loved her. What she did with that was up to her. If she wanted to continue to be mad, that wasn't my problem.

Emboldened by the new clarity I'd found today, I decided I'd use the same strategy for my issue with Devon. I'd come clean about my panic attacks and the fact that I couldn't travel with him. I'd also tell him about my past relationship that had scarred me. If he understood and still wanted to pursue something further, great. If not, I would let that go, too. My heart squeezed at this thought. I let myself feel the panic and the need to hold on to Devon, and then with a deep exhale, I released my death grip on that thought also.

OK, now I could concentrate on Ira's problem. As I sliced

a cucumber and marveled at how easy having a good, sharp knife made the job, I realized this was not just Ira's problem. There was a killer on Moon Key so it was everyone's problem. Until he was caught, no one was safe. A chill ran up my arms, and I suddenly became self-conscious of being in this large house alone. I walked over and locked the sliding doors.

I sat at the kitchen island eating my salad so I could watch the sunset through the window, safe from any lurking killers. It didn't disappoint tonight with its show of fluorescent oranges and yellows. This was paradise, but I really needed to start looking through ads for apartments in Clearwater. I was starting to feel pathetic not having a place of my own. I made a mental note to pick up an apartment guide while I was at the supermarket tomorrow.

Devon's camera bag was lying open on the island. After staring at it for a few minutes, I decided he wouldn't have left it sitting out if there was something he didn't want me to see on it. Curious, I fished his camera out of the bag and flicked it on while I chewed. After a few tries, I found the button that let me scroll through the images.

I came to the photos of me he'd taken the first night he brought me here. *Wait, was that me?* Staring at the girl with sparkling eyes and a blush, beaming happiness at the camera, I barely recognized myself. It wasn't the same face I saw in the mirror every day. This one was looking on with kind eyes full of joy.

Frowning, I moved through more photos. There were some action shots of Petey playing in the ocean and then the fashion show ones were next. I flipped through, smiling as I relived the event. The close-ups of the dogs in costume were especially cute.

'Look at you, Ghost,' I chuckled to myself at a photo of Ghost hiding in Violet's skirts. Devon had captured Violet's amused grin perfectly. I stopped at a close-up of an Italian greyhound I didn't recognize. I did, however, recognize the tiara. It was a replica of the Spencer tiara Princess had been modeling in the photo now hanging in my studio. So many diamonds. *Were they all real?*

And then like a lightning bolt, it hit me. I dropped the camera and stared out into the kitchen, my attention focused inward. 'Oh my god.' *Could it be? Yes, it had to be.* I knew who the killer was.

TWENTY-SEVEN

I paced frantically with my phone in hand as the dogs' gazes followed me. I had left a message for Devon to call me, but he was probably at the airport by now. I should call Detective Vargas, but what if I was wrong? It was just a gut feeling at this point. I really needed to run it by someone first. I had also left a message for Hope, telling her I think I figured out who the murderer was and to call me back ASAP. *What now?* I stopped. I had to warn Bonnie to be careful.

Scrolling through my phone, I dialed her number. It rang and went to voicemail. 'Why doesn't anyone answer their phone?' I growled. 'Bonnie, this is Elle. I hate to leave this kind of message, but I want to make sure you don't meet with Jamie alone. I think he's been selling you fake tiaras. Celeste had gotten her jewelry appraised and the tiara she had for Princess was only worth twelve hundred dollars.' I plopped on to the sofa, having exhausted my nervous energy with the pacing. 'Which means there was probably only a handful of those stones that were real. Celeste probably realized this when she saw the appraisal and confronted him. I think Jamie is the one that killed her.' *He definitely looked like a man who was familiar with Botox and other plastic surgery procedures. Plus, he was sitting right next to me when I was on the phone with Robert. He could have easily overheard our plan to meet that night.* 'Anyway, we'll give this information to the detective on Celeste's case, but meanwhile stay away from Jamie Boccelli.'

I tossed the phone down on the sofa next to me and stared up at the ceiling. 'Boccelli. B . . . O . . .' The pieces were falling into place. At least I could stop Devon from meeting with him tomorrow. Or maybe Devon could set up the meeting and wear a wire to record their conversation. Try to get him to confess. Do they even do that in real police work? Or was that just on TV?

I closed my eyes.

A ding startled me. I sat up, my heart pounding. Night had descended and blanketed the house in shadows. The dogs were two lumps still stretched out on the floor. I must've fallen asleep waiting for Devon to return my call. Wiping the drool from the side of my mouth, a light on my phone caught my eye. *Did I miss a call?* Nope, a text message had just come in from Bonnie.

Opening the message, it took me a few seconds to comprehend what I was looking at. 'Oh my god.' My heart leapt into my throat as I stared at the image of Bonnie, her eyes wide, a gag tied around her mouth.

The accompanying message said: 'This is Jamie. As you can see, I have Bonnie. Meet me at 34 Sandhill Drive in 30 min or she dies. No cops or she dies.'

I leapt from the sofa. 'Oh god. Oh god.' She must have confronted him. *Why didn't she listen to me?* I groaned and, bending over with my hands on my knees, did some deep breathing. *Focus, Elle.*

Why that house? Because it had been sitting empty since the fire, that's why. I recognized the burnt cabinets in the background of the photo. So he wasn't trying to trick me. She was there. In that house. Did he know I was only three houses away? Probably not. That was my only advantage. He wouldn't be expecting me so soon.

I stared at my phone. OK, no cops. Maybe I should call island security? No, I didn't trust Alex Harwick to understand the gravity of the situation and handle it appropriately, nor were any of them trained to handle hostage negotiation. Plus, they'd call Clearwater police. I had to go. Alone. There was no choice. If he killed Bonnie because I was too much of a coward, I couldn't live with that. But, I wasn't going there without telling Devon where I was. I dialed his number. Voicemail still.

I squeezed my eyes shut and concentrated on steadying my voice. 'Devon, if you get this, I'm at the house three doors down, the one that's for sale. Bonnie's been kidnapped by Jamie, and he's going to kill her if I don't go. He said no cops, or he'd kill her. I don't have a choice. I . . . I'm sorry.'

There were a million things I wanted to say to him, but not in a message. That would have to do.

I had to hurry now, to catch Jamie off guard. I kissed the dogs and had one foot out the door when I realized I shouldn't go there unarmed. My gun was gone. Devon usually carried his on him or in his Jeep. Then I remembered the bottle of Botox in my bag.

Racing back to the kitchen, I dug through my bag with shaking hands. It seemed to be taking forever, but I finally got the needle into the bottle and pulled up the plunger, filling the whole syringe. I placed the plastic stop on the end and put the syringe full of the deadly toxin on top of the contents of my bag and slung it over my head and under one arm. Time to go.

The moon was full and cast a soft blanket of light on the beach so I didn't dare take the easiest route where I could be noticed. Instead, I crept the back way, between the road and the high bushes of the neighboring bungalows. Tiny rustling noises had my guard up. Just lizards I was dislodging from the grass by my movement, but my senses were so heightened by the cocktail of fight or flight chemicals coursing through my blood, I was jumping like they were dinosaurs. Plus there were so many frogs and other Florida night creatures singing, the night was far from quiet. The noise assaulted my senses and made it hard to think.

Nerves jangling, I made it to my destination's backyard. There was no way to breach the wall of thick bushes, so keeping low I jogged around the side of the house to the driveway. Bonnie's silver Jaguar convertible sat there quietly. Abandoned. The sight of it brought home how real this was for me. Crouching in front of the car, I tried to catch my breath. It was so shallow, I didn't even feel like I had lungs.

What are you even doing? You're not going to be able to save her. I could feel the edge now; that place where I lost control to the panic and it took over. I forced my thoughts away from it with effort and a laser-like focus. This was life or death. Panic attacks were not an option. As I moved around the corner of the garage, I saw warm light pouring from the large kitchen picture window.

Something snapped in my brain. Like a cord had been cut loose, I suddenly felt detached from the situation and from my fear. My heartbeat slowed, and I could take a deep breath. I stopped mid-step. *Was I in shock?* No time to analyze this new feeling. I picked my way through the landscape bushes, barely registering the tiny pokes from a cactus, and braced myself against the stucco wall. I peered into the bungalow.

Bonnie sat there at the kitchen table, still gagged, her hands tied and resting on the table in front of her. Her head was down, chin near her chest. A different kind of heat rocketed through me. Rage. *She better still be alive.* Moving to the right a bit, I scanned the rest of the house. No sign of Jamie. Maybe he'd gone to the bathroom. It was now or never.

Half-leaping, half-falling, I managed to untangle myself from the lower foliage around the Bird of Paradise bush and made it to the front door. Pushing down on the brass handle, it gave way quietly under my touch and the door swung open. An alarm went off in my head. *This is a trap.* I hesitated only for a second. No turning back now. Shoving the warning thought aside, I moved into the entranceway, leaving the door open behind me for a quick escape.

I paused just long enough to listen for any sounds of footsteps. Then, I rushed into the openness and vulnerability of the living room. I had half been expecting to be ambushed. Nothing. I ran over to where Bonnie sat lifeless at the table.

'Bonnie?' I whispered frantically. 'Bonnie, please talk to me.'

Panic began to awaken again in my chest, unfurling new wings. Pressing two fingers under her jaw told me she was still alive. *OK. Good.* But, now I had another problem. How was I going to get her out of here? There was no way I could lift her. First thing's first. I worked frantically in between glances around the house to untie the rope around her wrists.

'Bonnie!' I dared a bit louder. 'Come on, you have to wake up.' I rubbed her wrists, then her arms, then pushing her long hair away, I slapped her face lightly. 'Please, I can't carry you.' The desperation fed the anxiety which began to claw at my lungs. Then a moan escaped her lips and hope bloomed. 'Yes, Bonnie, wake up!'

I threw her arm around me as she began to come to. Her

head rolled, and then I felt her tense. 'It's going to be OK but we have to hurry. He could come back any minute.'

Resting her full weight on my own shaking legs almost caused me to collapse, but I managed to keep us both upright. *Come on. Come on. Please let us make it.* Every step toward the door seemed like it took a thousand years but we were almost there. I could see the moonlit beach beyond the doorway. Then suddenly Bonnie planted her feet and stopped.

'Oh, hang on, Elle.' Slipping out of my grip she stumbled over to the kitchen.

'Bonnie,' I shrieked under my breath. 'We have to go now!' *What was she doing?* Had Jamie hit her over the head, too? Maybe she doesn't remember where she is or that she's in terrible danger.

She grabbed her purse off the counter.

'Bonnie—'

She turned around and my words were cut short by confusion . . . then disbelief . . . then despair. My heart sank like a rock tossed into the ocean.

In her hand was my gun. And she was pointing it right at me.

TWENTY-EIGHT

As I stared at her in horror, she flicked the gun, motioning me back to the table. 'Have a seat.'

By the time I made it back to the table, my legs were shaking so badly I collapsed into the chair. 'Bonnie?' I whispered through a constricted throat. 'What are you doing? What's going on?'

She slid gracefully into the chair across from me and began to chuckle. 'Did you like my selfie? Oh, Elle. I have to hand it to you. I didn't think you'd come. Thought you'd have a panic attack and pass out right there in your boyfriend's house. You should have seen your face when I turned around with the gun. Priceless.' The amusement suddenly disappeared as she shook her head. The blue eyes that had comforted me so many times were now cold as ice. 'Glad you didn't, though. Then I would've had to come to you. So much messier.'

I was so confused by this change in her; I was having a hard time putting the pieces together. I stared at the gun still pointed at me. '*You* stole my gun? But why? I don't understand.'

'Well, let me enlighten you. You were right about the tiaras being fake. Only Jamie knew nothing about it. He placed them in my shop on consignment, and I got a cut from the sales. Not a big enough cut for my tastes though, so I simply had most of the gems removed and replaced with fake ones. Sold the real ones for one hundred percent profit. It was the perfect plan. If only Celeste wouldn't have got her tiara appraised. I mean, who does that?'

As she talked, it occurred to me that her explaining it all to me was a bad thing. She didn't plan on letting me live. My mouth had gone dry as cotton, but I managed to whisper, 'It was you? You killed Celeste?' I got a flash of the letters Celeste had written in the mud with her dying breath. *BO. She was trying to write Bonnie.* How did we not see that as a possibility? 'But she was your friend.'

Bonnie tucked a piece of highlighted gold bang behind her ear. Such a normal move in this setting just emphasized how crazy this all was. I had to stifle the urge to jump up and say, 'Hey, let's just forget all this and go back to reality. This isn't you!' But it was her. That was becoming clear, so I kept my mouth shut.

'Yeah, I really didn't think she'd make it that far. Thought she'd croak in the parking garage. I had to hurry back to the shop before anyone noticed I was gone so I couldn't watch her die. Thank god she didn't get further in her attempt to name me. That was a bit of luck.' Bonnie sat back in the chair. Something in her expression shifted. Hardened. She tapped the gun on the table. 'You're so naive, Elle. Celeste didn't care about me. None of those women do. They don't care about you, either. They only care about money.' She looked away for a moment. I thought about leaping across the table for the gun, but I wasn't so far gone I couldn't see the probable outcome of that dumb move.

'Did you know I grew up poor?'

The hard little smile was so unfamiliar; I was having a hard time recognizing the woman I'd known for the past nine months at all. 'No.'

'Oh yes. Not just poor. But in the worst, filthiest little gutter town you could imagine. I was a sewer rat. That's what the kids called me in juvie.' She examined her manicured French nails on the hand not holding the gun. 'Did you know you could dress up a sewer rat, Elle?' Her eyes flicked to mine and I saw a brief flash of pain before it receded behind her icy stare.

Only one thought right now was keeping me from a full-blown panic attack. The hope that Devon would get my message in time. I had to keep her talking. 'You were in juvie? That must've been awful.'

'You would think. But, besides the cruelness of the other kids, it was better than home. Three hot meals a day, a bed without lice, a working toilet.'

'What did you do to get put in there?'

'Oh that? I stabbed a girl.' She narrowed her eyes. 'Stole Johnny Ray's penknife right out of his pocket when he tried to force himself on me in the gym. A knee to the groin took care of him, but for dumping her garbage on my lunch tray and humiliating me, Trudie Hicksman deserved a much more severe punishment. I found her in the bathroom alone. She was washing her hands. I walked right up to her and when she turned to me with that sneer, I stabbed her. Right in the gut. You should have seen the surprise in those big horse eyes.' She began to chuckle again. If that was her idea of entertainment, I was in big trouble.

I could feel the blood drain from my face. Black spots started dancing before my eyes. *Don't pass out. Don't pass out.* I swallowed hard.

'I think she screamed more from the shock than the pain. She looked a lot like you did, Elle. Shocked.' She snorted and then she grew serious. 'When I got out of that town, I told myself I would find a way to never be poor again. I worked damned hard to create the life I have. To learn how to talk and dress and fit in with the rich. So you understand why I couldn't let Celeste ruin everything? And I certainly couldn't go to jail.'

Understand? No, you freakin' psychopath, I screamed in my head. 'I do, Bonnie. I understand. Listen, we could walk out of here right now. I consider you my friend, and you know I'd do anything for my friends. I won't say a word. It'll be our secret.'

Her stare became contemplative. She waved the gun and smiled. 'That was quite a show you put on in the parking lot with this thing. I thought you were going to give poor Mrs Obermeyer a heart attack.'

I felt myself cringe in embarrassment, which was ridiculous but I felt it nonetheless. 'You saw that?'

'Oh yes. I had just gotten in my car and saw you pull the gun. Surprised me, I gotta tell you. Little Elle with a gun. I stayed to see what in the world you were going to do with it.'

That's how she knew I had a gun then. 'So you stole it? To use it on me? You had this planned all along?'

'No.' She shrugged. 'I didn't plan for this. I just knew that you were hell bent on figuring out who killed Celeste to get Ira off the hook. And you running around with a gun could

be dangerous for me. You should have heeded the warning I
left on your car, Elle.'

'Oh god. You're the one who hit me on the head.' Whatever
detachment about my predicament I had achieved suddenly
evaporated. Like someone had just ripped my clothes off, I
suddenly felt exposed. Vulnerable. And quite mortal. I began
to shake violently.

Bonnie studied me with a calculating stare. 'Sorry about
that. Hope it didn't hurt too much. I do like you, Elle. I will
shoot you if I have to, but I'd like to find a less violent way
to kill you. After all, you did risk your neck for me, coming
here. Not very smart, but appreciated.' She pursed her lips in
thought. 'You didn't even contact the police before you came,
did you? Obedient little Elle.'

I shook my head. Maybe I could play on her sense of
empathy, if she even had any. 'The text said you would be
killed if I did.'

'So you told no one, not even your boyfriend about the
text?'

'No,' I lied. There was no way I was going to put Devon
in danger, too.

'Like I said. Not very bright if that's true.' While she contemp-
plated my demise, I tried to push through the red panic in my
brain and think about my survival. Going for the gun was
risky. She was bigger and stronger than me, and I had acquired
enough respect of a gun's power at the range that I wasn't
willing to take the chance. *But the syringe full of Botox in my
bag?* That I had control of. I just needed an opportunity to
get it out of the bag. I needed to distract her.

'But, I did leave the front door open, remember? Anyone
walking along the beach can see it's wide open and call
security.'

Bonnie's eyes narrowed and she sat up straighter. 'Mm.' She
stood up, the chair scraping the floor loudly. 'Well, we don't
need anyone just waltzing into our little private party, do we?
I'm going to go lock the door. Please don't try anything. Like I
said, I really don't want to shoot you. It's painful.' She backed
up slowly toward the front door, gun still held on me.

I knew I would only have a brief few seconds when she

would lose sight of me behind the foyer wall. When those seconds came, I dove my hand into my bag, snatched the needle and pulled it back out quick as a flash. Then I placed my hands back on the table. My heart was doing a fairly good impression of a jackhammer now.

She stalked back toward me, holding my gaze. I tried desperately to calm down. Not give away the prize in my hand. She stood right over me. I could smell her familiar perfume. Her expression was now pure determination. Her cold blue gaze was making me shake more. She suddenly grabbed my bag and shoved her hand inside. 'So, where is it?'

My throat closed, thinking for a brief, insane moment she somehow knew about the Botox I had.

But she pulled her hand back out empty. 'Where's your cell phone?'

I was starting to become suffocated by my own anxiety. I just shook my head. She sat back across from me and hit the table with her fist. I jumped.

'You left it there. I guess it's time for us to part ways then.' She cocked her head at me. 'Botox has been so easy, but I didn't have time to get more. You were an unplanned snag. Do you know why I chose this house for our final meeting?'

I shook my head, the only thing keeping me sane at the moment was the hope of being able to use the syringe gripped in my palm.

She pointed at the ceiling. 'Look up.'

I did as she said. Wires hung from a small hole in the high ceiling. I didn't understand. I guess it showed in my face because she enlightened me.

'After the kitchen fire, the Yateses decided to replace the whole fire and security system with some state-of-the-art mumbo jumbo. So convenient for me that it's not installed yet. The rich,' she snorted, 'they spend half their time buying things and the other half figuring out how to keep them.'

She rested her chin on her hand. The gun was still angled toward me, but her grip had loosened. I noticed this with a detached awareness, like I wasn't the person about to be killed, but someone outside watching all this go down.

'A few people at the spa have heard you express interest in

buying this bungalow since Nan Yates won't step foot in it again. So my plan makes sense. You thought if there was another fire, she'd just dump the place to get rid of it, and you could get it even cheaper. Only—' she shook her head sadly – 'the small fire you meant to set got out of control and . . . you died in it. Such a tragedy. But, look at the bright side. You will die in your dream house.'

I stared at her horrified. *Death by fire? I would rather be shot.* The thought brought me back into my body. I was suddenly struggling for air. 'You . . . can't . . .' The words were just whispers. The syringe was getting slick in my fist as I broke out in a sweat. 'Please . . .'

'Oh, don't worry.' She waved off my concern. 'You'll pass out from the smoke before the fire gets you, won't feel a thing.' She raised an eyebrow and shook her head. 'Unless you pass out from that panic attack first. Those may be a blessing in disguise for you after all.' She stood, pushing the chair away from the table and backed up toward the kitchen. Moving to the counter where her purse sat, she used her free hand to pull out a lighter, keeping the gun pointed at me.

I was bent over the table now, desperately trying to slow my breathing, even though what my body screamed for was to suck in as much air as possible. I was hyperventilating. I squeezed my eyes shut and tried to block out the situation I was in for just a moment. I needed to pull myself together. It almost worked. Then I smelled smoke.

Oh god. This was really happening. I thought of my mom. And Hope. And Buddha and . . . Devon. I didn't want to leave any of them.

My eyes flew open, and I flung myself back in the chair. Tears had now joined the sweat on my face and neck. I stared at the curtains framing the sliding glass doors. They were engulfed in living flames. Gray smoke poured from them, filling the room. The flames were already licking at the ceiling. I turned, frozen by fear and disbelief as Bonnie marched over to the wicker furniture in the living room. Picking up a pillow, she held the lighter to it until a flame caught and then she placed it on the sofa cushion. She walked around, lighting anything in the house that would burn easily. Black smoke

billowed from the living room. A thin layer of it reached me
at the table. Bonnie was already coughing. I knew she'd have
to leave the house soon. Gun or no gun, I had to make my
move.

Unnaturally calm for just setting a house on fire and about
to commit murder once again, Bonnie moved toward me, her
free hand lifting the collar of her shirt over her mouth and
nose.

I forced my weak, shaking legs to hold me up as I stood
and braced myself upright with my fists on the table. This
made Bonnie laugh. My whole body suddenly shook with
something other than fear: rage mixed with a need to survive.

The table was still between us as she grabbed the piece of
rope I had untied from her hands what seemed like a lifetime
ago.

'Your turn,' she said, holding up the rope. As she came
around the table she added, 'You should know, I have to go
get that cell phone. I can't have a record of that text message
getting out. And if your boyfriend's there, I'll have to shoot
him.'

With my gun. The gun he bought me the day he first kissed me.

A thicker layer of smoke floated toward us. When she got
within a few feet of me, I tightened the muscles in my legs,
pulling up my kneecaps and grounded myself to the floor for
balance. Something a decade of yoga had taught me.

I saw her reach for me out of the corner of my eye.

'I'm sorry, too.' I swung my right arm as hard as I could,
knocking the gun from her hand. I heard it hit the floor and
slide. Taking advantage of her surprise, I raised my left
hand and tried to plunge the syringe into her throat. Her
surprise didn't last long enough, however. Her arm shot up
and knocked the syringe out of my hand. I cried out in
frustration. Then in pain as her fist hit me square in the jaw.
My shoulder crunched as I hit the tile floor hard, knocking
my head on the table on the way down.

Black spots mingled with the smoke in my vision. Fighting
the sharp influx of pain in my head, I tried to stay conscious.

'Guess I don't need the rope after all. Good. More like an
accident. Stupid girl.' Muttering to herself, she gave me one

last kick in the stomach. Any hope of fighting back was now gone. I sputtered and gasped for air, only managing to suck in smoke, starting the coughing fit all over again. Dropping to her knees, she crawled away toward the direction the gun had slid. *Stay awake, Elle.* I coughed and choked. I fought to keep my eyes opened. They burned now. Along with my lungs. I felt myself drifting. Suddenly Bonnie's face was in mine. Her smile manic. Her face a sheen of sweat. She poked me in the cheek with the gun. She had recovered it. I was already too far gone to care. She growled, 'I'll tell him you said goodbye.'

Then she was gone. I heard the door slam. Like the lid of a coffin.

I was alone. I stared at the tile next to me through watery eyes. It was as far as I could see. Everything else was an opaque gray. I could hear the crackle of the fire and a whoosh as it consumed something new. The tile was cool against my cheek. A nice contrast to the heat now reaching me. My breathing had slowed. Become shallow. My throat burned. My stomach ached. Then, suddenly, it didn't. A calmness came over me. A peace. I let my eyes close. It felt so good not to fight any more.

TWENTY-NINE

A muffled bark, millions of miles away touched my awareness. I felt the sun on my face. And Buddha was there. Grief washed over me like the tide as I wrapped my arms around him one last time. 'Goodbye, my friend.' As I held him, the barking grew more insistent. Then a feathery pressure, like a tongue lapping frantically at my eyelids. My cheek. My mouth.

A violent cough assaulted my lungs and throat. My eyes fluttered open.

The world was a blur. I could still feel the sun on my back. A sharp bark sounded right in my ear. Between bone-rattling coughs, I tried to get my bearings. Something was tugging at my shirt. I wanted to close my eyes again. But, the infuriating barking wouldn't stop. Then the licking started again. Licking. Barking. I fought my way to consciousness once again.

Angel's sweet face came into focus. Her sharp bark echoed in my head.

I smiled at her. Are we in heaven together? Wait . . .

My eyes opened wider. Unless heaven was paved with Saltillo tile, I wasn't dead . . . yet. I had to get out of here. I pulled my T-shirt up over my mouth and began the slow belly crawl toward the front door. My stomach and head were throbbing. Angel had disappeared in the smoke. Then she reappeared to my right. *Had I gotten disorientated?* I decided that was a possibility and pulled myself along in her direction. My hand hit something small, and I realized it was the syringe. Unbroken. I palmed it in case Bonnie was lurking outside, making sure I didn't get out. A coughing fit slowed me down. Then I suddenly remembered her last words. 'I'll tell him you said goodbye.'

Devon! She was going back for my phone. *How long had I been out?* Was that sirens in the distance? With a cry of frustration, I pulled myself along the floor with one hand, holding the syringe and my T-shirt over my face with the other.

I could see the flames through the smoke now. But, I could also feel the change of tile signaling the front entryway. With one last bit of determination, I launched myself forward and my hand hit the door. Frantically, I lifted myself to a kneeling position and found the handle. When the door swung open and I tumbled out into the fresh salty-air, euphoria washed over me. A gratefulness to be alive that made me want to kiss the earth. But there was no time for that. I crawled away from the front door and pulled myself upright on the outside stucco wall. Bonnie's car was gone. There wasn't a part of me, inside or out that wasn't bruised or singed. My breathing was still mostly coughing and hacking. But, most importantly, my heart was being torn apart not knowing if Devon was safe. Pushing off the wall, I let the momentum carry me forward down to the edge of the sand. I had lost my flip-flops somewhere in the house so the shells were digging into my bare soles. The pain was welcomed. It kept me alert. Unlike the dull pain in my head and stomach that made me want to crawl into a ball and pass out. I swiped at the tears rolling freely down my face. I could definitely hear sirens approaching now.

The moon hung, round and full above. I let that be my focus as I forced my legs to carry me back to Devon's house.

The first thing I noticed was Devon's Jeep wasn't in the driveway. That was a good thing. He hadn't come back yet. And Bonnie's car wasn't in the driveway either. But then, the second thing I noticed was the dogs barking. Coming from the backyard. I had left the dogs in the house. Someone had been in there. All the scenarios raced through my head.

Would Bonnie wait there to ambush Devon? *No.* She wouldn't need to kill him if she could grab my phone and leave before he came back. That's all she wanted. The evidence of the text gone. I needed to see if my phone was still on the counter where I'd left it. I muffled a cough with my arm and holding my stomach, snuck through the bushes to peer through the kitchen window. I had a clear view of the counter. The phone was gone.

My head dropped in frustration. *Now what?* Trying to think clearly after someone tries to kill you is not the easiest thing in the world to do.

The sirens had grown in pitch and shut off. The dogs were still barking. I could see red flashing lights over the bungalow roofs. The fire department then. At least we had one of those on the island. If Devon had normal neighbors, I could ask them to use their phone. But, I knew they only came to stay there in the winter. I'd have to go back and ask the firemen for help. But then, what if Bonnie is hiding in the house and Devon comes home when I leave?

Think. Think. Think. If she checked the phone, she'd see I had actually called him before I left. That would put him in danger. The dogs' barking sounded like a warning. If Bonnie just went in, grabbed the phone and left, they wouldn't still be barking. I had to make sure she wasn't in there. I still had the syringe full of toxin for protection. My decision was made. I'd sneak in and search the house. I couldn't go in the front door though, in case she was waiting for Devon to come home. Luckily, old habits die hard, and I had left the guest bedroom window unlocked. We didn't use the air conditioner much growing up so I always had a window open and still slept better with a window cracked to let in the fresh air, despite the summer heat. I'd have to thank Mom for her frugalness if I ever saw her again.

I snuck around the side of the house and, shoving the syringe in the waistband of my pants, I removed the screen and pushed open the window. It slid it up quietly to allow me entrance. The bedroom was various shades of shadow. I could only hope one of them wasn't Bonnie.

Grabbing the edge of the dresser for balance, I stepped over my suitcase then tiptoed toward the door. With just one eye and my nose exposed, I peered down the squat hallway. A faint light from the kitchen beyond the living room was the only illumination in the bungalow. I could now hear the dogs scratching at the glass doors.

Taking a deep breath, I stepped out into the hallway and slid along the wall. A cough began to tickle my throat, and I had to use superhuman concentration to keep it at bay. I was directly across from the guest bath now. My heart jumped, and I almost screamed. Then I realized it was just my sweat-and-smoke-covered image reflected in the bathroom mirror.

OK, calm down, Elle, you've got this. Look at what you've survived already.

Pep talk over, I stepped out of my hiding place and began to cross the living room. What happened next seemed to be out of a slow-motion movie.

The front door flew open and Devon was suddenly standing there, his face streaked with black smoke, his gun gripped in both hands, his face a mask of unchecked fear.

'Elle!' I heard the surprise and anguish in his voice. 'Get down!'

A laugh echoed behind me. And then a *BOOM!* Came from the same direction. The impact rattled my eardrums. At the same time, I saw Devon hit the floor. In horror, I whirled around and saw Bonnie standing behind the sofa. A swirl of gray smoke was still coming out of the barrel of the gun in her hands. Her eyes were full of rage as she swiveled her stance to now aim at me.

Something dark and primal ripped itself from my grip. I launched myself at her, not caring whether she planted a bullet in my chest. She had shot Devon. I would get my revenge before I died. My right foot hit the sofa, and I flew over it and into her, screaming like a wild animal, knocking us both to the floor.

The dogs' barking intensified. The gun went off again, next to my ear. I screamed again, not in pain, but in surprise. As she grabbed me by the hair, I reached between us, flicked the rubber end off of the needle full of Botox and plunged it into her neck.

Her eyes bulged. Then I felt her body go limp. I scrambled, pushing myself off of her. Wiping the sweat and smoke from my eyes, I stared at her as she began to laugh. She laughed so hard, she dropped the gun and wiped at her own eyes. Then she plucked the needle from her neck.

'Nice try, Elle.'

I stared down at her, confused. It didn't work?

'It's not that simple,' she explained between her laughing fits. 'You have to—' she clutched her stomach – 'to hit the oesophagus.'

Panic rose again but then I followed her gaze. Devon stood above us, his gun pointed at Bonnie with one hand, his cell phone in the other. Blood had soaked through his white shirt on the arm holding the gun. It dripped and puddled on the floor. I watched this with detached fascination. I'd never seen so much blood.

'Elle? You all right?' he asked without taking his eyes from Bonnie.

His voice was so raw, so gentle, it broke me. Brought me out of the numbness. 'Yes,' I managed to whisper before I collapsed into a sobbing ball against the back of the sofa.

I felt him instantly at my side. A strong arm pulled me in close. He made the necessary calls while I shook beside him. I heard him call Moon Key security first, then Salma. I also heard him trying to explain the impossible situation of Bonnie being the killer and attacking us and finally just giving up and saying, 'Get here ASAP.'

After he hung up from Salma, I finally got the tears to stop and the courage to look at Bonnie. She lay on the ground, staring up at the ceiling, her hands folded on her stomach. She was still chuckling and whispering to herself. Even though she had killed two people, tried to burn me alive and shot Devon . . . still, now that the terror and rage had subsided, I felt sorry for her. I knew I would miss the woman I'd gotten to know and trust. I knew that the caring woman who helped me through some major panic attacks was still in there somewhere. Or maybe I just hoped she was.

Buddha and Petey had stopped barking but they were both sitting on the other side of the glass, panting hard and watching us all with confusion. For some reason, this made the tears and shaking start again.

THIRTY

The two detectives actually arrived before island security. Apparently Devon had called Salma as soon as he got my message at the airport, so they were already on their way.

Devon gently moved me to the sofa, as a uniformed officer with the detectives cuffed Bonnie and led her out of the bungalow. It was so surreal, watching the detectives and uniformed officers move about a place that had been my and Devon's private space just a few hours ago.

Devon came back with a towel tied around his arm where he'd been shot.

I eyed it, cringing. 'You OK?'

'Yeah. Clean shot, went straight through. I'll be fine.'

Detective Farnsworth heard this and ordered one of the uniformed officers to find the bullet.

I looked up at Devon. 'Would you mind letting the dogs in?' I suddenly needed Buddha. Needed his warm, comforting presence and needed him to know I was OK.

'Sure.'

'I got it,' Alex Harwick said suddenly. He'd been standing around and seemed grateful for something to do. Devon moved to get up anyway.

'Thank you, Alex,' I said, holding Devon down in the seat. 'Stay with me.'

The dogs came scrambling in, tails whipping, mouths foaming. Buddha launched himself on to the couch next to me in an impressive feat of bulk defying gravity. His nubby butt squirmed as he proceeded to clean my face of the grime. I couldn't help but smile through my tears. 'I'm OK, boy. Good boy.' I pushed him down to a sit and nuzzled my head into his neck. As I rubbed his ears the way he liked, he began to calm down and eventually lay, pressed up against my thigh.

Devon pressed himself closer against me on the other side.

Good thing I wasn't claustrophobic. Then again, I couldn't think of any other males I'd rather be stuck between.

'Hello, Petey,' Detective Vargas said, reaching down to pet the blocky, brown head that was planted in her lap. Petey accepted the pats and then came to lie at Devon's feet.

In the back of my mind I wondered how she knew Petey's name and how many times she'd been here to Devon's house. But, right now, I was too exhausted to care.

The two detectives sat quietly on the love seat facing us, their notepads out. Devon and Salma shared a look and then Devon slipped his hand into mine and squeezed gently. 'Can you start from the beginning, Elle? What happened tonight?'

At first, I didn't even know where to start. Was it only one night? It felt like a lifetime. But once I started telling the story at the point I received the threatening text message, which I thought was from Jamie, it just tumbled out. I could feel Devon tense up when I reached the parts about Bonnie pulling the gun on me and then lighting the place on fire.

After I told them how and why I snuck back into Devon's house, I heard Devon mutter a 'Jaysis, Elle,' and saw the detectives glance at each other with raised brows. I brushed off their disapproval when I remembered something.

Turning to Devon, I asked, 'Where's your friend you picked up from the airport?'

Pushing my damp hair off my forehead, he smiled gently at me. 'I couldn't very well put him in danger, too. I left him to get a hotel and rushed here. Though I could've swum faster than that bloody ferry.'

I was still confused. 'So, how did you know to come into the house with your gun drawn? And why do you look like you were in a fire?'

He ran his thumb along my hand, shaking his head. 'I tried to call you back, but you weren't answering. I was goin' out of my mind trying to get back here. When I finally made it, I did see the strange Jaguar parked up on the street behind the house, but I didn't pay it any mind at first because your message said you were going to the house three doors down. When I saw the fire there, I just lost it. I managed to get inside the house—' he grimaced – 'I owe a few firefighters an apology.

They pulled me back out and convinced me the house was empty. That's when I remembered the strange car and raced back to the house. When I heard the dogs barking outside, I knew something was wrong. I saw Bonnie stand up from behind the sofa as soon as you stepped into the living room.' He stopped suddenly, his eyes meeting mine. I saw a glimpse of the raw fear again before he masked it.

'I'm sorry,' I whispered.

He palmed the back of my head gently and pulled me into his chest. I didn't even care that my head hurt where it made contact with his body. I could feel his heart beating against my cheek. His lips pressed into the top of my head and I felt him sigh deeply. 'You're alive. That's all that matters.'

'OK. We're going to go check out the other crime scene,' Detective Vargas announced. They both got up to leave. She stopped in front of us, her expression a neutral mask while her eyes blazed with emotion. 'I'm glad you're both OK. We'll talk about this more in depth, Devon.' She went to leave and turned back. 'Is this your friend from Ireland that's in town?'

The way she said 'friend' seemed like he was more important than just a visitor. Devon nodded.

'Good. We can discuss that, too.' She glanced at me. 'If you still want to?'

Devon adjusted the towel on his arm with a wince. 'Yes. Of course.'

She nodded, eyeing his arm. 'Go get that looked at.'

'She's right,' I said when they left.

He looked me over and nodded, probably deciding a trip to the hospital was in order for me, too.

We didn't return to Moon Key until the wee hours of the morning. Devon had gotten stitched up and found it very amusing that I got my head examined. Literally. Besides some bruising and smoke inhalation, I was good to go.

I'd used Devon's phone to call Hope, since they confiscated mine as evidence, and gave her and Ira the good news. Hearing her grateful tears made my water works come again. I had a feeling it was going to take a while to sort through the tangles of emotions this whole experience wove within me.

Besides being so exhausted I could barely move my arms, there was another reason I was quiet on the drive back. I glanced up at the stars for strength and luck. Then turned to look at the man I was about to open my heart to.

'Devon?'

He blinked like I had startled him from his thoughts. 'Yes?'

'I know this isn't the best timing, but there are a few things I need to tell you. Are you up for it?'

Devon immediately pulled the Jeep over on the quiet road beneath a palm tree. Turning to me, he took my hand in both of his. His eyes were suddenly animated like the stars above us. 'You can tell me anything, Elle. You have to know that.'

So, taking a deep breath, I told him all about my college relationship and how that experience left me afraid to be vulnerable again. I confessed my deepest shame about the panic attacks and how I'd love to travel to Ireland with him, but knew it would be a challenge I may not be able to overcome. I told him about my fear that I would be a fling and that my heart would break when he left to travel again.

At this, his jaw tightened and he suddenly started the Jeep and pulled back out on to the road. We drove the remaining few minutes in uncomfortable silence, and I was left to wonder if he was angry or hurt or had just had enough of my drama. By the time we walked into the house and were greeted by the dogs, I had convinced myself it was all of the above.

'Elle.' Devon stood, leaning against the kitchen counter, his arms crossed. 'Come here.'

Unsure what to expect, I walked timidly over to stand in front of him.

Slowly, he reached up and cupped my face in his hands. Making sure I was looking right in his eyes, he said, 'Apparently I haven't been clear in my intentions, so I want you to listen to me very carefully.'

I nodded as best I could.

'Elle Pressley, while it's true that I have been avoiding relationships my entire adult life, I do not want just a fling with you. I've fallen madly in love with you and am willing to go through hell and back to explore that. Do you understand?'

I didn't have to hear the words. I saw the dead serious truth in his eyes. Tears pooled in my own eyes but didn't fall. 'Yes.'

'Good,' he whispered, bringing his mouth down on mine with a hunger that pulled me into him like gravity on steroids. His mouth was warm and strong and I felt my heart explode as his kiss swept through me, body, mind and soul. When we finally released each other, a tentative smile touched the corner of his mouth. 'I'm not saying it's going to be easy, but we'll work it out together. We do make a good team. Agreed?'

I let myself smile as I nodded. Then, not trusting any words I attempted could explain how I felt the same way, I simply took his hand and slowly led the way to his bedroom.

'Stay,' I said to the dogs as they hit the threshold behind us. For once Petey sat down beside Buddha. 'Good boys.' I smiled, closing the door.

'Impressive.' Devon grinned at me, humor and something much more mischievous sparkled in his gaze.

I pushed myself off the door and into his arms, grinning. 'Oh, I've got talents you've never seen, Devon Burke.'

With a sudden burst of laughter, he scooped me up, only wincing once as my weight stressed his bandaged arm and carried me to the bed. 'Well, let's remedy that right now, shall we?'

Releasing all the emotion of the evening in a fit of shared laughter, I wrapped my arms tightly around his neck. 'We shall, Irish. We shall.'